LEGENDS
OF THE SKY

LEGENDS
OF THE SKY

LIZ FLANAGAN

David Fickling Books
Scholastic Inc. / New York

First published in the United Kingdom in 2018 as *Dragon Daughter* by David Fickling Books, 31 Beaumont Street, Oxford OX1 2NP.

davidficklingbooks.com

The publisher does not have any control over and does not assume any responsibility for author or third-party websites or their content.

Library of Congress Cataloging-in-Publication Data available

ISBN 978-1-338-34966-5

10 9 8 7 6 5 4 3 2 1   19 20 21 22 23

Printed in the U.S.A.   23

First edition, October 2019

Book design by Shivana Sookdeo

For my daughters,
with love and admiration xxx

ARCOSI
and the surrounding seas

SARTOLA

ARCOSI

THE SHADOW STRIP

THE PALACE

THE GARDENS

THE DRAGON HALL

THE PALACE GATE

THE COURTYARD

THE YELLOW HOUSE

THE HIGH STREET

THE ORCHARDS

THE CITY WALLS

THE WAREHOUSES

THE CITY GATE

THE MARKETPLACE

THE SEA WALL

THE DOCKS

THE WATERSIDE SHRINE

THE HARBOUR

Part One

Part One

CHAPTER ONE

M illa was hiding in an orange tree on the day the dragons returned to Arcosi. She was busy ignoring anyone
who called for her, just as stubbornly as she ignored the twigs
that were poking into her back or scratching her arms or tan-
gling her curly black hair. She was small enough to be completely hidden by the dense green foliage, making it the ideal
hiding place right there in the middle of it all, between the
main building of the Yellow House and its kitchen building.

If she turned her head, she could gaze down over the garden wall to the city rooftops below and count the ships
approaching the harbor. She breathed in the hot, busy smell
of Arcosi, the city she loved: dusty stone, foul drains, rotting
fish, salt, spice, and blossom.

Being hidden brought Milla the first rest of the day. She
felt the wobble in her legs and an airy, untethered feeling that
told her she'd missed a meal. She reached out and picked
a sun-warmed orange, peeling it with her dirty nails and

sucking the juice from the flesh till it ran down her chin, before throwing the evidence over the garden wall.

She began to feel better. She was sure no one meant to give her too much work. It was just that the moment anyone saw the youngest servant, they'd say, "Milla! Job for you!"— not realizing half a dozen others had already said the same thing. It was a point of honor never to say no, never to say she was too tired. She made herself useful. Indispensable. She would never find herself out on the streets like a stray cat. For in these strange days, when the duke's soldiers roamed the streets day and night, and rumor flew faster than a hawk sighting prey, the whole city felt like some great beast, waking hungry from a long sleep. At twelve years old, Milla already knew that everyone needed a place of safety. Somewhere to belong.

Just then, Milla heard voices approaching. For a change, they were not calling her name.

Two figures paused almost directly below her. She saw Lanys, the other servant girl, and a strange man wearing a dark blue, salt-stained cloak pulled low over his face. Lanys must have been covering the gate while the guards took a break by the well.

"Wait here, sir. I'll fetch the master, if you pass me the token?" That was Lanys, being careful. Everyone knew you didn't let any old traveler through your gates, not these days.

"Take it. Give it only to Nestan." The stranger's deep voice shook slightly. And the accent? Milla couldn't place it, rare for her. It sounded rusty, unused to the long vowel sounds of Norlandish, the official language of the island of Arcosi.

"Please, be seated." Lanys indicated the carved stone bench next to the fountain. "I'll bring refreshments when I return."

But the stranger didn't sit.

Milla nearly yelped when his hand brushed through the branches right next to her left foot. His hand was tanned deep brown, wrinkled as a peach stone, and holding an oddly shaped bag, something like a double pannier for a mule, only smaller. The man blindly hooked the bag around the same branch Milla was sitting on, but he kept checking behind him and didn't notice there was a girl roosting in his chosen hiding place.

She stared at the bag: there were four deep pockets of woven silk, two now hanging either side of the widest branch. They were roundish, as if they contained water jars. It was the most beautiful thing she'd ever seen, and she was drawn to it like a moth to a candle flame. She prodded one carefully— firm and well padded—and tried to guess what was inside. What needed hiding so urgently? Rubies? Poison? Firepowder? She pulled her hand away swiftly and checked that the bag wasn't going to tumble down and blow her and the orange tree to ash and bone.

A new voice spoke below her, and she almost fell off her perch. Milla was known for her finely tuned hearing, but this person must have feather feet to creep up so silently.

"Where is it?" the new voice hissed, so low and so menacing she could barely make out the words. "Give it to me."

Who was it? She peered through the dark green leaves.

A gloved hand pressed a knife against the cloaked man's throat.

5

"Now!" the newcomer said. He was dressed all in black, with a black-and-gold mask covering his face, as if he was on his way to the evening's entertainment at the palace.

The first man didn't speak. He jabbed his attacker in the ribs with one elbow and tried to twist away. Milla caught fleeting sight of a strange tattoo inked on his inner wrist: a circle and something like a bird.

The masked stranger was quicker. His knife dug into the flesh of the man's neck. A thin trickle of blood ran down the blade.

Milla gathered herself, preparing to swing down feetfirst—with enough force, she could probably send them both flying—when she heard the master's voice in the distance, raised in anger, ". . . and my daughter knows very well that we're due at the palace after sunset . . ."

Her fingers gripped the branch so hard that her knuckles showed pale. She should move. Now. But no part of her body obeyed her.

"Sir, let me go and look for Lady Tarya, while you meet with—" Lanys's words came to an abrupt halt. She and Nestan must have reached the arched entrance to the courtyard.

Milla heard the whisper of steel as Nestan drew his sword. His war injuries might slow him a little, but Milla wouldn't want to bet against Nestan in a fight. She craned her neck, trying to see through the leaves.

The masked man spun around to face them, pulling the inert body of the other with him.

The first man managed to gasp against the blade: "Never!"

It was his last word.

Afterward, Milla was glad they'd turned from her.

She still saw the sudden spray of scarlet against a terra-cotta pot. She heard the heavy slump as the body hit the ground. She saw a blur of black as the assassin fled.

Lanys screamed, piercingly loud, drawing guards from the kitchen yard.

"Catch him! A man in black, masked, with a knife!" Nestan bellowed the alarm and rushed down the stairs from the house. "Quickly! He's getting away."

Milla heard the clattering of boots as the household guards ran out of the gate in pursuit. She heard Nestan approaching, the metallic scrape as he sheathed his blade.

Milla had her eyes screwed shut. She clung to her branch, concentrating on just breathing and trying not to be sick. It needed all her attention. She'd seen plenty of dockside brawls, or city folk being dragged off by the duke's soldiers. But she'd never seen someone killed before. She could have stopped this. Why hadn't she acted when she'd had the chance? She'd hidden, like a mouse. Now a man was dead.

She opened her eyes and took a long, slow, shuddering breath.

"He knew," Nestan said, half to himself.

Milla watched him through a gap in the leaves.

He was staring at the growing pool of crimson by his feet, turning a coin over and over between left fingers and thumb. "He knew to send this coin so I would come. Now we won't learn what message was worth dying for."

"He—he—he knew the password," Lanys stammered slowly. "That's why—that's why I unlocked the gates." She bent forward, her auburn hair bright in the sunshine as she sank down onto her knees, her hands flying up to her face like startled doves. "I don't know how the masked man got through . . ." she whispered. "I'm sorry."

"Yes, that's the real mystery here. The assassin knew exactly when my guards would take their break today. *I wonder . . .*" Nestan's voice trailed off.

Milla was a loyal servant: she should tell the master what the stranger had hidden in the tree. Something worth killing for. Something worth dying for. But, for once, she was speechless. Her mouth felt dry and sour with shock, while her stomach turned over. She sat there, trembling and clinging to the branches.

One of the guards who'd given chase jogged back into the courtyard. "Sir, we lost him. In that crowd: no chance."

How clever the assassin was! Tonight was the duke's Fifty-Year Ball: the streets were full of the city's revelers in their finest clothes, all wearing masks. It would be impossible to find this man again, Milla realized.

Nestan's wondering came to an abrupt halt. He snapped his fingers to Lanys and the guardsman. "Clear this up, before the twins see it. Double the watch on the gate." He limped away, shouting, "Where are my children, anyway? Isak? Has anyone seen the Lady Tarya?"

Lanys got up and stumbled after the master, and they both vanished into the cool interior of the house. The guardsman bent and lifted the cloaked man's body under his arms, dragging him away and leaving a bright scarlet smear on the stone tiles.

How could the duke's ball be more important than a man's life snuffed out before their eyes? Milla felt dazed.

The strange pannier hung there, gleaming. It called to her, like a sweet and tempting song. She touched the silk with one shaky finger. She wouldn't lift it down; not now, with the house in turmoil: Lanys would only snatch it from her immediately.

"I'm coming back for you later," she said, and jumped down from the tree. Knees weak, she staggered, then caught herself, blinking the stars from her vision.

She took one long moment to look down at the blood, to stare straight at it and bear witness. This was real. This had happened. And she wondered who would mark this stranger's passing? As nausea rose again, Milla felt the narrowness of her life, her duties closing in on her like a snare.

She did the only thing it was in her power to do: "I'm sorry. I'll look after your bag, I promise," she whispered to the man's spilled blood.

Then she ran to warn the twins that they had to move fast.

CHAPTER TWO

O ne glance at the western seas showed Milla she didn't have long. The sinking sun stole color from the sea till it was as pale blue as a blackbird's egg.

If the twins were late for the duke's ball . . . If Nestan thought it was all her fault . . . Milla ran, even though her legs still shook. She darted along the polished floor of the master's favorite room, with huge arched windows facing southwest so Nestan could look down on his ships and warehouses far below.

Lanys was lugging a huge jar of water and a handful of rags back outside. Her face, white as curdled milk, mirrored Milla's shock back at her.

"Where have *you* been?" Lanys snapped, with more venom than usual. "The twins have to get ready, but I've an urgent job for the master, so you'd better jump to it." Even in the midst of horror, Lanys managed to make this about point scoring. "Remind me again, why does he keep you?"

"I'm looking for the twins right now!" Milla was used to ignoring her meanness. Her stomach turned over as she realized what job Lanys had been sent to do. "Have you seen them?"

"Well, I thought Isak was in the practice yard." Lanys tilted her head, listening. "But then who's the master yelling at upstairs . . . ?"

Milla didn't wait for the rest. She rushed through the house, taking the stairs two at a time, following the sound of raised voices. She flattened herself against the wall outside Isak's room and peeked through the open doorway.

"And you tell me this now?" Isak's voice was almost unrecognizable. Hoarse with held-back tears. "You can't just . . ."

Milla heard Isak gulp down a sob. Was he crying over the dead man? She edged closer.

Isak was standing by the window with his back to his father, all stiff and hunched over. His breathing was still wheezy from being ill last year, and his eyeglasses were slipping sideways. He took them off: two little circles of glass, connected by wire, that sat on his nose. Nestan had brought this rare device home from a long voyage, and Isak wore them all the time. She saw him knock back a little glass vial of his medicine, scrub at his face with his knuckles, and put his glasses back on.

With her heart still turning somersaults of alarm, Milla chose to do what she did best: she listened.

"Better?" Nestan checked his son, the in-out, in-out of Isak's labored breathing growing gradually smoother. "But I

11

told you as soon as it was arranged. And yes, *I can*. That's just it." Nestan's voice rose in volume. He reached out, as if to grasp Isak's arm. Then he changed his mind and rubbed his hands over his beard so it rasped.

Milla felt suddenly cold, even in the muggy corridor, and wrapped her arms around her rib cage. What had he arranged? Something so important it rattled even Nestan, who could look at a dead man with detached calm. Her thoughts circled back to the murdered man, to his mysterious bag. She pictured it, hanging there, waiting for her. She tugged her thoughts away, catching the end of Nestan's next words.

". . . I want to give you what I didn't have. What I had to work for. Why can't you see?"

"Maybe because I'm not you?" Isak spoke in gasping phrases. "Because I want something else? And you'd know that if you ever bothered to talk to me."

Milla winced, but it was true. Nestan was either traveling or busy with work, and rarely sought out either twin. Their mother, Vianna, had died ten years ago. Since then, they'd run wilder than any other merchant's children, till Nestan finally noticed and imposed a new regime of lessons they both hated.

"How did I end up with such a spoiled child? Will you not see how lucky you are? It's not a punishment, Isak!" Nestan roared at his son.

"You sure? That's exactly what it feels like. Punishment for not being the son you wanted!" Isak spun on his heel, backlit so Milla couldn't see his expression. "I see how you look at us—sickly son, bold daughter—as if you'd like us to switch places."

Nestan gasped as if he'd been struck.

Milla covered her mouth with clammy fingers so she didn't gasp, too. Isak never yelled. He was quiet. Dry. Funny. Kind. Hearing his raised voice only added to the horror and unreality of the day.

Father and son faced each other, barely a handspan apart. At thirteen, Isak was already as tall as Nestan.

"And when you tell Tarya what you've got planned for *her*, she's going to feel exactly the same. We're not kids anymore. We're not your pet chickens, to be bred or bartered away. You'd better watch out, Dad. Or else one of these mornings you might just find we've flown the nest."

No, no, no! Tarya and Isak couldn't fly the nest! What was he talking about? Milla shook her head, trying and failing to piece together the fragments of the argument.

"Are you threatening me?" Nestan's voice dropped now. He edged even closer to Isak, and one hand moved again to the sword at his belt.

"I don't believe you." Isak shook his head in disgust. "What, are you going to lift your sword to me? We all know how well that works in this city." His voice dripped with bitterness. "You're not even a soldier, not anymore. We only have your word that you ever were. You probably hurt your leg falling down drunk outside a tavern."

Nestan stared.

"Oh, forget it. I'm leaving."

"You can't. We're due at the palace. You know what this means . . . You can't risk it!"

Isak shouldered past his father and strode out of the room.

Milla put her hand on his sleeve, whispering, "Wait!"

But he ran down the stairs without a word, leaving her reaching after him.

A noise made Milla turn. She saw Nestan stagger backward as if he'd been hit, folding down into Isak's chair. He gripped his left leg with both hands, hissing as he eased away the cramping stiffness in his old wound.

Milla darted down the steps after Isak. There was no sign of him. Instead, Lanys stood there, wide-eyed, now spilling red-tinged water from her water jar and stained rags. "What's going on? What've you done now?"

"Where'd he go?" Milla blurted. The scent of the blood-stained water filled her nostrils, making her retch. She fought not to be sick right there.

"Out." Lanys pointed to the main gates where four guards now stood in a row. "But . . . ?"

Milla had no time to explain it to her. Instead of chasing after him, she spun away and took a high-speed shortcut through the kitchen, which made Josi, the cook, swear like a sailor.

"Sorry, Josi," Milla gasped. "Tell you later!" She wanted to throw her arms around Josi's broad waist and sob out the tale of what she'd just seen and heard in the last hour. The image of the dead man still filled her mind's eye: that pool of thick red blood spreading, spreading, spreading.

14

Instead, she commanded her feet to keep moving, crossed the kitchen yard, leaping over Skalla, the massive kitchen tomcat, and ignoring his hiss. The hens scattered in her wake, scolding her with a flurry of indignant clucks. The orchards spread away to the west along steep terraces, and the goats tethered there stopped grazing long enough to glare at her through yellow eyes. Milla used an ancient gnarled olive tree as a ladder to scramble onto the wall of the practice yard. She knew better than to open the gate unannounced—you lost fingers that way.

She paused to catch her breath. The image of the dead man rose before her once again, and this time the tide of nausea won. She turned and vomited down the practice-yard wall. Afterward, she spat hard, panting, and wiped her mouth on her tunic sleeve. She hoped no one would notice the watery, orange-flecked mess, and then she focused again on her task.

Two people were fighting in the walled yard. Their swords sang and clashed; their feet danced and scuffled in the sandy earth. They both wore helmets and practice leathers that covered their chests and thighs. Richal Finn, Nestan's head guardsman, was dueling with his best-trained student. The student was almost as good as Finn. Milla knew, because she'd been talked into being a duel partner when Finn wasn't available. She had the bruises to prove it. Milla watched as Finn's blows were blocked, dodged, and matched.

Milla made a small move with one hand, tilting her head backward, to draw Finn's attention and remind him what his student was actually supposed to be doing right now. It worked.

Finn narrowed his eyes, focusing harder. He saw his

chance and took it, lunging faster and flipping his opponent's sword away with his, so it clanged against the stone wall.

"That'll do for today," he said. "I'm needed by the master. *Sir*." He took off his helmet—showing his bronzed and balding scalp—and bowed briefly, before slipping past his pupil. He looked up on his way out and caught Milla's eyes with his intense blue gaze. He seemed to be assessing her, checking for something.

Milla nodded to thank him. Finn was no fool. He'd been teaching both twins for more than ten years. He knew exactly what was happening here. The new regime of lessons permitted only Isak to learn how to fight. So, out of loyalty and affection for the twins, Finn kept up the pretense that he was teaching only Isak. If he was challenged by Nestan, he could always claim not to have known the truth.

Finn nodded back and left.

"What? But we've only just started, Finn! You were late!" his student called after him, arms wide, baffled at the abrupt end to the session. The helmeted figure caught sight of Milla crouching on the wall like a cat. "What are you doing up there, Milla?"

"It's time, we have to hurry!" Milla jumped down into the yard and started unbuckling the leather armor. Concentrating helped her feel calmer. She could almost ignore the tremor in her legs. She could almost ignore the way the silken bag called to her. "I'm supposed to be dressing you for the ball! What are you doing down here, today of all days?"

The warrior lifted the leather helmet, freeing a mass of

16

tousled blond curls framing the beautiful face of Tarya Thornsen—dressed as her brother, Isak.

"I'm sorry, I know how important today is—I do! I just lost track of time. I didn't mean to cause you trouble. But if I have to behave like the perfect young lady all evening, I needed to let off steam first. Now you can dress me in pearls and silks and I'll be good, I promise!"

"The thing is, Isak's just run off. He was shouting at your father."

"Isak was? Are you sure?" Tarya asked. And then, more gently, "Hey, what's wrong? You look terrible."

"Nothing," Milla lied, and ducked her head, fumbling with a stiff buckle. There wasn't time for this now. Besides, she'd whispered a promise to a dead man's blood. In Milla's mind, promises were binding.

"Right, but leave the armor; I can run in this. We'll have to hurry if we're to find Isak in time."

CHAPTER THREE

B ilge buckets!" swore Tarya. "Why now? He picks his moment, that brother of mine!"

Headstrong was how Nestan described his daughter. *Stubborn* was what Isak called his twin. *Fiery*, the servants might dare, as they rolled their eyes. Milla would choose different words: She'd say *loyal*. She'd say *brave*.

Tarya's eyes were as blue as the darkening sky above, as she checked how late it was. "Usual place, you think?"

Milla nodded. They both knew Isak was happiest on board a ship or, failing that, at the harbor.

"I can be there and back before sunset. Maybe. If we're not on time for the duke's stupid ceremony, we're all blacklisted."

"You're not coming," Milla said quickly. "I'll go. You need to get ready: I've laid the rose silk out on your bed . . ." The thought of running down to the harbor and back again made her sway with exhaustion, but she gritted her teeth. "Besides, there'll be patrols out. You don't know all the shortcuts." Milla knew the winding streets of Arcosi like a cat, all the snickets and secret ways.

"No, I'll do it!" Tarya said. "He's my twin. It's my family's reputation at stake. Besides, you're trembling like a leaf and you've got sick on your tunic. Are you ill?"

"I'm fine, and that's just orange," Milla lied again. She didn't want to be left at home tonight. She stood up straight, willing her legs to stop shaking.

"Fine," Tarya huffed. "Don't tell me what's wrong! But at least let me come with you. Me and my friendly blade?" She tapped the pommel of her sword, eyebrows raised. She was still humming with energy from her unfinished fight with Finn.

"Fine," Milla echoed. "Follow me." She led Tarya back up onto the practice-yard wall, circled away from the house, and showed her the jutting stones they could climb, two stories down to the next street. "But we'll need to go the quick way."

"How did I not know this secret entrance to my own house?" Tarya demanded, starting after Milla.

It was usually an easy climb, but Milla's legs still trembled slightly, and her left foot slipped, leaving her hanging by her fingertips. "You know it now. Come on, we need to run." She dropped the last stretch, landing lightly and throwing herself onward down the narrow lane.

Milla stuck to the shadowy back routes. Without Isak's helmet, Tarya was far too recognizable as her father's daughter. Almost half the city had worked for Nestan at one time or another, and he had loyal friends in every quarter who might challenge them now and ask why Tarya was heading in the opposite direction of the palace.

"Wait!" Milla said, as they neared the main street that encircled the island like a coiled snake. "We have to cross here," she told Tarya. She took her hand and started walking down the wide paved roadway, feeling exposed. They joined people in their best clothes: some headed up to the palace for the ball, others down to the docks for the street party.

"It's fine. We have every right to go for a walk," Tarya said, tossing her head back. "Two friends, out for evening air . . . What's wrong with that?"

Milla glanced at her friend. Did Tarya really believe that? She stayed quiet and hoped her happy illusion wasn't about to be shattered.

A man's voice yelled the words Milla was dreading: "Patrol! Get back."

The noise of marching feet echoed off the high sides of the houses lining the road.

Milla dived back against the wall, pulling Tarya after her, and tucked her arms and feet in tight. Next to her, a young mother ran forward and dragged her toddling daughter out of the roadway, clutching her tight to her chest and scolding her in relief: "Don't you ever wander off again. You see soldiers, you stay close to me, all right?"

The little girl started bawling loudly.

The soldiers marched toward them with no break in their rhythm, adjusting their stride to the steep hill. They faced unswervingly forward, in silence but for the thump of their boots and the metallic clank of sword and shield. Milla stared at the soldiers as they approached, trying to see them as individuals. She knew they were only people—that young lad with the sunburned neck, that burly older man with the bushy beard—but in this large mass they seemed like something else: something more powerful and more terrifying than ordinary men.

They were almost upon them. Just one more moment; in another, they'd be past. As long as no one moved, or gave them reason to—

"Halt!" the captain ordered. "Checkpoint formation." The men stopped as one. Turned, stepped sideways, stopped again, blocking the street just above them. "Citizens! Show papers!"

Milla cursed under her breath, sending up a hasty prayer for inspiration. They were trapped, unless she could find a way out quickly.

The woman next to her sighed and rummaged under her cloak. "Again! Third time today. As if I've had time to put a foot wrong when they keep checking on us constantly."

The soldiers acted like a human barrier, sweeping slowly down the main street, checking papers as they went, challenging each person to prove their name, address, and family origins.

"What do we do? I've brought no papers with me," Tarya hissed, gripping the hilt of her sword. "I didn't know I was leaving the house. If we're arrested now, we'll never make the ball, and my family will be blacklisted for sure."

"Norlanders, blacklisted? Never . . ." Milla said, cursing herself for leaving in such a hurry. She never forgot her papers.

"It happens!" Tarya said. "My friend Anna's family lost everything."

"Let me go! Get off me. I've done nothing wrong," a young man protested as two soldiers grabbed his arms. He looked barely older than Isak, with a mess of dark brown hair that fell in his eyes.

"No proof of identity? That's an offense under the duke's law, as you well know. Sir." The captain added this last word as a taunt.

"It was in my pocket. It must have fallen . . ." The young man started begging as he realized what this meant. "I can show you where I live. You can ask my parents! They can't afford the release fee. *Please!*"

"Bring him in." The captain didn't even watch as his men dragged the boy away, struggling and protesting his innocence. He'd already turned away to the next terrified citizen, his hand out for their papers.

Milla glanced around the woman's shoulder. There were only four more people to be checked before the soldiers reached them. She looked in every direction, searching for an escape route. There! Between the houses. There was a tiny gap, just wide enough to fit through. Not for the first time, Milla blessed the original inhabitants of Arcosi, who'd laced the city with smugglers' secrets and hidden passageways.

"This way!" Milla grabbed Tarya's arm and tugged her backward into the gap, where a tiny alleyway zigzagged back on itself, leading to a steep flight of stone stairs, squashed between the houses. "If we're fast, we can beat the patrol and loop around it on the way back." Her feet pounded on the worn steps, and they flew down, tumbling out at the harbor.

"There he is!" Tarya overtook Milla with a final burst of speed.

As they had predicted, Isak was leaning on the harbor rail, staring at the newest arrival moored before him: a sleek, two-masted schooner, still being unloaded. Gulls scrapped and screamed over a basin of fish waste dumped from the market stalls that fringed the upper quayside.

"Isak, what are you playing at?" Tarya didn't waste any time on greetings. Her anger melted into concern when he didn't answer. "Hey, what's wrong? Are you all right?"

Isak turned and eyed his sister up and down, the sunset reflected in his glasses. "And you're dressed as what, exactly? Warrior scarecrow? You'll be turning heads at the duke's ball, all right."

Behind Isak, the protective arms of the harbor wall held dozens of boats safe: Arcosi's fleet of fishing boats and the taller merchant ships. Through the harbor gates, Milla saw the last bright sliver of sun drop below the rim of the sea, like a coin into a pocket. "It's sunset. Hurry!"

"Oh, so it didn't just slip your mind, then?" Tarya was saying, running both hands through her curls and shaking out the dried leaves and stalks that she found there. "Because I didn't spend all month practicing dance steps and helping you learn that oath for nothing. Now hurry up, or we'll be late and have to spend the rest of our miserable lives regretting the insult to the duke."

"Since when did you care so much about it?" Isak lashed out. "What's in it for you? I haven't noticed you sticking to any rules lately, unless it pleases you . . ."

"Stop it! What's wrong with you?" Milla put herself between the twins. They didn't do this. They took each other's side. Always. She longed to tell them everything she'd just witnessed, but they were upset enough, and time was running out. "Look! Sunset. We don't have time for this!"

"I'm coming," Isak said. "Well done, little goatherds . . ."

That stung. "We didn't have to come after you."

"Sorry," Isak mumbled, not meeting her gaze.

Tarya grabbed Isak's hand. "Just stay close to me." She spun on her heel and started striding back toward the smugglers' steps. "There's a patrol headed this way, which I think we'd rather avoid."

As she hurried after them, passing the newly moored ship, Milla paused, then caught the sleeve of one of the boys unloading crates. "Hey, did you bring in a passenger?" she whispered. "An old man in a dark blue cloak, carrying a large silk bag?"

"Yeah, glad to see the back of those two! Bad luck. Brought us an east wind. Not surprising, they was jumpy as cats the whole sailing," the lad muttered back, pulling away from her.

Those *two*? Milla wondered. Who had the murdered man been traveling with? And where was this person now?

CHAPTER FOUR

M illa led the twins home using the smugglers' steps and hustled them upstairs to get changed. Nestan was pacing by the front gates, leaning on a finely carved, silver-topped walking cane. He spun around when Milla and the twins finally emerged, dressed in their finest clothes. Richal Finn stood waiting by the wall, in the formal suit of a sword-bearer, his cropped hair gleaming with moisture as if he'd just dunked his head in the well.

"And just where have you been?" Nestan asked quietly.

Milla knew that tone. Nobody answered. The three of them stood very still on the upper level, clutching their masks and trying to steady their breathing.

Nestan's searching gaze passed over each of them in turn. Tarya was wearing her best rose-silk dress. Milla had hastily tamed Tarya's blond curls into a high knot threaded with a string of glass beads, and clasped her mother's pearl necklace around her neck. Isak stood stiff and resigned, looking handsome but uncomfortable in his cream silk shirt and formal suit, holding another glass vial of his medicine in one closed fist.

Milla tugged her plain purple dress straight. Even maids had to look their best tonight, so she had borrowed one of Tarya's outgrown gowns. It was the finest thing she'd ever worn, with matching shoes that didn't quite fit. Her fingers lingered covetously over the silky fabric.

Milla peered back at Nestan from under her lashes, praying they would all pass his scrutiny. Isak and Tarya needed to be at the ball. Milla didn't. With one snap of his fingers, he could summon Lanys instead.

Lanys would love that. She was always flirting with Richal Finn.

"You look well, Tarya," Nestan said finally. "The pearls suit you."

Isak stood straighter, waiting for his word of approval.

"Isak? Don't disgrace us up there."

Milla felt him slump with disappointment next to her.

"Your faith in me is *so* reassuring," Isak muttered under his breath.

"Shh," Tarya whispered back. "He didn't mean that."

"Sounded like it." Isak's face was crumpled and miserable, but Nestan didn't seem to notice. His gray-bearded jawline was clenched tight. He wore the usual sword at his belt and a not-so-usual spare blade bulging slightly under his best cape, the midnight velvet.

Seeing Nestan dressed for trouble made Milla's empty

stomach churn again. But if he'd decided not to worry the twins tonight by telling them about the murder, then she must be brave enough to follow his example.

Her fingers flew to the gold medal around her neck, as they did whenever she was anxious. It was her only true possession. She traced the outline of a dragon in flight beneath a full moon, stamped onto the worn metal.

"We're late," Nestan snapped, turning.

They'd passed! Milla was actually going to the palace. A smile danced over her lips, then vanished again as she remembered the dead man. She vowed to stay close to the twins tonight and be on guard, for their sakes.

"Ready?" Tarya danced down the steps, took her father's free arm and squeezed it, disguising her breathlessness as excitement.

"I've been ready for some time," he said dryly. "Now, put your masks on and let's go!" Nestan gestured to the guards to open his gates.

It was dark, and the moon hung low over the horizon: almost full, and round as a pearl. They didn't need lanterns tonight: the whole city was ablaze like a birthday cake, with beacons, flares, and bonfires from the poorest dwellings, built into the lower seawall, to the palace of the four winds, right at the top of Arcosi. Milla glanced down over the light-filled streets, wondering where her other friends were right now. They'd be gathered on the docks, she guessed. Thom would be perching expectantly on the harbor wall, waiting for the fireworks. Rosa had been making spiced cakes and planning to *borrow* a bottle of sweet Sartolan wine from her parents' stall for the street party.

And Milla was here, joining the throng of Arcosi's first families, all dressed in their best silks and velvets, dripping with jewels and gold, wearing sequined and feathered masks. Her eyes darted around till she felt giddy from all the glitter and gleam. Then she winced as the shoes rubbed her heel, reminding her that she was a sparrow trying to blend in among the peacocks.

"Are you all right?" Isak asked, noticing. "Has something happened?" He offered Milla his hand, looking down at her with gentle concern.

What if she blurted it all out? *Someone was killed, right under my nose. I didn't stop it and now a man is dead. He hid something valuable and I haven't told your father.*

She didn't want to worry him. He needed to be calm to play his part at the duke's ball. "No," she said smoothly, but she leaned gratefully on his arm to stop herself limping, just for a few steps.

A portly Norlander woman in a bulging red satin dress scowled in puzzlement over her shoulder, her eyes moving from Milla's short black curls and golden-brown skin to the purple dress—a few seasons old but still fine quality—and on down to her borrowed shoes.

Milla knew she had become a strange, mixed-up creature who often confused outsiders. Keeping Tarya company, she'd learned a bit of everything: how to fight, how to dance, how to speak like a lady, stretching her vowels in the elegant

Norlander style. But some would always judge by first appearances.

Now she caught this woman's glance of disapproval and braced for the inevitable comment.

"Is the duke letting anyone in this evening?" the woman asked loudly. "Norlanders only, I thought?"

Nestan said nothing, but he stepped very deliberately between Milla and the woman, blocking her view.

Cheeks burning, Milla quickly pulled away from Isak, pointing ahead. "Look! We're there."

People were tipping their heads back, mouths open, eyes wide, awed by the size of the smooth brick wall that reared above them: a daily sight turned majestic now that they saw it at close quarters. The crowd walked, ten at once, through the grand stone gateway, flanked by watchtowers, which arched above their heads. Milla examined the guests around her, glaring at every black-clad man she saw, homing in on each black-and-gold mask to see if one matched the assassin's from the garden. It was hopeless. There were too many. She'd never recognize the right one, and he'd probably switched disguise long ago. But she couldn't relax, knowing that a killer roamed among them.

Inside the palace grounds, an excited twittering rose from the crowd, like the murmur of a thousand starlings.

"Come on, you two. Isn't it beautiful?" Tarya came and took their hands, tugging them along wide avenues, flanked by trimmed lime trees hung with oil lanterns. They walked under elegant pergolas draped in jasmine. On either side lay ornamental rose gardens, and the warm night air was scented with their perfume.

"Oh, look, there it is!" Milla pointed, forgetting her watchfulness for a moment. Lit with strings of lamps, like fallen stars, the Palace of the Four Winds was more beautiful than she had ever imagined.

The main building was braced with stone arches like the rib cage of a huge beast. From each corner rose a tall tower, one facing north, one east, one south, and one west, reaching up into the night sky, light spilling from dozens of windows. A tiled courtyard led to the palace steps, inlaid with the image of a massive black dragon breathing fire.

She paused, unable to believe she was really here. Images of dragons were everywhere on Arcosi—on almost every lintel of every house—but she'd never seen anything on this scale before.

They were all ushered into the building beside the palace.

"It's the dragonhall of the ancient kings, it must be!" Isak breathed as they followed Nestan and Finn through the enormous double doors. He wrinkled his nose to keep his glasses in place as he stared up at the high vaulted ceilings, covered in tiles.

"Like a stable, but for dragons, you mean?" Tarya asked, gazing around in astonishment.

"Finest stable I've ever seen," Milla said, her eyes drawn to the faded murals and ancient tapestries hung around its curved walls. "Look!" She pointed at the nearest wall hanging: a dragon in flight, a female rider on its back, with long black hair streaming behind her.

"It's a woman!" Tarya said triumphantly. "Looks like they got some things right then, whoever they were . . ."

"It's just a story . . ." Isak sounded doubtful.

"They were real! They lived right here, in our city." Milla knew the old songs and legends, she'd seen the basking places built into the crumbling walls of the main square, but this was different, this was vivid proof. She wished for the hundredth time she'd lived back then, in the days of the dragons.

She looked around, trying to imagine real dragons living here, but the dragonhall had been turned into a ballroom. Tonight, the hall was warmed by dozens of burning braziers, scented by lilies in tall crystal vases, and one whole side of the room was filled with tables laden with delicious-smelling food. There was roast lamb; gleaming black olives; plump salad grains dotted with pomegranate, coriander, and raisins; smoked fish; warm loaves fresh from the oven; and her favorite: baked peaches, oozing juice. Milla's mouth watered, reminding her how long it had been since she'd eaten.

Just then a fanfare sounded and a herald cried, "Make way for His Grace, Duke Olvar Refarson!"

Guards came first, row after row, all dressed in the duke's black ceremonial livery. The deep, dark beat of marching feet filled Milla's ears, drowning out her thoughts. She clutched for Tarya's hand as she swayed, suddenly off balance.

The guards stood to attention, making a pathway. Everyone turned, expectant.

Milla blinked away the dizziness, eager to see the duke she'd heard so much about.

Three people walked between the lines of guards, drawing every eye: the duke, the duchess and their son.

The duke's wiry bone-white hair stood on end like a crown, making him even taller. He smiled, and Milla heard sighing in the crowd around her. The duke had the palest blue eyes she'd ever seen, and his face was lined but still handsome.

They stepped up onto a little platform marked out with golden ropes and lit by flaming brass torches.

"Welcome to my Fifty-Year Ball." Duke Olvar seemed golden, luminous, in the circle of light. He nodded down at the crowd, as if they were all his children, and not just the tall, dark-haired young man at his side.

"That must be Vigo, his son," Tarya whispered to Milla behind her hand.

"As handsome as they say?" Milla teased. She felt as if she'd walked into a story or a dream, finally seeing these people with her own eyes.

"Maybe." Tarya sounded unconvinced.

"Hmm, I'd say so," Isak said on her other side, as if it were a tricky equation to be puzzled out.

As if he could hear them, Vigo's curious gaze fell on the twins.

Tarya and Isak collapsed in giggles, heads close together, getting shushed sternly by Nestan.

Next to Vigo, his mother smiled warmly down at them, hearing the laughter. She was popular in the lower town. Everyone knew Duchess Serina had wealth of her own, which she spent on healers and midwives throughout the city. She was even said to do healing work herself. The dancing light caught the coil of smooth ebony plaits and the white lily she wore behind one ear. In her bright orange dress, Serina was a spark of color in the sea of black uniforms surrounding them.

A herald stepped forward and cleared his throat nervously. "To mark the occasion of his fiftieth birthday, His Grace will be known henceforth as the First Dragon Duke of Arcosi," the announcement came.

"Dragon Duke?"

"Did he say *dragon*?"

The crowd buzzed like a swarm of bees at this news.

Milla dug her fingernails into her damp palms, trying to battle against the heat and a heady, hungry feeling that overwhelmed her now. It was too late. Milla's vision started breaking up in a sea of colored dots, and she grabbed at Tarya's hand as if she were drowning.

CHAPTER FIVE

M illa! What's wrong?" Tarya held her up. "Are you all right?"

She couldn't faint at the duke's ball. She was here to help Tarya, not the other way around. Milla fought the dizziness, bending down and shaking her head to banish the fog. "I'm fine," she whispered to Tarya. "Just hot." Her face and neck felt clammy, the purple dress too heavy and damp. She took long deep breaths and made herself focus on the duke's words.

"Today is not just my birthday," the duke said. "Tonight we celebrate fifty years in Arcosi. Fifty years since our fathers and grandfathers fled famine and plague in the Norlands and made it safe to these shores. Fifty years since our prayers were answered and we found Arcosi waiting for us. Arcosi: our haven, empty as a new shell waiting for the hermit crab . . ."

They all knew this story: Arcosi's own personal fairy tale.

Tarya turned to Milla. "Bet he skips the interesting bits . . . like how his family ended up in the palace!"

"Shhh!" Milla said, with a quick glance to check no one had heard. That was lower-town talk, the kind that could get you arrested. Everyone knew there were no dukes on those broken, wind-battered ships fifty years ago. Duke Olvar's ancestors had simply been the ones who had talked loudest, fought hardest, and took the best of the deserted island city for themselves.

"What? Everyone knows he's not noble, not like the duchess," Tarya hissed back. "She just had to marry him to seal the peace."

"Not the time. Not the place . . ." Isak told his twin between gritted teeth. "The guards are looking!"

"What?" Tarya repeated. "It's the truth!"

Milla squeezed her hand again, hoping she'd get the message. There was a fine line between fearless and reckless, and she was used to Tarya dancing all over it, but the stakes were higher tonight.

Nestan turned and glared at both twins, hawklike in his dark mask.

"We filled the ancient city with life once more," the duke was telling them. "And we were blessed in our endeavors. Our ships multiply and we prosper. Our children grow up without fear."

Some of them do. Milla felt uncomfortable contradicting this golden duke in her head, as she watched Tarya stifle a yawn.

"To mark this day—my birthday and the day our fathers

35

arrived here—I adopt the symbol of Arcosi, birthplace of dragons."

At that magic word, complete silence fell. Milla held her breath to listen.

"I take as my emblem this proud image of the city's past. The dragons are dead, like the former people of this place, perished in mystery . . ." The city was full of images of the lost dragons: carvings, statues. None of the wind-worn engravings showed where they'd gone.

"We remember them. We honor them." The duke's expression turned sorrowful. "But we are now the children of this city." He brightened. "We are the children of the dragon. And I am the Dragon Duke."

At that, dozens of trumpets sounded and actors trooped in, carrying aloft on wooden poles four enormous paper puppet dragons, lit from within so that each one seemed to be alive. The crowd murmured in delight.

The colors were dazzling. One was as blue as a peacock's feather, one as yellow as a cracked yolk, one as red as the blood Milla had seen spilled that day, one as green as a new spring leaf. The paper dragons spread their wings and danced around the duke in curving, sinuous flight, casting shadow dragons on the high walls. She saw the muscles stand out on the arms of the young puppeteers.

Finally, the duke clapped his hands and the dragon dancers all stopped, arranged around him. "Please," Olvar commanded, "enjoy the entertainment, the fireworks. Then, I will receive the young men's oaths of allegiance. Afterward, I invite you to feast, drink, and dance, here in my home. Tonight my doors are open to the people of Arcosi!"

The crowd paused. People were smiling, hands raised, about to applaud.

In that blink of an eye, a strange noise began: a high, keening wail.

Was this part of the show?

The wide grin vanished from the duke's face.

"You are *not* the Dragon Duke," a woman's voice screeched, as loud and yowling as a cat in the night.

Who was speaking? Milla peered around as the crowd held its breath.

The duke motioned with his hands, and his guards slipped from his side, moving silently through the bodies to find the unseen speaker.

"You are thieves! Interlopers. This is not your city!"

It was as if they were all turned to stone, all these gathered Norlander noblefolk.

"Keep your paper dragons! That's all you'll ever know."

Everybody stayed frozen, listening.

"We are the children of the dragons. This city was ours . . ." The woman spoke with the same rusty accent as the murdered man. "Our people were imprisoned. They died as they fled. Our blood is on this stone. Our ghosts haunt your beds. Can't you hear us?"

"Find her!" the duke roared. His face had turned paler than ever, except for a red patch on each cheek.

Milla pushed her way forward, ignoring the twins, to get

a closer look. She saw who was speaking: an old woman in the middle of the crowd.

The woman opened her arms and circled on the spot, apparently unafraid. She had gray hair shot with silver, gathered in a loose knot on her head, revealing gold hoops in her ears. Her skin was rich brown; her face was as weathered as a piece of driftwood. Her bearing was proud and straight, even as the guards pushed closer, hunting for her.

Milla saw the same black tattoo inked on her inner arm as she'd seen on the blue-cloaked man before he died. And the fabric of this woman's robe? It matched the dead man's exactly. Had they traveled here together, on that newly docked ship?

As the guards elbowed guests aside to reach her, the woman spoke faster: "We were ripped away from here. But I have returned to my home. And I am not the only one. Your days here are ending, you'll see . . ."

Her voice rose to a new volume, loud and clear, so no one missed a word: "We are coming home. The dragons of Arcosi will return! And they will *never* belong to you!"

Then the woman pulled her hood over her head and started moving toward the back of the hall.

"A reward for the capture of that woman!" the duke shouted. "Which way did she go?"

Milla watched the guards searching and said nothing.

As she passed, Milla locked gazes with the woman. Her bright, beady brown eyes held Milla's and she couldn't look away.

He's dead! Someone killed your friend. You're not safe!

Milla wanted to grab the woman and tell her what she'd seen, but her mouth seemed full of sawdust and no words came.

The woman's gaze dropped only for a moment, down to the gold disc around Milla's neck. The woman gasped and her eyes widened. Surprise, joy, fear: they flashed across the woman's face in rapid succession, like cloud shadows over the sea.

Milla's own face burned, under her mask.

The woman backed away, but kept her eyes fixed on Milla's as if she was trying to tell her something.

Her nearest neighbors turned to Milla, curious, to see what the woman was staring at. Milla ducked her head, grateful for the purple mask that covered her face. She started shuffling backward. Then she turned and tugged off the mask, shoving it in the pocket of the dress so it couldn't mark her out. She reached the platform where the duke and duchess stood. She circled around the platform surreptitiously, hoping no one would notice her.

Duchess Serina spoke quietly at her husband's side. Even frowning hard, she was stunningly beautiful, with clear tawny skin, high cheekbones, and expressive eyes that seemed black in the dim light.

"Call off your guards?" Serina asked the duke. "That woman looked elderly. Alone. She is no threat to us."

"My dear." Duke Olvar's tone was perfectly controlled and barely audible. He stared down at Duchess Serina. "Leave it. Let the guards deal with this . . ."

Behind the platform, Milla was close enough to see the

knuckles on the duke's hand turn white where his fingers gripped his wife's arm.

A flicker of movement caught Milla's eye. While everyone else was distracted, watching the guards search through the crowd, the old woman had reached the back of the hall, her dark blue cloak almost invisible in the shadows. She tugged aside a wall hanging and disappeared behind the tapestry.

No one else saw her go.

Milla felt the words rise in her throat. *She's there. She's escaping!* But she recalled the bright gleam of recognition in the woman's brown eyes and stayed silent.

CHAPTER SIX

The interruption had wrecked the timings. Fireworks started going off outside the hall. Milla could hear the wail and fizz as they shot up into the sky. People swarmed through the great doors of the hall to watch the display: sparkling golden blooms exploding in the air and shimmering down over the island. Milla stumbled, carried along by the crowd, as everyone poured out into the garden.

People tipped back their gaudy masks to see better, revealing rigid smiles pasted over shocked expressions. It didn't help that they were tinted gold, green, and pink by the light of the fireworks. Duke Olvar's face seemed carved in stone. Everything took on a tense, nightmarish air.

Milla found Tarya and Isak.

"Who was that old woman?" Tarya whispered under the noise of the fireworks. "Did she say *dragons*?"

"She can't mean real ones. She was just speaking in symbols,

41

like the duke. Wasn't she?" Milla still felt addled with heat and hunger.

"What did she mean, about the people who lived here once?" Isak looked horrified at the idea. He pushed his glasses up his nose. "It can't be true they're coming back!" His breathing had turned hollow and fast again.

"Breathe with me, Isak. Come on, let's sit here." Tarya put her hand on his back and took deep slow breaths for him to match. "That's better." Her face was all focus and concern for him.

"Well, someone must've built the city. And then vanished," Milla said. "What did you think?"

"She was angry. But it's not our fault!" Isak said in breathy gasps. "How could it be? The city was empty when our people arrived. And we were *born* here." He tilted forward, one finger on his eyeglasses to keep them in place. His breathing settled at last, as he stared down over the palace gardens and out to sea, where the last of the fireworks were reflected in little points of light. "This is our home. It's not our fault, whatever happened before."

"Well, where are these people?" Tarya said, still with one arm around her brother. "If it belongs to them, why don't they come and get it?"

"She didn't say it was our fault," Milla cut through them. "Just that people died. She wasn't blaming us—"

"Who cares about blame, what about *dragons*?" Tarya interrupted. "She said they're returning! People searched for years . . ."

Milla was saved from more questions by a new announcement from another tense-looking herald.

"The young men of Arcosi will swear their oaths to the Dragon Duke!"

"Now?" Isak asked. "I'm not ready, Tarya." The duke had invented an elaborate oath for the occasion of his birthday, and everyone would be listening.

Tarya helped Isak stand, took his mask, then straightened his glasses and smoothed down his shirt. "You can do this. You know the words. We all know those words, back to front and in our sleep. Right?"

Isak managed a weak smile. "Right."

"Good luck!" Milla called.

He nodded, looking unconvinced, and went to take his place in the line.

Milla moved to the back of the hall with the other servants. The Norlander maids edged away and looked down their noses at her, but she ignored their whispers, keeping her eyes fixed anxiously on Isak.

He recited his oath perfectly. He even stayed on the platform a little longer, chatting with Duke Olvar. When he walked back to his place, wearing a pewter medal inlaid with a black enamel dragon silhouette on a chain around his neck, he seemed energized after speaking to the duke. That was Olvar's talent: he drew people to him. He was their sun and they all turned their faces to his light.

Milla hurried to bring the twins platefuls of food, stealing a few discreet mouthfuls along the way so she could tell Josi it wasn't as good as her cooking. It was delicious, and she began to feel stronger again. After the guests had eaten, the palace musicians stepped up, and soon the old dragonhall was full of music.

"Time for the dance . . ." Tarya stared longingly toward the polished wooden dance floor, decorated with another fire-breathing black dragon. "But you'd better not risk it, Isak. You should rest. We'll just watch."

"I feel fine now. I'll just dance this one," he said, gulping. "It's the duke's ball. I owe it to him. He was so kind when he spoke to me. Did I tell you he asked me to sail with him?"

"Yes, three times already." Tarya rolled her eyes, but she was smiling.

"Here, hold my glasses for me, Milla?"

So it was Milla who watched, holding Isak's eyeglasses and Tarya's shawl and fan, one foot surreptitiously tapping out the beat. The twins were the best dancers here, Milla saw with pride. She watched Isak dance with a girl in a silver dress with long, blond hair and diamonds glittering at her neck. He moved smoothly, with perfect rhythm and control, and whatever he was saying made the girl laugh. You'd never guess how much it cost him.

Now Tarya swung past: she tackled dancing with the same energy she tackled everything else, and Milla couldn't help smiling as she watched her.

"She's beautiful," a voice spoke in her ear, making her jump. It was a tall young man, wearing a green feathered mask and a matching green silk jacket embroidered in silver thread.

"Yes, and that's not all she is . . ." Milla retorted protectively.

"So I hear." He stood very close, speaking so only she could hear. "That's good. I could do with a challenge." He drawled the long courtly Norlandish vowels, sounding just like the duke.

"You'll get it, dancing with Tarya Thornsen." He must be next in line on Tarya's dance card, but Milla didn't like the way the stranger's hungry gaze followed her friend around the dance floor. "She's no ordinary merchant's daughter, you know? She speaks three languages, she's practiced in archery, skilled with a longsword, and she throws a short dagger better than her father. She can brew a healing draft, draw a good scale map, and she's more fun than anyone in this room!" Milla drew breath, feeling her cheeks burning. She hadn't meant to say all that.

"Better and better." The tall young man pushed his mask up onto his forehead and smiled down at her.

Her mouth fell open. It was Vigo, the duke's son. Just like Skalla, the kitchen tomcat, he had a spoiled, languid air and a lazy fluid grace. He was much taller than Milla, with short, curling dark hair and very green eyes, adding to this catlike impression.

"And are you part of the package, little wildcat?"

Making her mind up in an instant, she decided to pretend he was just the same as anyone else. Otherwise she'd just stand there gaping like a goldfish and the guards would come and steer her away.

"No," Milla snapped, before remembering to add, "Your

Grace." She knew from city gossip that Vigo liked pretty girls, and they tended to like him right back.

She looked up at him, trying to decipher his words and his expression. There was keen interest in those green eyes, and something else, more disdainful. Did he think Tarya was beneath him? Then she noticed something. "Why aren't you wearing the dragon medal, like the others?"

"Did you hear me swear loyalty to my father?"

"No, Your Grace." Milla spotted Duke Olvar in the crowd. Isak had stopped dancing and was talking intently to the duke.

Vigo switched to Sartolan, lowering his voice: "I might have had the misfortune to be born his son, but it doesn't mean I have to like it. Although he does have some good ideas," he murmured, keeping his glance on Tarya. "Please, excuse me," he said to Milla, slipping through the crowd to the dance floor.

Vigo tapped the shoulder of Tarya's current partner. Apologizing charmingly, he took Tarya's hand and bowed to her. Milla was too far away to hear what he asked, but she saw Tarya's nod in reply.

Vigo and Tarya started to dance.

The other couples noticed the new pair and left space around them. The dance suited them both: fast and complicated, it demanded tight control. They spun around the floor, gathering speed, perfectly matched.

Milla watched with an uncomfortable premonition gathering weight in her chest. Without losing the formal steps of the dance, Vigo added moves to surprise Tarya. She followed his lead, keeping pace and adding flourishes of her own. Already a combative dance, it became a kind of duel, as both dancers stretched its formal pattern to the utter limit.

Tarya held herself very straight and tall. In perfect time to the music, she snapped her head around as they changed direction, then kicked into the air, as high as her dress allowed.

Vigo tipped her backward, and for a moment she resisted, almost falling, then she gave in and allowed him to take her weight on his arm.

Milla couldn't look away.

Tarya was glaring at Vigo. He smiled down at her, lip curling in that catlike way.

A plump woman with wine-reddened cheeks said, "Well, if he chooses her, at least she is a Norlander." She lowered her voice to whisper, "Not like his mother . . ."

"Hush! You can't say that!"

"Why not?" the woman said. "It's what we're all thinking. About time he was betrothed, too. And she'll bring a fine dowry, Nestan's daughter."

Nestan wouldn't promise Tarya to Vigo, not without telling her first! But Milla's sinking feeling plummeted ocean-deep at those words. The woman was right. If the duke wanted to fund his growing army of soldiers, who was richer than Nestan? Milla knew the rumors. Nestan had saved Olvar's life in the last war—almost losing his own. Olvar paid him in guilt money afterward. Nestan used that gold to buy his first ships, and now his wealth was unparalled.

But a betrothal? It made sense of Isak's angry words to his father.

Milla had to warn Tarya, quickly, before anyone else did. She took one step forward, ready to dart in with some excuse. She was too late.

Tarya and Vigo stood together in the middle of the dance floor, perfectly still, face-to-face. His lips were moving.

Tarya pulled back from Vigo, snatching away her hands.

There was an audible intake of breath from the watching crowd.

Tarya looked furious. Noticing the stares fixed on her, she forced a smile and fanned her face with a hand. "Sorry, please forgive me, Your Grace, I need air." She fled from the hall.

Turning to run after her, Milla caught sight of Nestan's face. He looked up and met her eyes and for a second he looked guilty. What had he done?

Milla caught up with Tarya in the garden. She put one hand on her shoulder, feeling her skin, hot under the flimsy silk sleeve of her dress.

"Leave me alone—" Tarya began, spinning around. "Oh, it's you. I didn't mean you." Her face crumpled. "Milla . . ."

Milla saw the tears on Tarya's cheeks, silvered in the moonlight. She reached up and opened her arms to her.

Tarya pulled her close and sobbed into her curls. "Father's promised me in betrothal . . . to him!" Then she lifted her face and wiped it, shaking the tears away angrily. "And Vigo just loved telling me. What an arrogant, smug, spoiled . . ."

So it was true. This was Nestan's plan for his daughter— the one he and Isak had been fighting about earlier. "It's all right, shhh!" Milla hugged Tarya, finding words of comfort, even if she didn't believe them yet. "We'll find a way through this. It's going to be all right."

"I won't do it." Tarya's anger seemed to win now. "You're always telling me there are choices, Milla, and this is mine."

"What do you mean? What's your choice?"

"Even if I have to jump from the palace walls on my wedding day, I'm not . . . marrying . . . *him*."

Milla kept her arms around Tarya, staring up at the pearly moon above them, wondering how her world could change so much in one single day. Her secret burned inside her, but she stayed silent, for now.

CHAPTER SEVEN

They got home just before sunrise. The sky was fading to a mist-shrouded blue, and even Tarya was yawning and stumbling as they walked through the gates of the Yellow House. Milla had persuaded her to return to the dance floor—"Come on, Tarya! Show him. Show everyone your kind of courage!"—and she had stayed there all night, avoiding Vigo's gaze.

Even though she was exhausted, Milla sat up, waiting for everyone else to fall asleep. Her pallet bed was tucked in a corner of the first-floor hallway, in case Tarya called for her during the night. She changed back into her usual tunic and leggings, trying not to make a sound. Then she crept down the main staircase, listening hard. She paused in the hallway, by the portait of Vianna, trying not to feel as if it was watching her disapprovingly. She heard nothing but deep breathing and gravelly snores, and some distant music from parties in the lower city.

Only then did she creep back out into the garden.

It was time to discover the truth about the hidden bag. It felt strange, doing something so entirely for herself, something only she knew about. But if the bag held something dangerous, better it should hurt only one person. And if it held rubies, then there was an escape route for Tarya and Isak and for her.

She hoisted herself again into the orange tree, pushing through the leaves and branches to that little cave of greenness, feeling that it might be the last time. It didn't feel like a safe haven anymore.

She unhooked the pannier and placed it carefully around her neck. Two of the padded pockets hung down near her shoulder blades, the other two rested on her chest. They were lighter than she expected, and there was no sloshing liquid as she moved, only a strange, gathered density centered in each pocket. It was beautiful, the main strap embroidered in gold thread with a pattern of leaves or flames. Each of the pockets was a different color: subtle, jeweled shades of crimson, kingfisher, primrose, moss. The bag alone was worth more than she'd ever own, never mind what was inside it.

She reached out and pushed some of the orange tree's branches aside, letting more light into her refuge. Then, with trembling fingers, she reached down and struggled to unhook one carved ivory button from its tiny loop. Finally, she freed the lid on the blue pocket. Just at that moment, the first rays of the sun slanted through, dappling her with brightness.

She held her breath. How did firepowder ignite? She sent a prayer out into the pale morning and peered down.

Milla saw a smooth, gleaming expanse nestling in a deep velvet surround. There was a rounded dome inside, a light turquoise blue, dotted with dark gold speckles like the first drops of rain on stone. Gently she wiggled her fingers down the sides and lifted it out.

It was smooth and egg-shaped. It was larger than both her hands: she held it between her palms and stared. Was it real? Surely it was too big to belong to a bird. Perhaps it was an ornament?

She tapped it lightly with one fingernail: it sounded neither hollow nor solid, but something between the two. It could be a rare bird: an eagle for the duke to hunt with, perhaps?

She bent down and touched her lips to it, finding it surprisingly warm and slightly damp. It wasn't made of stone. It felt full of potential. Alive and quickening. A pulse of excitement fizzled up her spine, as an incredible idea took shape.

The old woman at the ball had spoken of dragons returning to Arcosi. A man had been killed. If these were dragon eggs, it would explain why.

Dragon eggs?

It couldn't be. She was tired. She was dreaming. Didn't Josi always say her imagination was too wild?

Men had fought and died and sailed to the ends of the earth in search of dragon eggs. No one brought back even a rumor of seeing one.

It must be treasure. A gemstone, maybe lapis, or quartz?

But her heart said otherwise.

"Hello, you," she whispered, feeling ridiculous for speaking to the thing. But she felt a pull toward it that she could not explain. She sat there for a long while as dawn became day, cradling it against her chest, like the beat at the heart of her life.

Finally, swaying with exhaustion, she almost fell from the branch. Reluctantly, she eased the blue egg back into the safety of its pocket before she could drop it. She opened all the other pockets and checked—three more eggs, each a different shade, just like the pockets themselves: yellow, red, and green.

She knew she should go straight to Nestan and tell him what she'd found. That was what a good servant would do. He would know what these eggs were. He would know what to do. But she'd have to admit she was there—that she'd seen the murder and done nothing. What if he blamed her? Her sleepy thoughts felt muddled and confused.

She'd ask the twins, she decided, yawning. As soon as a good moment came along. When Tarya had calmed down, she'd ask her advice.

For now, Milla had a promise to a dead man to keep, and a new, deep protectiveness welling up inside her. "I'll look after you!" she whispered. Whatever they were, she couldn't give them up. She knew it as well as she knew her own name.

Guarding the eggs as carefully as a newborn baby, with one arm clasped across the front pockets, she climbed slowly down, one-handed, trying not to jolt the pannier. With her heart beating hard underneath the padded fabric, Milla stole across the garden. She circled the kitchen building, moving as silently as Skalla when he was hunting field mice. The smokehouse leaned against the rear of the main oven's chimney stack. She drew aside the leather curtain that sealed the wooden door and slipped inside.

The smoke caught at her throat immediately: rich, pungent, and gently acrid, carrying the aroma of curing fish and cheese. She reached up in the darkness, fumbling past the heavy sides of fish, to the large bunch of sage leaves she'd hung there yesterday. She took them down, hooked the pannier up high, and then replaced the herbs on top.

"There, you'll be safe." There was no reason for anyone else to come in here and look up into the dim, smoky warmth. Even if they did, you could barely see the bag.

She stumbled to her pallet bed. Now she lay awake, staring at the ceiling, trying to decide what to do, till the exhaustion won and she fell into a shallow sleep.

CHAPTER EIGHT

M illa dreamt of blue. Deep endless blue, like the sea. In her dream, she soared over blue water. She flew through misty blue air. She was lifted and held by blueness. There was music, too. She sang out, loud and clear. The same repeating notes, going up and then down again. The tune came echoing back to her. And in her dream she was happier than she had ever been. She was bathed in joy, like hot sunshine. And it was all because of—

"Milla! Where is she? She's late!" Lanys's angry words floated up the main staircase, getting closer.

Nearby, she could hear Isak singing, for the first time in days: maybe that explained the music in her dream.

Milla scrambled to her feet and fled down the steep back stairs. She went straight out to check on the eggs, still half-asleep. She blinked up at the bright blue sky, trying to wrap herself in the dream and hug that perfect feeling to herself a little longer. She pursed her lips and blew, to capture the tune before it faded. Those five plaintive notes . . . Too late, it was gone.

In the gloom of the smokehouse, she eased each egg from its hiding place. She greeted them in turn, lingering over the blue one, checking for damage, and then she carefully hid them all again. She emerged, squinting against the late-morning sunshine, while her thoughts chased themselves in circles.

Her gaze fell on the kitchen window, and what she saw jolted her wide-awake. Inside, Nestan and Josi stood in a tight embrace. As Milla watched, Nestan pulled away and wiped Josi's damp cheek tenderly.

"Where have you been?" Lanys demanded.

Milla jumped guiltily and spun around. "Just checking on the new cheeses," she lied, barring the entrance to the smokehouse.

"Here, you take this. Breakfast is your job. Just because they took you to the palace, don't get any ideas." Lanys scowled at Milla, pushing a tray of dirty plates at her.

Milla took it, too stunned to reply.

Even her silence enraged Lanys.

"Go on, then, laze around all you like. You know what last night's news means? After the twins leave, they won't need two maids anymore. They found you in the street and that's where they'll dump you, just you wait and see." Lanys hissed these last words and then strode back into the house.

Feeling winded, Milla stumbled toward the kitchen with the heavy tray.

"All right, Milla?" Nestan emerged, looking as troubled as she felt. "Did you sleep at all?"

Milla mumbled incoherently, robbed of words.

"You'd better get in there . . ." Nestan patted her arm and left.

Milla went in and put the tray down.

Josi was standing at the workbench with her back to Milla, her short black hair tucked behind her ears. She was hacking with a cleaver at a joint of lamb that really didn't need such savage treatment. Above her head hung the empty pans, two hares waiting to be skinned, a plaited bunch of onions, and some fresh basil, just picked, scenting the air with greenness.

Just standing in the kitchen made Milla feel better. If the Yellow House was her home, the kitchen was its heart. Everyone came here sooner or later, drawn by the warmth and the irresistible smells that poured from its window all day long. Josi's temper might be legendary, but so was her cooking and her wise advice.

"Josi?" Milla asked, trying not to startle her. They always spoke Sartolan together, ready to switch to Norlandish the moment anyone walked in.

With a loud thwack, the cleaver buried itself in the wooden chopping board.

"What's wrong?" Milla was shocked to see tears streaming down Josi's face. She'd never seen her cry before. She'd never seen Nestan and Josi together like that. The ground seemed to shift uneasily beneath her feet.

"Nothing—just onions!" Josi said curtly, throwing the meat in the pot, clattering the lid down.

That wasn't true. Milla caught sight of the onions, all

57

cooked through with thyme and garlic, well past causing tears.

"What are you doing up?" Josi demanded. "I sent Lanys to serve breakfast so you could rest." She wiped her face on her apron.

"I know."

"I think you mean thank you," Josi said tartly, but her dark eyes were warm and dancing with life again. Then she noticed Milla's expression. "What is it?" She came and put her hands on her shoulders, those bright perceptive eyes searching Milla's.

"Oh, Josi," Milla began, sensing a torrent of words threatening to spill out, about the murder, the eggs, the duke's ball last night. She longed to ask Josi for advice: the words sprang to her tongue. She must know about the man who was killed, right outside her kitchen door.

Then she froze. If Josi was with Nestan now, it changed everything. They wouldn't be equals anymore. Josi would be lady of the house. People married out of their own community all the time; even the duke had done that. And her friend Thom's mother was Sartolan, his dad Norlander. But Nestan and Josi . . . Milla had not seen that one coming. So Milla bit the words down, like bitter medicine. If she told Josi, she'd tell Nestan, Nestan would tell the duke, and the duke would be given the bag and its precious contents before the day was through.

"It's all right, kitten." Josi pulled her into a hug. "You can tell me."

But Milla tugged herself free. She wasn't sure of anything

anymore. She sat down on the little stool by the fire. Skalla the kitchen cat came and meowed loudly, till she let him jump onto her lap. She stroked his black fur absentmindedly.

"Here." Josi passed her a heel of bread smeared with goat's cheese, followed by a bowl of warm milk with nutmeg and honey stirred into it.

Milla stared into the flames and dipped the bread in the milk, comforted by good food and Skalla's warm purring bulk, anchoring her.

"So, are you going to tell me what's wrong?" Josi tried again. "Is it about Lady Tarya's betrothal?"

She nodded: it was a safe place to start. "Lanys said they won't need two maids when Tarya leaves for the palace. What's going to happen to me? Will Nestan"—she whispered it—"get rid of me?"

"Is Lanys in charge of this household?" Josi snapped.

"No."

"So why would you listen to her? Lanys is just jealous. You and Tarya have been friends since the day you arrived, and nothing is going to change that. You'll always have a home here."

Josi's words warmed Milla like the heat from the fire. She let Skalla lick the crumbs of cheese off her fingertips, smiling at the feel of his small rough tongue.

"What's going to happen?" Josi was saying. "Honestly? I don't know."

"They probably won't want someone like me in the palace, will they?" Milla asked. "But if Tarya is married, she'll still need me."

"She will, love, she will," Josi agreed. "But needing and getting are quite different things, as you and I both know." She started shaking fine wheat flour into a bowl.

Milla felt stupid for not guessing this might happen one day. "But . . . but, if Tarya goes, will I go, too? I don't want to leave you, Josi!" Everything was changing so suddenly, she felt dizzy with it.

Living here, working here, it was all Milla had ever known. It was different for the twins: their memories of their mother faded gradually, like the beautiful mural portrait of Vianna that covered one wall of the entrance hall. And just as the portrait was retouched with fresh paint to keep it vibrant, so the stories about Vianna kept her memory alive.

Milla had no memories of anything else. No stories. No mother.

With a jolt, she remembered how the old woman had stared at her last night. She lifted her medal on its golden chain and rubbed the skin-warmed gold against her bottom lip, feeling the tiny outline of the dragon and the moon. Lanys's words were painfully fresh in her mind. "Josi, where did the twins' mother find me?"

Josi's voice softened. "I'm sorry, kitten, we don't know. When Vianna died, your story died, too," she said, her hands busy now rubbing fat into the flour.

"So when was that? How old am I?"

"You know all this!" Josi said, not meeting Milla's eyes. "We guessed you were two then, so you're twelve now. Thirteen next spring."

"It's not a proper birthday, though, is it? Just one you made up."

"It felt right," Josi said, looking down very deliberately.

Milla watched her keenly. What wasn't she telling her? "So my family could be anyone?" She'd thought about this a lot. She imagined a wealthy family on the mainland of Sartola, dark-eyed brothers and sisters who looked like her. Or a sailor's family, at sea in all weathers. Or a trader's clan, seeing the world, bartering, bringing back spice and silk and ceramics.

"Could be," Josi said. "But why do you need to know? You've a place to sleep, people who care for you. That's more than some. Isn't it enough?"

Once, Milla had loved hearing these stories, believing they bound her to Josi, to the twins and Nestan. But on this bright morning, the day after everything had changed, suddenly it wasn't enough.

Milla needed to know more.

CHAPTER NINE

W hen Josi sent her to market, Milla wanted to disobey. *No!* she almost cried. *I can't leave the eggs. Don't be ridiculous*, she scolded herself. *What are you, a mother hen? They aren't yours, and they might not hatch anyway.* But as she stood, reluctantly, the thought of the four eggs tugged painfully at her heart.

On the storeroom shelves, Milla found two baskets and the worn slips of stamped parchment that would identify her. She started to wind a scarf over her hair to keep the sun from her eyes, sore and gritty with exhaustion.

A shadow fell through the doorway, and she leapt around with a yelp of alarm, suddenly convinced it was yesterday's assassin come back for her.

"Steady, Milla," said Richal Finn. "What's wrong?" He filled the doorway, solid and dependable as ever.

"Sorry! Jumpy today." She put her hand on his arm, relieved it was only him. "Just tired, after last night."

"Strange evening," he agreed. "But don't worry, you're safe now." His tone turned almost gossipy, as he asked, "And what about Lady Tarya and the duke's son?"

Milla glanced at him, curious. That wasn't like Finn. Was he checking on her, or Tarya? "She'll be fine. She just needs some time, you'll see." She turned and crossed the courtyard, with Finn by her side.

Lanys was in the doorway, watching, a look of furious envy on her face as Milla chatted easily to Richal Finn. Milla chose to ignore her.

"Should I expect her down the practice yard later, you think?" he asked. "Better get some thicker armor while she takes out her frustration, eh?"

"Be ready for a beating, Finn." Milla smiled in spite of herself, picturing it. "Rather you than me. I'll have a skin of ale cooling in the well for you afterward, shall I?"

"Cheers, Milla. You going down into the city? I'll come with you; I'm headed that way," Finn said, opening the gates.

"Sure." She was glad to have Finn by her side: tall, calm, and undemanding. They set off down the main road and hit a patrol almost immediately.

"Papers!" the first guardsman yelled when he reached Milla. He caught sight of Finn and modified his tone slightly. "Do you have permission to walk in the upper town?"

She watched how differently they treated Richal Finn, because he was Norlander. Well, she might not know who her family was, but it was evident to everyone that she was not of Norlander descent, and she braced herself for an interrogation yet again.

"Yes." She produced her papers and recited the information wearily: "I work for the Thornsen family. Second-generation Norlanders. Yellow House." It was a daily ordeal, but today Milla felt unhinged with tiredness. She had a sudden crazed urge to shout her suspicions out loud: *I found dragon eggs! The dragons are returning! They're already here!*

People would scream and rush forward, shouting, *Where? I want to see the dragons!* She'd be crushed, surrounded by desperate, eager faces. The guards would drag her away, for questioning by the duke himself.

She blinked, and the daydream vanished. That's all it was: A dream. A mirage. Wishful thinking, nothing more.

The guard waved her through, and Milla called goodbye to Finn when they went separate ways at the busy docks and the marketplace.

Traders called out their best prices. Their rhythmic patter filled the air like birdsong. She heard bickering and bartering in Norlandish, in Sartolan, in dialects she could only guess at. There were Silk Islanders with their neat jackets and brightly printed skirts; merchants from the far south, wearing thick gold armbands that glinted dully in the sunshine. Arcosi was a jewel of an island, where all the main trade routes crossed, so its marketplace was always full of riches: intricate gold jewelery, fragrant spices, precious glazed ceramics, and the softest leatherwork. One sailor had a tame bird riding his shoulder, its feathers as red as blood, and one yellow eye beadily watching Milla as she slipped past.

She reached the main marketplace and breathed in deeply, half closing her eyes, enjoying the familiar smell of the market: sweet cinnamon doughnuts frying in a large pan to her left, strong dark coffee brewing in a tall metal pot on a stall to her right, the warm stink of pack mules patiently waiting in the shade. But when she opened them, blinking, Milla saw there was something wrong. People huddled in tight groups, looking around uneasily.

There were too many guardsmen here, spreading out through the marketplace like a dirty stain. Their black uniforms outnumbered the colorful hotchpotch of ordinary clothes.

Milla speeded up, heading to her friend Rosa's stall. As she jostled her way through the crowd, a guardsman turned and sneered, "What's your hurry?" He paused to stick one foot out, very deliberately.

Too late to avoid it, Milla tripped. She sprawled forward, baskets flying, skinning her palms on the loose gravel. Hot and humiliated, she spat away dust and wearily climbed to her feet.

"Oi! You bully. Haven't you got anything better to do?" Rosa was there, helping Milla to stand and dust off her tunic.

The guard was smirking, still enjoying Milla's fall.

"Leave it, Rosa, it's not worth it," Milla hissed. She'd seen people beaten and arrested for less.

But Rosa bawled out, so loudly that everyone stopped to stare, "Oh, wait, don't tell me, that's the only way you can get a girl to notice you?"

Snickers of amusement passed through the crowd.

Milla saw the guardsman flush crimson. His eyes narrowed as he glared at Rosa.

She watched in horror as his hand flew to the hilt of his sword.

CHAPTER TEN

Thinking fast, Milla reached out and tickled the hind leg of a tethered mule with the scratchy handle of her basket. The mule kicked out, knocking over a tall jar of wine, which spilled in the dust like blood. The stallholders began arguing, voices raised, hands waving. In the hubbub, no one was looking at the girls.

Milla tugged Rosa quickly away through the crowd, back to her stall. "You shouldn't antagonize them." She knew Rosa's family couldn't afford the release fee if she was arrested.

"I'm sick of it! Who do they think they are? He wouldn't dare trip a Norlander maid. Are you hurt?"

"I'm fine, really." She ignored the pain in her hands and glanced backward to check no one was following them. "But thank you."

Now that they were safe, they turned and hugged each other hard.

"How are you? How was last night?" Milla demanded.

Rosa grinned broadly and wiggled herself up to perch on the wooden planks of her family's stall, laid out with fruit, cheese, and Sartolan wine imported from the mainland. "You should've come down here—we missed you at the street party . . ."

"You *did* take some wine!" Milla whispered. "I knew it!"

"I shared it," Rosa said mock-defensively. "Made me some new friends, that bottle did. And not all of them were boring." She told Milla about her evening, making her laugh for the first time that day.

"I wish I'd been there . . ."

"Did they leave you behind again?" A shadow of concern passed over Rosa's beautiful heart-shaped face. She had huge brown eyes, usually full of laughter, and her tight black plaits stuck out sideways from under her red scarf.

Milla said, "First, tell me, what's all this about?" She tilted her head surreptitiously toward the duke's soldiers. "What are people saying? What's going on?" Gossip flowed downhill in Arcosi, like the spring water, gathering momentum along the way. Rosa always knew the latest.

"Haven't you heard? They say the duke had an unexpected guest at his precious ball, doom and gloom all around." She retold an exaggerated version of the old woman's outburst at the palace. "It's the curse of Arcosi, Dad says, just like the old days."

"What curse of Arcosi? That's rubbish! No one ever said the city was cursed before last night." Milla shivered. She didn't want to hear about curses, not today.

"You know—the legacy of mad Duke Rufus? Last duke of

68

Old Arcosi? Won the war against Sartola on his dragon, then vanished?" Rosa asked. "Every kid knows that one."

"I work for Norlanders; they have different stories." Milla watched the soldiers moving from stall to stall. "So, is that who they're looking for? That old woman from the ball?" She remembered the duke's offer of a reward for her capture.

"Nah, watch them. They're looking for something quite small, something that would fit in those crates."

Milla felt the blood rush to her cheeks at this news. They must be searching for the eggs.

With her heart banging out a protest, Milla watched the soldiers rummage through the stall opposite them. Had they searched the Yellow House yet? She gripped her baskets tightly, resisting the urge to run home and check. She hoped her flush didn't show.

"See how nice they are with the Norlander marketfolk." Rosa swore at them quietly. "Bet we get it worse. Sartolans always do, even when we outnumber them. Especially then . . ."

"I'll stay with you," Milla said. "And to answer your question, no, they didn't leave me behind. I was there . . ."

"What? You saw the duke?" Rosa almost fell off the stall. "What's he like? And his son—isn't he gorgeous?" She put a hand on Milla's sleeve, smiling now as she remembered. "I did see him, last year, lovely eyes . . ."

Milla glanced away from the soldiers for a moment, thinking of Vigo, and immediately of Tarya. If the betrothal took place, Tarya would be talked about like this. Every dress, every gesture, every word would be commented on, till she was something both less and more than a real person. How would Tarya live with that kind of scrutiny?

Rosa was watching and misread her hesitation. "Oh, well, if you don't want to tell me—"

"It's not that," Milla said quickly. "I was thinking of something Vigo said . . ."

"*Vigo?* Oh! First names, is it? You didn't really speak to him?"

Milla nodded, seeing Rosa's expression change.

"Oh, so you don't need to hear all this from me if you were actually there!" Rosa snapped, hurt. "Well, just make sure you don't forget your real friends, next time you're dancing at the palace with the duke's own son . . ."

Milla started saying, "*I* didn't dance with him—" but she was interrupted by the duke's soldiers reaching them.

"Open these crates up, quickly now," the officer said, banging loudly on the wooden slats of the stall.

One of the younger soldiers lifted a box of fruit awkwardly and then dropped it again.

"Hey!" Rosa shouted. "You'll bruise the fruit. Careful!"

The officer cuffed the younger man around the ear, growling, "Did you forget the duke's orders? This cargo is fragile. Anyone breaks it, anyone hides it, they pay with their life, got it?"

With their life? Milla's mouth felt as dry as sunbaked sand. The duke really wanted those eggs. The assassin must have been working for him. He must have reported back to the duke. Perhaps they were searching the Yellow House right now. Whose life would they take if they found the eggs there?

70

She licked her dry lips and managed to ask hoarsely, "What is it you're looking for?"

"Hold your tongue, missy. None of your business!" the man shouted at her, muttering about Sartolans as he turned away.

The younger soldier met Milla's eye. He wasn't Norlander either: as the duke's army expanded relentlessly, it was forced to let others in at the lower ranks. *Sorry!* he mouthed, and hurried after the older man.

"Oi, what about the peaches? You can't just ruin them and walk away!" Rosa called after them. "Mom and Dad will go mad." She jumped down and gathered up the fruit that had been spilled.

"Look at these, all bruised now. I bet we don't even cover the cost of the stall today. It's so unfair. One day," she said hotly, "one day soon, I'm going to do something about this." Rosa stood up carefully, with her apron full of dusty peaches, glaring across the marketplace with open resentment. "I swear I will!"

The shady side was reserved for stallholders of Norlander descent: the coolness protected their wares. Milla could have shopped there—Nestan's paperwork permitted it—but she stayed loyal to Rosa, knowing how tough times were. She'd never heard Rosa sound so bitter, so ready to snap.

"Josi wants a load of stuff; just add those in, she'll stew them up tonight," Milla said, giving Rosa her list. With an effort, she made her voice sound normal. "Thanks, Rosa. You know, I wish I'd been here with you last night, don't you?" It was mostly true. "Promise? I'll see you next week."

71

Milla had a half day's rest every second week and she always spent it with Rosa and Thom.

She kissed Rosa on both cheeks and hurried away, balancing a basket on each arm, heading for the smugglers' steps to avoid more patrols. As she rushed along the crowded dockside, a piercing whistle split the air.

"Milla!" Thom Windlass was standing on the dock next to his father's fishing boat, the *Dolphin*, poised by the thick coil of rope that bound it fast. His wide, handsome face lit up at the sight of her.

"Thom!" She couldn't help grinning back.

"Hey, stranger! Where were you last night?"

Smiling at Thom, with the sparkling sea behind him, this morning's dream resurfaced briefly: that sense of freedom, that fleeting tune. It faded again, leaving Milla aching for it.

"I was at the palace, with the twins." She gestured up the hill. "Anyway, what are you doing, going out at this time?" She caught sight of the empty crates he'd just loaded, and teased, "Late start, is it, after the parties?"

"Gotta be joking, Milla. Going out again, you mean. Dad would never sleep in; it's in his blood to be up before dawn." Thom looked tired. His large brown eyes were ringed with shadows. "Great party, though. Those fireworks! Did you see them, from up there?"

"Sure. But why two trips today?" Milla knew Simeon Windlass was hardworking, but this wasn't right.

"Winds are changing. Storm coming, Dad says. First of the autumn, and big, too. We won't put out of harbor for days, so we got to do double till it brews."

72

"I'll let you get out, then," she said. *"May the winds be swift and the tides be kind,"* she added, using the old sailors' blessing. She put her baskets down and rummaged in one. "Here, Rosa gave me extra peaches—catch!"

"Thanks," Thom said. "You take care in the storm." That was typical of Thom, thinking of her when he was the one who'd be out in it.

"Now, Thomsen!" Simeon roared suddenly, all his preparations complete.

Thom jumped to obey. He uncoiled the heavy rope and twined it in a loop around his arm, then leapt the growing gap between dock and boat. He cleared it easily with his long legs.

"When?" Milla thought to shout, just as she reached the steps. "How long before the storm?"

Simeon looked at the sky. "By dawn tomorrow, it'll be here."

"Home safe, both of you!"

Thom nodded in farewell, the peach clenched between his teeth as his hands worked to stow the ropes.

Milla dashed for the steps. She turned, briefly, just as the *Dolphin* passed through the massive harbor gates—the sea suddenly came alive and the boat was tossed around. It crested one wave and then disappeared into the trough of the next.

Then she turned her back on her friend and ran to see if her secret had been discovered. The officer's words kept echoing through her mind: *they pay with their life; they pay with their life.*

73

She didn't stop running till she reached the smokehouse. Forgetting caution, she dropped her baskets outside and dashed straight in to check on the eggs.

She sighed and patted the pockets gently. "Hello there, how are you?" she whispered, opening the blue pocket first.

She sang to the blue egg, the half-remembered tune from her dream, lingering there in the gloom till people started yelling her name and she was summoned back to work.

CHAPTER ELEVEN

T he storm hit Arcosi in the night, just as Thom and Simeon had warned. Milla jerked awake, startled by the rain on the roof like pattering feet.

The eggs! What if they got wet?

She must have checked on them a dozen times yesterday. Now she padded down through the darkened house. When she opened the door, the wind almost wrenched it from her grasp. She held it with difficulty, cursing in whispers, stopping it before it slammed against the wall and woke everyone inside. Moments later, in the velvety darkness of the smokehouse, she lifted down the bag with the eggs and placed it around her neck. They were dry. They were safe.

It was a risk, but she curled her body carefully around the bag and dozed through the night with them. The dreams returned.

She was back in that perfect blue, speeding through mist, hair streaming behind her. She sang the five notes: up and down again. Then she threw her head back and laughed, letting the wind snatch her breath away. When she looked down, her hands touched cool blue scales . . .

Milla woke with a start. She sat up, breathing hard. The bag was there.

"Morning," she whispered, bending down to stroke the blue egg with a fingertip. "I'm glad you're inside, out of this storm. You stay here and no one will find you."

The eggs were warm, maybe even warmer than yesterday, which seemed odd. Milla had let the smokehouse fire go out because of the storm. But perhaps the eggs retained heat?

She spoke quietly to the eggs: "Wish me luck, stuck inside today with the twins and their father, all of them in moods as dark as that sky.

"Tarya's protesting her betrothal—not sure how long she'll keep that one up. Isak's not speaking to anyone, and that's even worse."

She rocked them slowly, absentmindedly humming that five-note tune again. "Nestan's feeling guilty about them both. That always makes him grumpy, so he's shouting and fussing and we've all got to jump to it . . .

"Looks like that killer got clean away, too. No one's seen him since. You're safe here, don't you worry. At least the soldiers haven't come to search here yet."

On she crooned, telling the eggs everything that was on her mind. It felt good to be speaking honestly to someone, even if they couldn't reply. What had life been like before the eggs? She could barely recall: it was as if they'd always been here. At the back of her mind, the need to decide what to do with them flapped anxiously, trying to get her attention, but she looked away.

She heard a movement in the kitchen on the other side of the chimney. Josi was awake, hanging the kettle on its hook to boil.

"Bye-bye, eggs," Milla said. "See you soon." She walked, yawning, into the kitchen, as if everything were normal, as if every bone in her body didn't scream to stay there in the dark with the eggs. She'd never had anything of her own to look after before.

That must be why she thought of them every waking hour. Every breath. Every heartbeat.

When Milla had left the smokehouse, from deep inside the pannier came an answering noise: *Tap! Tap, tap!*

Milla built fires, carried water, washed clothes, and wrung them out to dry. She cooked breakfast, washed plates, chopped wood, and fed fires. It was still only the middle of the morning when the duke's soldiers arrived.

Milla was crossing to the kitchen door with a handful of hen's eggs she'd just collected from the chicken roost, when Finn opened the gate and let the guards file in, six tall men in the duke's black livery.

This was it. They'd found her. They knew about the bag. Everything seemed to move in slow motion: her fingers dropping the hen's eggs, the bright splash of yolk across the slick wet tiles.

"Milla? Are you all right?" Finn put a gentle hand on her arm.

The soldiers were blocking the gate. There was nowhere to

77

run. "The twins," she managed to croak. Surely there was time for goodbye, before they took her? She ran for the stairs.

Tarya was playing chess against herself, in the middle of her crumpled bed, but she jumped up when Milla burst in. "What's wrong? You look like you've seen a ghost!"

There was a boulder on Milla's chest, stopping her from speaking. Instead, she put her arms around Tarya and hugged her hard for the last time as tears came spilling from her eyes.

"Hey! What is it?"

Lanys knocked at the door. "It's Her Grace the Duchess Serina and His Grace Vigo Refarson, to see Lady Tarya . . ."

Tarya pulled away as if she'd been stung.

Relief flooded through Milla. The soldiers weren't here for the bag of eggs! They weren't here to take her away. That ebbed as she realized they were here to take Tarya away. Maybe not now, but one day soon, it would happen. She sniffed hard, wiping her eyes on her sleeve.

"No! Not here!" Tarya began pacing wildly, like a newly caged bird. "Milla, I can't talk to him." Her eyes were wide with distress and her hair stood out in crazed tufts, like a ruff of feathers. As she passed the low table, her nightdress caught a plate and swept it to the floor with a crash.

Milla swooped to remove the shards before Tarya stood on them. She came back to herself with a rush: she had a job to do, right here. Tarya needed her.

"Shh, go steady, or you'll hurt yourself." She moved fast now, pulling a dress from Tarya's clothes chest. "Here, let's get this on." Then she knotted a scarlet wrap around Tarya's shoulders and replaited her thick hair. "There, that'll do." Milla put her hands on Tarya's shoulders. "He's come out in a storm to see you. You can't leave him waiting. Ready?"

"Well, I bet he came in a carriage—you just check if his feet are dry." But Tarya raised her chin and stood tall, shoulders braced back. "Ready as I'll ever be. Don't leave me, Milla?"

"I won't."

They walked down into Nestan's favorite room, where the tall glass windows showed the raging tempest outside. Huge, white-topped waves flung themselves at the island, battering against the harbor wall, furious at being locked out. Serina and Vigo were indeed perfectly dry, in their silks and velvet cloaks, sitting in the best chairs while Lanys served them drinks. Nestan and Isak were both watching Tarya approach, as if she were a keg of firepowder and Vigo held a flame.

Nestan stood, clearing his throat. "Ah, here's my daughter, Lady Tarya."

When all the formal greetings were done, Serina asked, "And this is?" She was smiling at Milla.

"Ah, yes. This is Milla," Nestan said. "My daughter's maid and companion. She's been with us almost all her life."

Lanys glowered at this warm introduction.

Milla was grateful for the welcome, ignoring Lanys's glare and that tricky little word—*almost* all her life. When would she ever learn about where she came from? She pulled her thoughts out of this well-worn track and busied herself handing around a plate of Josi's famous almond cake.

After a while, the chatter petered out. Duchess Serina stood, asking, "May I go and compliment your cook on her cake? I'd like her recipe."

Nestan offered her his arm. "Of course, Your Grace, I'd be delighted to introduce you." They left the room.

Isak coughed and stood, adjusting his glasses. "Excuse me. I need to go . . . and check on . . . something. Lanys, can you help?" He backed out of the room, staring hard at Lanys till she followed him.

Tarya sprang up, keeping her back to Vigo. *Don't you dare!* she mouthed at Milla. *Don't leave me!*

Milla met Tarya's eyes and nodded once, then went to tidy the drinks tray in the corner.

"So," Vigo began, standing, too, "I don't think I made myself clear at the ball. That is . . ."

"No, you were very clear," Tarya said softly.

Uh-oh, Milla thought. She recognized that tone, soft as a cat's paw, right before the claws came out and slashed you across the cheek. *Tell him! Tell him you don't want to marry him, and we can stay together, like always.*

"That is, I thought we could start to . . . spend . . . er, time. Get to know . . . each other. Before . . ." Each word sounded effortful.

Tarya laughed, but it wasn't a pleasant sound. "You're not great at this, are you?" She eyed him curiously. "Do you have any actual friends? I mean, people who aren't being paid, or living in fear of your father, or trying to snare you in marriage?" She counted off the categories on her fingers.

Milla glanced at the duke's son to see how he'd take this.

Vigo flushed, but it only made him look more handsome, the color spreading across his bronze cheekbones. "That's hardly my fault. There's my cousin Luca in Sartola—he's a friend. And there used to be Jonas, the head stableman's son, but his family was blacklisted. I think they live in the lower town now."

"You think? Didn't you check?" Tarya asked him.

"Should I have?"

"A friend would check."

"Well, anyway, what about you? What friends do you have?" Vigo turned it back on her.

"I don't have friends," Tarya said simply. "I have Isak and Milla. That's all I need."

"And how's that different from me?" Vigo pushed.

"We've known each other all our lives, haven't we, Milla?"

Milla nodded, warily.

"Yes, but she works here, right? So she can't disagree with you. Not really. Not without risking her job."

Tarya paused, looking thoughtful. "You tell me, don't you, Milla? When you think I'm wrong? You just did!"

"Yes, of course."

"See!" Vigo said. "That's exactly what I mean—she's never going to say you're wrong. That's what it's like for us. That's why we get so . . . lonely." He was being honest now, Milla saw, and she almost felt sorry for him. "I talk to my mom, my cousin, my horses. Everyone else just tells me what they think I want to hear."

Tarya stepped closer, listening. "You have horses? How many?"

"Two. My old pony that I've outgrown, and the new chestnut colt I'm training. Do you ride?"

"When I can. My black mare, Greti. It's hardly fair on this island, riding in tight circles, like trapped rats. Oh, I'd love to ride on Sartola one day: gallop along the plains! Have you done that?"

"Yes! When we visit my uncle."

"What's it like?" Tarya's face grew animated as they talked about riding.

". . . and you can use the palace riding trails," Vigo said, "when we're married—"

"*When?*" Tarya jerked back.

"Yes, you can bring Greti and—"

"Oh, I can, can I? Wait a moment," Tarya said frostily. "You haven't heard my answer. You've barely asked the question. Or do you think I'll be another one of these people who just tells you what you want to hear?" Now she let rip, at top volume. "Well, I'm afraid you're wrong about me, Your Grace. I make my own decisions. I won't trot along and do as I'm told. Not now, and not ever!" Tarya ran straight out of the door, heading down the steps, past the assembled guards, and out of the gates into the street.

"Excuse me, Your Grace, I must follow her." Milla bobbed a quick curtsy and turned to dash after Tarya.

But when she'd glanced up at Vigo's face, he wasn't upset by Tarya's tirade. He looked delighted. He looked relieved.

CHAPTER TWELVE

Tarya!" Milla kept her head down, squinting against the rain, almost blown sideways as gusts caught her. The streets of Arcosi were empty, streaming with fast-flowing water. Soon she was cold and soaked through, but she followed Tarya's fluttering red scarf, catching glimpses to guide her way. She was heading right into the north of the island. There was a narrow neighborhood of abandoned houses no one had ever moved into, in the very north where the sun never reached. People called it the shadow strip. People said it was haunted.

Tarya darted ahead, slipping into the garden of one of these abandoned villas.

"Wait, Tarya!" Milla yelled. "Wait for me! Where are you going?" She followed her under a crumbling arch into the walled garden. To her right, a house reared up. Once elegant and gracious, it looked strange and dejected, one gaping window sprouting weeds and ivy. Milla watched a bird fly in through a jagged hole in the roof.

"So a haunted house is less scary than the duke's son?" Isak's voice made Milla jump, startled. "Sounds like my sister."

"Oh, Isak, you came, too! I didn't hear you." Knowing that he'd come after her made Milla feel less cold suddenly. "I think she's gone in here. Let's get out of the rain."

His cheeks were pink, his glasses steamed up, and his hair was dripping wet. But he grinned at her. "Come on, let's find her." He offered his hand.

Milla took it, finding comfort in the warmth of his fingers.

They walked deeper into the garden. Tarya was there, her dress and scarf soaked through, her hands tracing over the intricate stonework of the ancient wall. "Hey, you two. Come look at this. Dragons!"

"Where?" Milla asked quickly.

"Look, here! Ah, they're so beautiful."

Milla ran up and touched the stone images—the proud necks, the powerful wings—ignoring the rain that ran down her sleeve.

"Hey, this one, this is the first. It's a dragon sitting on its eggs." Isak beckoned them over to the panel farthest from the ruined house. He took his glasses off and wiped them on his wet shirt, peering closer.

Milla looked hard at the carvings. Her heart started thumping in her chest. What about her eggs: had a dragon laid them? Looking closer at the image, she traced her fingers lightly over its lines. "What else is it sitting on?" Below the eggs, there was a kind of nest, made of smaller round shapes. "Pebbles?" Maybe she should make a nest for her eggs— perhaps they needed it?

"No, don't you remember? Dragons love gold. It's in the old songs you hear," Isak said.

Milla's hand fell down. Here was proof: if they were dragon eggs, then they weren't meant for someone like her. Dragon eggs needed gold. They needed a dragonhall, a palace. She could be hurting them, hiding them in a smokehouse, of all places. They might die and it would be all her fault.

"Gold! It can't be. There's piles of it . . ." Tarya turned away to the next image. "Look, here it's hatching!"

The next panel had the unmistakeable shape of two halves of the dragon egg, and the outline of a baby dragon.

Milla's hand crept back and stroked the carving. Were her eggs going to hatch? How would she keep hiding them if they did? What would she feed them? Suddenly, she longed to tell Tarya and Isak about the eggs right now. They would have ideas. They could help her look after them.

The urge to share her precious secret grew irresistible, and she gathered up her courage. "Come on, let's sit down for a bit."

They found a sheltered spot underneath two broad apple trees. The three of them huddled together for warmth.

"Cozy," Tarya said sarcastically.

"Better than being at home," Isak said. His face was pale now, but his breathing was quiet and steady.

Milla took a deep breath, getting ready to speak.

"So," Isak got there first, his tone warm and gentle, as if

Tarya was a spooked foal, "what did the duke's son say to make you run screaming out into the storm?"

"No. You first." Tarya nudged her brother. "Tell us, now that we're alone. What did Dad say to you that was so awful on the day of the ball? You've barely spoken since then."

"He's sending me away, after your betrothal," Isak said in a rush, looking down at his wet boots, as if he couldn't bear to see his sister's face as he told her.

Tarya flinched at that word, *betrothal.* "He really wants rid of us both, then?"

The wind lifted Milla's hair. Everything was changing too fast. She felt as light and insubstantial as a dandelion seed, as if this storm might blow her away, too.

"Nah," Isak whispered. "He thinks it's for the best. He thinks it's the right thing. He's never known what people need, has he?"

"Where?" Milla said. "Where is he sending you?" Maybe it wasn't far. "Maybe Thom could bring us to visit on his fishing trips?"

"The Silk Islands," Isak said. "Two weeks at sea each way."

"No!" Milla wailed. Her dreams vanished, like pictures drawn in the sand.

"You get to go away!" Tarya said, sounding envious.

"You get to stay here!" Isak cried. "The thing is," he said, "Dad actually thinks he's being generous: setting me up to learn the trade from his partner out there. That's why he's so angry with me, his ungrateful son. Such a disappointment."

"Why can't I come, too? He can't send you away from

me," Tarya wailed, knotting her arm through his. "I need you every day, not twice a year, if I'm lucky."

Me, too, Milla thought. *I need you both. You're my brother and sister, too!* She threaded her arm through Isak's other arm, and huddled close, shivering, still feeling the buried warmth of his body through their sodden clothes. The three of them clung to each other, as if they feared separation any moment.

"Wh-wh-when?" Milla made herself ask. "Has he said when you'll be betrothed, Tarya?" She needed to know how long they had left.

"A betrothal next spring, to get it signed and sealed, then a wedding when I turn sixteen," Tarya said, her voice high and brittle. One strand of hair had escaped her plait and curled against her cheek. She narrowed her eyes and frowned. "Just don't expect to find me here! I'd take your path any day, Isak—you get to sail away." She sounded wistful. "You get freedom, your own work. You'll get choices . . ."

"That's not true!" Isak interrupted. "I didn't choose this; Dad did. I don't see what you're complaining about," he went on. "You'll get to stay here, see Dad, see Milla."

Milla squeezed his arm in response.

"Haven't you realized?" he went on. "One day you'll be a duchess! You'll live at the palace. You're the one with freedom and choices."

"It's just . . . I never thought he'd make me marry someone." Tarya's voice didn't change, but her cheeks glinted with tears. "I'm not his daughter. I'm just useful, like a boatload of grain, nothing more. He didn't even tell me! Some excuse about waiting till I'd met Vigo, as if I'd swoon obediently into place."

"Same here." Isak tightened his grip on his sister's arm.

Suddenly, Milla wasn't so sure. A cold thread of fear started curling its way through her thoughts, dark as squid ink. She was a listener and a watcher: she'd learned to read people. She'd seen Nestan's face when he'd argued with Isak, and he was worried. He was expecting trouble. What did Nestan know, that Isak needed to be shipped away and Tarya placed safely behind palace walls?

"You and me both," Isak went on. "I mean, I always wanted to travel. But not like this. Not so far away, without you." He turned to Milla. "Both of you."

"I don't want this either," Milla managed to choke out, not mentioning her fears to the twins. "I don't want to be left behind. If I could split myself in two, send half of me with each of you . . ."

"I won't leave you," Tarya said, but all her exuberance had faded.

The wind howled more strongly, as if it were mocking them. They stayed like that, listening to the rain, holding each other.

Milla moved first. She saw something to Tarya's left, glinting with moisture. She stood up, stiff and damp.

"Did you drop something? I saw—" She bent to rummage on the floor.

"What is it?" Isak asked.

"Dunno." Milla turned her fist over. Something hard, cool, heavy in her palm. She rubbed it against her tunic, wiping the crusted dirt away. It gleamed when she held it up. A coin. A golden coin, stamped with a name and the outline of a king's head.

She read aloud: "Rufus. Wasn't he the mad duke? My friend Rosa told me that." As she held it, a cold shudder of dread went through her, as though a vast shadow passed over them.

"Looks like gold," Tarya said. "Old, though, from before."

"Keep it safe," Isak told her. "You found it, Milla. It's yours now."

The horrible icy feeling deepened as Milla turned it over between her fingers. "I don't want it," she said firmly, throwing it down again. "It's unlucky. Old Arcosi was cursed." As soon as it left her grasp, she felt better.

Tarya jumped up and retrieved the coin. "What if we just left," she said, "as soon as the storm blows out?" She paced restlessly, rubbing the coin with one thumb.

"We have no money," Isak said.

"No, but we could use this gold, and we could work?" Tarya said, oblivious to the fact she'd never done a day's work in her life. Her voice was hopeful and fragile. "At least we'd be together. All three of us."

Tarya's words warmed Milla through. Here was proof that someone trusted her. That she mattered: not just as a servant, but as a friend. It was time to make her decision. She wasn't powerless. Not anymore. She cleared her throat and began, "We can't leave."

"So, what are we going to do?" Isak asked. "Milla? You're always the one with a plan."

Both twins looked at her expectantly.

Milla met their eyes, looking from Tarya to Isak and back again. She would tell them. This was the time to put her trust in them, as Tarya had in her. If they really were her family, she needed to prove it.

Milla's stomach flopped and twisted like a landed fish. She started speaking, fast and quiet, before she lost her nerve. "The thing is, something's happened. It changes everything. On the day of the ball, a man hid a bag in the garden of your house."

"So?" asked Tarya impatiently. "What bag?"

"The bag contains four large eggs. This big." She showed them with her hands. "And he was killed for it." Milla described what had happened that day.

"Right there, in our garden?" Isak interrupted, suddenly ashen. "Are you sure?"

"I saw it happen," Milla said, looking at their stricken faces.

"But why didn't you say?" Isak asked, bewildered. "A man was killed? That's awful!"

"I didn't want to scare you that night. You had enough to think about."

"Milla, are you serious?" Tarya whispered, clutching her arm. "Who would do that? We have to find them!"

"Your father tried . . ."

"When you say eggs . . . that size," Isak spoke slowly, "you don't mean . . . could they be—?" He tipped his head toward the carvings.

"Dragons!" Tarya breathed, her eyes sparkling.

"I thought they might be precious stones, but they're not." Milla was babbling now. "They're *alive*. I'm sure of it. They could be birds . . . but the colors! They're blue and green and red and yellow. I've never seen a bird's egg those colors." She took a deep breath. "What else could they be?"

There was a long silence while the twins absorbed it.

"So they're still here?" Isak asked. "You mean there are dragon eggs at our house, right now?"

"Show us!" Tarya said.

"I will. I was just waiting for the right time to tell you. But promise me you'll keep it secret?"

They nodded solemnly.

"I promise," Tarya whispered eagerly.

"I promise," Isak echoed.

As they spoke their vows, Milla shivered. She felt as if the world was listening and had witnessed them.

"Let's go home, and I'll show you," Milla said. They ran back to the Yellow House and immediately slipped around to the smokehouse.

"Wait here." Milla opened the smokehouse door and crept inside. She felt around in the darkness, eager to find it, eager to see their faces, eager to start making plans. Her hands reached out.

Something was different. "No!" With a sickening jolt, like waking from a dream of falling, everything changed.

"They've gone! The eggs have gone!"

Part Two

Part Two

CHAPTER THIRTEEN

The eggs were really gone. Milla searched the whole smokehouse frantically, but they'd vanished. She staggered back to face the twins, but their father had summoned them to his study.

She saw the look on Isak's face as he turned to walk away: uneasy, embarrassed. He didn't believe her.

She went back inside the smokehouse and searched again, with tears pouring down her face.

"Milla!" Josi yelled from the kitchen, calling her back to work.

Milla swallowed down a sob and scrubbed at her cheeks with her sleeve. Her hair was still wet: she could pretend her tears were just rain.

"Take this tray to the master. He's called the twins to hear some news. As if they've not had enough—" Josi stopped abruptly when she saw Milla's face. "What's wrong?" She put the laden tray down to feel her forehead, clucking her disappointment. "You are cold as snow and soaked to the bone. Didn't I say you'd catch a chill?"

Milla did feel frozen inside. Her mind was still stuck on that awful endless moment when she reached up for the eggs and found nothing. Someone had taken them. Her heart felt as raw and bruised as the scraps of meat Josi had been chopping.

"It's nothing," she mumbled. "I'll take the drinks."

Milla picked up the tray, vaguely aware that her hands were trembling and making the cups clink anxiously against one another. Maybe the master had the eggs. She would soon see for herself.

"Make sure you come straight back here and warm up," Josi shouted after her.

When she pushed the study door open soundlessly and walked in, Milla cast a searching glance around the room and found no trace of the pannier. The master was sitting at his desk, with Tarya and Isak opposite him, Lanys standing to the side. Even from here, Milla could see the rigid tension in all four.

Nestan knew about the eggs! He must. The atmosphere in the room was charged, like the air just before the storm broke. The door closed behind her, and they all looked up with a start.

Lanys flashed her a mocking grin. A moment later, a mask of false solemnity was pasted over it.

So Lanys had done this. Milla felt it like a slap. She'd

resented Milla for years, jealous of her friendship with the twins.

"Why, Milla?" Nestan asked accusingly. "Why did you hide this from us?"

Milla dropped the tray with a crash. The cups smashed into jagged shards and the pewter flagons spilled, red wine and water mingling in a dark pool on the floor tiles: a dirty, guilty stain.

"Leave it," Nestan ordered as she moved to pick it up. "This is more important. Come here." He clasped his hands together. In his high-necked, dark jacket, he looked somber.

Where were the eggs? Milla went to stand next to the desk. Her heart was thudding in her chest, and her mouth felt dry.

"Lanys brought the bag to me." Nestan sounded quietly furious. "The twins have told me the rest."

So much for their promises.

Lanys must have noticed her going into the smokehouse too often. Milla cursed her own carelessness.

"They said you witnessed the murder? And found the eggs?" Nestan's anger was white-hot and controlled, not blazing. It made it worse.

She nodded again.

"And yet you chose to keep them hidden all this time?"

She couldn't move.

"You'd better have a good explanation for deceiving us."

"I . . . I don't know." The words burned: it hadn't felt like deceit. "I didn't mean it that way. I didn't know what they were."

"Really?" His voice grew louder now. "A man was murdered for a bag of eggs, and you didn't guess what they were?"

So it was true: they were dragon eggs. Milla put one hand out to steady herself.

"I just wanted to keep them safe." She looked straight at Nestan, meeting his glare, hoping he'd see she was telling the truth.

She heard Lanys stifle a snicker behind her.

"Safe? For whose purpose?" Nestan demanded. "Did you see the murderer?"

"He was masked. I could hardly hear him. Spoke Norlandish, though . . ."

"Did you know him?" And before she could answer, something else occurred to him. "Did someone pay you to do this?"

"No! Of course not!" Milla cried out at his accusation. "It was horrible! I told you, he wore a mask, the man who did it. I don't know who it was. I was scared afterward. I wasn't thinking. And then we rushed out to the ball."

"What were you going to do with them?" Nestan kept firing out the questions. "Sell them?"

"No! I wouldn't. I couldn't. I wouldn't do anything with them." Milla realized how stupid she'd been, hoping she could keep the eggs hidden forever. "They were right here. I kept them safe! I was looking after them."

"I know what you're like," Nestan said, softly now, "always wandering down to the lower town. Who paid you? Who are you working for?"

"For you! I promise." Tears sprang to her eyes. "Sure, I know lower-town folk. But I'm loyal—ask Josi! Ask Finn!"

She was shaken to the core by Nestan's questions and his doubts.

Nestan continued to glare at her. "You've lived in my household almost all your life, Milla. I thought I could trust you."

Milla stared at him through her tears. She felt something else behind his anger, but she was too distraught to work out what it was.

"You can! You can trust me," Milla said, begging now. "Please!" The whole conversation felt as unreal as a nightmare. She felt Tarya take her hand and that was the first thing she could believe in.

"It's all right, Milla." Tarya's fingers squeezed hers. "She already told us about the eggs. She didn't know what they were! She's telling the truth, Dad. Unlike you." In Milla's defense, she went on the attack. "Why didn't you tell us someone was killed in our home?"

Distantly, Milla was touched by Tarya's fierceness.

"I hoped to protect you," Nestan snapped.

"And maybe that's what Milla was doing, protecting the eggs?" Tarya shot back. "So what if she hid them? They were safe here, weren't they?"

"Why us?" Isak spoke next, raising his voice to be heard between the yelling. "I don't understand why that man chose to bring the eggs to us instead of the duke."

"Who knows?" Nestan barked. "I didn't get to hear the traveler's message before he died, did I? But there's no question about it, we will take them directly to the duke now."

"No, you can't!"

"I *can't*?" Nestan said, in a slow, incredulous voice.

"It's mine!" Milla cried from her aching heart before she could help herself. "I mean, it needs me." *The blue . . . Just the blue one.*

Lanys laughed out loud at this.

"It *what*?" Nestan was looking at Milla with a piercing intensity that went right through her.

"I don't know." Milla struggled to put it into words: that deep instinct to protect them. "I'm sorry, I just felt so . . . I needed to care for them. I can't explain it, but I didn't mean any harm. Please! You can't give the eggs away!"

"I have to take them to the duke," Nestan said tightly.

"Why?" Tarya rebelled.

No! Not the duke. Olvar mustn't get the eggs. Milla prayed that Nestan would listen to his daughter now.

She heard the master's curse as he exhaled impatiently and spelled it out to them: "He is the ruler of the city and commander of the army. Isak and I have publicly pledged our loyalty to him. Our families are about to be allied through marriage. Besides, you know how he is about dragons. *Since Lanys brought the eggs to me*," he said, with a hard, bitter edge in his voice, "it's more than all our lives are worth not to take these eggs straight to the duke."

Milla felt sick at the thought.

"Couldn't we keep just one?" Tarya said. "Say it broke."

Yes! Milla found herself wishing. *Just the blue one. Please!*

"And what do we do if it hatches? Think it through, Tarya."

Milla felt a sudden lurch of anxiety at the idea of the eggs hatching without her there.

"We could hide them, take them away to the Silk Islands," Isak suggested.

"Impossible." Nestan was curt. "They must hatch here."

"Why?" Isak challenged his father.

"What's wrong with you both?" Nestan ignored the question, raising his voice. "We take them straight to the palace. The timing works—we've been invited to a feast there this evening to announce your betrothal to Vigo."

"And when were you going to tell me?" Tarya stood up— Milla heard the sharp scrape of the heavy chair across the tiled floor.

"Today!" Nestan's anger was finally blazing now. "So you didn't have time to work yourself up into this kind of state."

"You have no faith in me," Tarya accused him.

"So earn it!" Nestan bellowed, and even Tarya flinched. "Act your part. And as for you, Milla: you may leave us, while I think this through."

Milla let out a sob. She slammed one palm across her mouth to stop any more escaping. Vision blurring with tears, she ran from the room.

Lanys said, "I'll go after her."

In the corridor, Milla felt a yank as Lanys grabbed her sleeve.

Lanys heaved her up against the wall, almost tearing her tunic. "You're finished," Lanys hissed, spraying spittle. "Now I'll be first, like I should always have been."

Milla tried to turn away, but Lanys held her close.

"I'm the Norlander maid, after all. You're nothing but a

thief." Her eyes were narrowed, her freckled face twisted with rage.

Milla felt that cut deep, like a knife in her side. She prised Lanys's fingers loose, tugged herself free, and ran away from them all.

CHAPTER FOURTEEN

It was hard to run and cry at the same time, but Milla couldn't help it. She had to get away. She kept seeing Nestan's look of disappointment, Lanys's hatred. Would the twins defend her? All those days, months, years of hard work—how much would they count for, in the light of this mistake? This *deceit*, he'd called it. Eventually, she could run no more. She bent double, resting her hands on her knees and sobbing out her pain, while the rain soaked her through.

Looking after the eggs had been a new reason to wake. Her first thought and her last. She'd never had anything of her own to care for. And now they were gone.

She sobbed harder.

Soon Tarya would marry Vigo and go to live in the palace. Milla would see her from afar, in the crowds on feast days. And Isak would go to the Silk Islands, to learn his father's trade. He'd come back next year to visit: tall, tanned, transformed.

And the eggs? The idea of them hatching without her actually hurt. She didn't know why. All she knew was that her whole body ached with loss.

When she lifted her head and looked about her, she was back at the shadow strip, near the ruined house with the garden. She needed solitude: no surprise her feet had brought her here. Her teeth were chattering and she felt the shivers begin. She had to find shelter, fast.

She crossed the overgrown garden of the ruined house. It reared above her, vast and intimidating. It had a large sunburst tile on the front and crumbling lettering that read VILLA DORATO. Slowly, cautiously, she put one hand against the paneled wooden door and pushed. With a deep groan of rusted hinges, the door gave way.

Milla stepped through and paused in a dark entrance hall. It smelled damp and musty, and then worse, like a dead thing rotting slowly. Her eyes adjusted. She made out the ruined staircase, the proud curve of a slender banister strangled by a creeping vine. There were doorways on each side. She tiptoed to the right and peered in: a broken window shutter let in daylight. It was a dining room, with a table and six chairs. She stopped by the table covered in dust.

What had happened here? This was once the home of an Old Arcosi family: prosperous, settled. They'd fled in sudden fear, or worse.

This was the perfect place to hide. Like an injured animal, she needed somewhere dark and silent to lick her wounds. No one would look for her here.

The wind blew through the shutters, and the ragged

remnants of the curtains fluttered like an empty sleeve. Milla shuddered, suddenly afraid of what else she might find: dry bones, flesh turned to dust . . .

Just then, she heard a noise: a whisper of movement, hushed into silence.

She yelped in surprise, then felt ashamed, squeaking like a mouse. *Come on, Milla, don't be afraid.* There were no ghosts. *What, just like there were no dragons?*

If something happened to her, no one would ever know. She could vanish from the face of the earth. She would become one of the disappeared. Just another spirit of this island.

Milla made her feet move toward the sound. "Hello?"

A cool draft of air against the back of her neck, like the breath of a ghost.

"Who's there?" She found a door near the back of the house, and pushed it open. "Where are you?" she whispered hoarsely.

There was a fire burning in the grate of a huge iron cooking range. There was a stone table with a chopping board, laid out. A peeled apple: fresh, intact. A knife. "Hello?" She lifted the knife and held it ready.

She heard a sudden noise: a violent clamoring of wings. She jumped and spun around, back to the hall. It was only a crow, she told herself, nesting in the roof. Hadn't she seen it, the other day? But she couldn't quell her fears now. She imagined the people who'd lived here, rising around her like wraiths. Their ghostly hands in her hair. Pleading for justice.

Her fear grew, heartbeat speeding.

Something touched her shoulder.

Milla screamed.

Turning, she stood face-to-face with the old woman from the duke's ball, looking as terrified as Milla felt.

A while later they were sitting together by the fire.

"What are you doing here?" Milla spoke Sartolan, guessing the people of Old Arcosi spoke it, too. "I saw you at the duke's ball."

"I've come home," the woman replied in the same language, huddling into her cloak. She still looked alarmed, with none of the fiery defiance from that night at the ball. Maybe she'd caught a chill, living here, all alone. She didn't seem to recognize Milla, which seemed odd, till Milla remembered that she'd been masked at the ball.

"Where is home: do you mean Arcosi?" Milla asked. She should ask herself the same question. Did she even have a home anymore, after today? "Or did this house belong to your family?"

"Both." She was obviously reluctant to say more.

This was her family's old house? Milla looked around. In the corner, there was a threadbare cushioned bench. A stack of dry wood.

Milla would be the one begging her for shelter tonight. Beyond that, she couldn't think. Her future without the eggs stretched ahead of her, like a dark, starless sky. She shivered and edged closer to the fire. "What's your name? I'm Milla Yellowhouse." Since she had no family, that was the name written on her papers.

"Kara." The woman stared at Milla, solemn and round-eyed. The gold hoops in her ears gleamed in the firelight.

"The duke has men looking for you. We are supposed to bring you to him if we find you," Milla said. "Don't worry, I'm not going to!" she added hurriedly when Kara looked anxious.

"I'll be safe here," Kara said, though it sounded more like a question than a statement.

"That night . . . you spoke of dragons returning to Arcosi. Did you bring dragon eggs? You and that man? The one who—" Milla halted. She didn't know if this woman knew about the murder.

The silence expanded uncomfortably. Kara seemed frozen over. What could Milla say, to make her thaw and trust her? She took out her medal and showed it to her. "You saw this, before. Do you know it?"

The sight of the medal worked like a spell, transforming everything. Kara sprang to life.

"Where did you get that?" she asked with piercing intensity. "Is it yours?"

She leaned forward and grasped Milla's chin, tilting her face to the light of the fire.

"Yes, it's mine. It's the only thing that is." Milla shook her hand away, not enjoying the feeling of being examined like a young goat at the market. "I've always had it."

"So tell me! The eggs? What do you know of them, child?" Kara's hand shot out and this time grabbed Milla's arm, making her jump. "Did he bring them to you?"

"To me?" Milla gulped. "I saw them," she said, a wave of shame flooding through her, "but now they're gone. I'm sorry. I tried . . ."

"Where?" Kara squeezed her arm so hard it hurt. "Where have they gone?"

"Nestan took them," Milla said. "They'll be at the palace right now. They've gone, without me." Her voice wavered like a candle in a draft. "And I don't know if I'll see them again . . ."

"Why didn't you say? Hurry, child, hurry! Why did you let them out of your sight?" Kara's voice was so furious, it left no room for disbelief. "They'll be hatching soon— tonight's the full moon—and you must be there . . ."

"Wh-wh-at? *Why me?* How do you know?" A dozen more questions burned in her mind.

"We brought them home for this. They hatch at full moon and that means tonight. Time is running out. Go! Go now. Quickly, find the eggs and don't let them out of your sight again!"

"Now?" Milla struggled for words, her mind a turmoil of excitement and confusion. "What should I do?"

"Go to the eggs!" Kara issued a stream of instructions. "Listen to me: with no living parent, the hatchlings must bond quickly, and you must be in the room. One will choose you. When it hatches, go to it. Speak to it. Warm it, feed it meat, let it drink. The hatchlings must be kept warm. All will be well, but go now. You haven't got long. Hurry!" Her urgency spilled over into distress. "And don't utter a word of this! Tell no one."

"All right, I'll go. I'll keep quiet." Her words burned,

bright and vivid, in Milla's mind, spurring her on, showing her the path to her heart's desire.

Then she paused, looking back at Kara huddling there by the fire. She couldn't abandon her, alone in the storm. "But what about you?"

"What about me? There's no time!"

"I will do as you say, I promise, as long as you come with me. We need to get you warm and safe. You can't stay here, it's too dangerous, with the duke's men looking for you."

"And you can't wait!" Kara urged.

Milla shook her head stubbornly. "I won't go without you."

"You don't understand!" Kara looked ready to burst with impatience. "Oh, very well, then."

They both headed back out into the storm. Milla blessed the bad weather for keeping everyone else—including the patrols—indoors. The wind tugged at their hair and clothes, and Milla's mind felt stormy and wild to match.

Were the eggs really hatching? Either way, she burned to get back to them, but she couldn't turn up at the palace like this: they'd never let her in. As they stumbled away from Villa Dorato, a plan started forming in her mind.

She hurried home to the Yellow House and took Kara straight to the kitchen.

They burst in, wet and breathless, startling Josi, who dropped a jar of pickled plums, smashing ruby juice and pink flesh all over the stone floor.

"I'm sorry!" Milla's words poured out in a torrent. "This is Kara. Can you hide her here, please?" she begged.

It wouldn't be the first time Josi had hidden a fugitive

from the duke's idea of justice. Milla always pretended not to notice when the back storage room was suddenly out of bounds. She'd ignore the whispers in Sartolan; take care to keep Lanys out of the kitchen; and after a day or two, the invisible guests were always gone.

"The duke's soldiers are searching the island for her." She met Josi's gaze: they both knew what that meant. "Kara will explain. I need to run, to get to the palace . . . Please?"

Josi didn't say a word, her face shocked and silent. She just nodded and passed Milla the plate she'd been eating from.

Milla took it and rushed upstairs. She got changed into Tarya's old purple dress and a matching cloak, seizing all the scattered items Tarya had forgotten: scarf, pearl necklace, fan. She grabbed the food Josi had given her—a roll of bread and a slice of chicken—and tried to eat a mouthful. It was dry and she almost choked on it in her haste, so she stuffed it into the pocket of her dress for later. She lifted down a glass vial of Isak's medicine from the shelf and unstoppered it: checking its freshness, breathing in the scent of ginger and honey. Isak always forgot it. That's why Nestan kept servants: to remember the small things. Isak needed to take his medicine whenever the weather turned wet, or at times of stress or excitement.

He'd definitely be needing it tonight.

CHAPTER FIFTEEN

There was a break in the storm clouds. The moon appeared: full and bright, painting the island silver and black, showing Milla the way.

The eggs will hatch tonight! The eggs will hatch tonight! It was the strongest thought in Milla's mind, pulsing along with the beat of her blood. Stronger than fear, stronger than her worry about Nestan's reaction or the mystery of Kara's words. It kept her going, all the way up the steep road to the palace, through two checkpoints, all the way to the palace gates. They stretched above her: vast, iron-studded doors. Most definitely locked. The wind whipped her hair across her eyes, and she pulled it back into a knot, jutting her chin and stretching up to ring the bellpull.

"Yes?" A small window opened in the huge expanse of oak.

Milla could barely see the guard's face in the darkness beyond. She mustered all the courage she had, throwing her voice from the pit of her stomach, and copying Tarya in her most imperious mood. "I need to come in! My lady is here for the betrothal feast, and she needs me."

"Oh, she does, does she? I don't think so."

Milla kept her face steady, refusing to show how it stung, always, to be dismissed at first sight. She had to convince them she was more than she seemed. The stakes were too high to fail tonight.

"Who is it?" a new voice spoke from behind the first man.

"Another lower-town gannet. Always pecking around for scraps, that lot. Ignore her."

"Lady Tarya Thornsen won't be happy when she hears you kept her maid outside in the storm," she drawled, in her best Norlandish. "Every moment you keep me waiting, you keep her waiting. You know she'll be the next Duchess of Arcosi? Not such a wise move."

"Let me see." The second man came to the door.

Milla swallowed. If they turned her away now, that was it. She couldn't scale these walls. The eggs would hatch without her. She'd have to tell Kara she'd failed. The duke would own the dragons. Nestan would send her away. Her thoughts spiraled fast: she pictured a lonely life, living in the ruins, scavenging for food, begging Thom and Rosa for work. *No!* With her heart beating so fast she was sure the man could hear it over the wind, she raised her eyes to his and tried another tack.

"Evening, sir," she began again with this new guard. "The thing is, my lady changed her mind and sent me back for her favorite necklace. If I don't get it to her soon, I'm in for a beating," she lied, widening her eyes. She felt under her cloak and lifted out the pearls. "Look! See?" She watched the guard consider the evidence. "Please, let me through and I can dress my lady before the dinner, and no harm done," she said earnestly. "Also, I have Master Isak's medicine." She rummaged for the glass vial and held that up, too.

The guard hesitated. He scowled, ready to turn away.

"Wait!"

Milla's hand flew to her necklace, the habit of a lifetime. Her fingers stroked the gold medal with the imprint of the dragon and the full moon. Her only possession. The only way of tracing her family. She felt sick at the thought of giving it up. She couldn't do it.

The guard started closing the window.

She had no time and no choices left.

"Wait, please!" Milla closed her eyes, steeling herself. With reluctant fingers, she unfastened the necklace. She stared down at the gold medal in her palm, gleaming in a sudden shaft of moonlight. She brought it to her lips one last time.

Then she folded her fingers over it and held it out. "Take this," she made herself say. It was the only link with her past, and she felt it snap like a broken chain. She gambled her past for the sake of her future.

"For your trouble, sir," she said through gritted teeth, and handed over the ancient gold medal, blinking away tears.

"Let her through." The guard winked at her and palmed the gold. "She's right: they've only just reached the palace. Let her through, but escort her all the way, do you hear me?"

"Thank you, sir." Milla nodded her head demurely,

listening to the bolts being drawn back and the heavy gates swinging aside over the cobbles. Two more guards waited on the other side. She threw a smile at them, but it was like smiling at a stone wall.

They walked swiftly through the palace grounds. Last time, Milla was with invited guests, part of the jeweled throng. This time she felt like a prisoner. The guards marched her up the steps, through a vast hallway with a massive curving staircase and into the great hall of the palace.

Milla blinked, dazzled by the opulence: dozens of gold candelabras; a long dining table covered in snowy linen, laid with glass and crystal; a huge stemmed bowl dripping with purple grapes.

Nestan and the twins stood by an enormous fireplace with Richal Finn in attendance, all scrubbed up for the occasion.

"Milla!" Nestan exclaimed, steadying himself with two hands on his cane.

Was he angry, or relieved? She couldn't tell.

"Milla? What are you doing here?" Tarya cried out, coming over.

She felt the grip of a gloved hand on her arm. "Expected, were you?" the guard growled.

She had seconds left before they threw her out. Her eyes searched the room. There was a strange gilded table by the fire, shaped like a compass on a map, with four leaves pointing outward, and a little dish of water set right in the center. On each leaf there was a large silk cushion. On each cushion rested one of the dragon eggs: blue, red, green, and yellow.

The eggs were safe.

On either side of the table stood a burly palace guardsman gripping a lethal-looking pike and armed with longsword and throwing knife.

Her gambles had worked so far. Now she played her best card. "I brought your necklace." Milla passed the pearls to Tarya with a squeeze of her fingers. "*As you wanted*, my lady," she added.

"And the medicine for your brother . . ." She went to Isak and handed him the glass vial.

"Thank you, Milla," Isak said, taking it carefully from her shaking fingers.

"Just in time, I see," Nestan said dryly.

"I think you mean to thank Milla for her speedy return," Isak said. He swigged a mouthful of his medicine and came to stand so close to her that the guard had to release Milla's arm.

"Yes! What would we do without Milla?" Tarya said loudly, playing her part. "Quick, fasten my pearls, won't you?" She lifted her mass of curly hair and turned her back.

Milla fumbled with the clasp of the necklace, her fingers damp and trembling.

"That will be all." Nestan dismissed the guards.

She heard their footsteps receding beyond the door and let out a low sob of relief.

"*Are you all right?*" Tarya whispered, patting her pearls into place. "Where did you go? I was so worried! It didn't feel right, coming without you, but I wanted to stay with the eggs and keep them safe for you." She added quickly, "It doesn't mean I accept the betrothal! They can't make me do that."

"I'm fine," Milla breathed shakily into her ear so no one else could hear. "That plan you wanted? Be ready: I'll need a diversion. If it works, let's meet later, back at the ruined house?"

Tarya swung around, eyes glittering conspiratorially, and nodded. "I'll tell Isak."

Just then, the duke swaggered through an archway at the far side of the room, followed by Serina and Vigo.

"Friends, friends, friends!" Olvar greeted Nestan and the twins with a broad smile. His pale eyes slipped over Milla, and Finn next to her: as servants, they were invisible to him.

"What could be more perfect?" Olvar was lit up. A man who held his heart's desire in the palm of his hand.

Milla noticed that Serina and Vigo weren't smiling and wondered what they knew that she didn't.

"Nestan, old friend, I thank you again for this most fitting gift," Olvar declared. "On the day our families celebrate their union, we also celebrate the return of the dragons to Arcosi. It's a sign: We are blessed! You two are blessed!"

He turned to indicate Vigo and Tarya, standing awkwardly together, fidgeting under his gaze. He started applauding them loudly, till Nestan, Isak, and Serina joined in. The noise sounded hollow and echoing in the large room.

"Sit! Let's eat and celebrate this momentous day," the duke said.

Time was running out. Any moment now, Milla and Finn

would be dismissed, and she'd have to leave the eggs. She'd promised Kara she would stay with them. But how?

Vigo bowed to Tarya. "Shall we?" He indicated seats at the far side of the table. The eggs lay just behind them.

Milla darted to Tarya's side, pretending to adjust her hair.

She checked the guards: they were staring straight ahead, like two statues.

Next, she watched the duke, waiting for a moment when his attention moved away from the eggs.

She just needed a distraction, a smashed glass, nudged in error.

Her hand reached out . . .

Tarya looked up and smiled at Milla, and her plan fell apart.

Stealing broke all the rules of Norlander hospitality. If she stole this egg, Tarya, Isak, and Nestan would never make it out of the palace. They'd be arrested. Blacklisted. They'd lose all they owned—house, ships, possessions.

It wasn't fair! Milla had nothing of her own. Why couldn't she take the blue egg, just this one?

Not if it destroyed Tarya's life.

She drew her hand back from the table. She would need another plan, and fast.

Crack!

It was the noise of something fragile breaking.

Nestan glanced down at his glass.

Serina checked the windows.

Isak looked at Tarya, peering over his glasses.

But Milla was already facing the eggs. She moved closer to them and she was the first to see.

Crack! It came again.

The duke noticed Milla now. "Get back from there!" he bellowed.

The guards crossed their pikes, pushing her back.

"If you have damaged them . . ." Olvar roared.

"No!" Milla cried. "It's hatching!"

CHAPTER SIXTEEN

The blue egg was hatching.

In the chaos, everyone pushed forward.

"Get back," the duke was yelling, putting himself closest to the eggs.

"No!" She had to be there. Milla felt it like a fire in her blood.

The guardsmen dragged Milla away from the table. That was wrong; that was impossible. "No!" She twisted around to gaze down at the blue egg. Its smooth curve was now zigzagged by a giant crack.

"Let me go!" she shouted, trying to tug her arms free. "I need to be there. Careful! Don't scare it."

"Get her out of here." Olvar jerked his head toward the door.

"Your Grace." Nestan limped over and put his hand on the duke's arm. "She's my servant. Let me deal with her?"

"Let Milla go," Tarya cried. "She's with us. She needs to stay with us. Vigo, please? Can't you do something?"

"Father?" Vigo tried, but the duke was staring down at the eggs and nothing would avert his gaze now.

Milla shoved her heels down, but the guards' iron grip tightened.

"No! Please," she begged. "Wait." She slid unwillingly, resisting every inch of the way.

Crkk! A tiny nobbled lump appeared, right through the egg, pushing out a jagged piece of shell the size of her thumbnail.

"It's coming," Milla said. She struggled with all her strength, only causing more pain. "Let me see! Can't you just let me see?" she pleaded uselessly with the guards. Her neck protested as she twisted around.

The dragon made steady progress, with pauses to rest. *Tak!* Another larger piece of shell fell off.

They were almost at the door now. A few more steps. "I don't mean to leave you!" Milla shouted, praying that the little creature could hear her.

Then came a different movement: a rocking, shifting, gathering. Quite suddenly, the two halves of the shell fell apart.

"Ohh! Wait. Look!" Vigo's words stopped everything.

Even the two guardsmen halted to stare.

Curled on the cushion lay a damp, exhausted baby dragon, mewing faintly, next to the shards of its shell. Its body glistened with moisture, dark blue like lapis lazuli.

"A dragon!" Milla's heart blossomed at the sight. The color of the dragon unlocked something inside her: she recognized that blue. It was the blue from her dreams. This was meant to be.

Before she knew what she was doing, Milla put her lips together and blew. She whistled a short series of five notes, ascending, then descending. The song from her dreams. Loud and clear, it carried across the room.

The dragon heard. It lifted its little head and listened. Drained and limp as it seemed, it heard Milla and it responded with a hoarse *Ee-ee-ee-ee-eep!* as if trying to sing the same song.

She whistled again, the notes she'd been dreaming.

The blue dragon replied. Everyone heard it.

"I'm right here. Listen to me!" Duke Olvar prodded the dragon.

But the dragon only looked past him, trying clumsily to stand and failing. It had four scaly feet that seemed too big for its puny body, and it was weighed down by a lumpy damp mass on its back. It tried again and almost fell off the table, trying to get to Milla.

"Don't let it fall!" Milla said. "Let me go. Can't you see? It needs me."

Duke Olvar gave the slightest nod of his head, and the guards released Milla's arms. She darted across the room. The others parted for her, letting her through.

This time the dragon staggered forward, tripping over its tail. Then it got up, flicking its tail behind it, ridged with tiny blue bumps all along its length. It stood taller and stared at Milla through two bright unblinking eyes, fixed on her: two green jewels, each slashed vertically with a black pupil.

Milla and the dragon stared at each other and the world was remade.

She felt as if the dragon saw right into her soul; and her soul gazed back. She knew, without a shadow of doubt, that this dragon was hers. She loved it. She would live and die for it. Nothing in her life had ever felt so right or so strong. Tears blurred her vision, but she was smiling so widely that she couldn't manage her next whistle.

The hatchling's head drooped and it sank down, tugging at her heart, banishing the smile. She whistled again, and remembered Kara's words from earlier that night: she needed to feed it! Didn't she have meat and bread in her pocket? She whistled, faster, rummaging for it.

She held out a pale morsel of chicken. "Here, little one."

The dragon stretched up and took the meat from her fingers delicately, swallowing it down. Its whole body was about the length of her forearm.

She hurried for more meat and then, whistling and feeding, feeding and whistling, she lavished her entire concentration on these repeated actions, sensing the dragon growing stronger every moment.

At last, the hatchling was full. Milla noticed its small belly was now round and swollen with its first meal. It rested down with a little sigh.

The damp dark mass on its back stirred next, fluttering into life. Two wings sprang open, with shiny blue skin stretched taut between bones. Batlike, each wing ended in a tiny claw. They flapped once, and then folded again. The dragon set to preening itself, adorably inept, losing its balance now and again. It wobbled to the water bowl set into the table, put its snout down, drank deeply, then rested back.

Milla reached in and picked it up, feeling the ache in her arms where the guards had bruised them. The blue dragon was light and cool, drying out now but clammy with its egg sheen still on it. She draped it around her neck, its head in the hollow between her neck and her left shoulder, where the heat from her bare skin could comfort it. The dragon nestled into the dip of her collarbone, one claw hooked into the purple fabric of the dress. She felt it curl up and relax into sleep.

Only then did Milla look up.

Everyone else in the room was staring at her: spellbound, openmouthed, speechless.

Vigo was astonished; Isak delighted; Olvar thunderous.

Milla moved her hands to protect her dragon, prompting a sleepy scolding mew from the creature curled at her shoulder.

"Bring it here. Give it to me," the duke ordered.

The world seemed to pause. Everyone stared.

Milla's life tilted on this moment.

Either she was a good servant girl.

Or she held her dragon.

"No," she said. She was going to disobey him. "No. No. No." She wasn't used to saying that word. It flew from her lips like a flurry of black wings, a murder of crows, filling the room, taking the light.

She blinked hard, coming back to this new reality. She spoke again, sure and strong. "He needs to sleep, Your Grace. He'll be hungry when he wakes. We need more chicken."

The duke made a move as if to snatch the baby dragon from her. Then he halted. His gaze returned to the three eggs still waiting. Doubt rippled across his face, making him look like someone else.

"More chicken!" the duke ordered, and someone hurried from the room. Then, "He?"

The dragon stirred, raising its head to listen.

"Yes," Milla said firmly. "The dragon's a he." She knew this with the same instinctive certainty that she knew the song. The same way she knew they belonged together. And she knew another thing. "His name is Ignato."

Iggie growled lightly, answering her.

CHAPTER SEVENTEEN

Things might not have gone well for Milla and Ignato, except that the next egg began to hatch. The duke stopped glaring at Milla and pushed forward to stand by the red cushion. "Let me through."

Shakily, Milla crept nearer the fire. She peered down, keeping her hand cupped over her dragon. "Sleep, Iggie, sleep."

Just as before, the red egg was tapped apart from the inside, till a gap was wide enough for the dragon to crawl out. It lay there, exhausted, its sides heaving.

Duke Olvar copied what Milla had done, whistling and then humming with desperate eagerness. He bent low to the cushion. "Dragon! Dragon, do you hear me?"

But the little dragon's head sank down. It glistened, the color of raw meat, but the color was paling slightly, turning pinkish. Its breathing slowed.

Tarya called out the dragon's name. A two-beat cry, one high note, then a low: "Heral!"

Milla watched, trying not to grin too broadly as the dragon responded to Tarya. It stirred and tried to stand, quivering.

The red dragon stared at Tarya, and she stared back. The air seemed to thicken and pulse between them. Then the red dragon made a noise that echoed Tarya's call.

Tarya's eyes swam with tears.

"I don't believe it," Duke Olvar cried. "What's wrong with these creatures? I'm right here."

By then, a servant had brought in a silver plate piled high with more chicken, so Tarya was allowed through. She gently took the red dragon in both hands and lifted him to her face. They touched each other, nose to nose. Tarya was whispering to the hatchling constantly. Then she brought Heral to sit by the fire and reached for a piece of meat.

Heral growled and snapped it out of her fingers.

Tarya sobbed, laughing-crying with delight and pride.

The duke shrugged his shoulders and turned back to the table. "Still two to go," he said, wiping the disappointment from his face. For now, at least, he seemed to accept the dragons' choices.

The green egg was next, and this dragon was stronger. Milla watched as it got up immediately and hissed in the duke's face. Undeniably aggressive, its wings unfurled and flapped twice, creating a little draft.

The duke stepped back, shocked.

Vigo was by his side. He laughed, looking bewitched by the hatchling's determination.

It cocked its head toward Vigo, listening.

Something crackled between them.

Vigo laughed again. "Do you like that?" he asked, and slowly reached down and held open his hands.

The green dragon blinked its amber eyes and bowed its head, then clambered into Vigo's hands and curled there, purring like a kitten.

"She l-l-likes me!" he stammered in astonishment, all his usual poise melted away in the warm glow of his delight. "Hello, Petra." He seemed like a small boy on his birthday.

That left one egg. The yellow egg sat on its golden cushion, motionless. Duke Olvar leaned low over the table, one ear to its pale dome.

"This one must be mine! I can hear it." He picked up the egg in both hands and went to sit in a carved wooden chair at the other side of the fireplace. "Come on, then. I'm ready!" He sat there, almost bursting with impatience, staring down at the egg he cradled in his hands.

Milla's heart sank. That wasn't the right way. She didn't know *how* she knew, she just did. When a dragon and a person stared at each other and bonded, everything changed for them both. She'd felt it happen. She was a different person now. She'd been made new when Iggie hatched and found her.

Her hand still cupped Iggie's sleeping head. With every moment that passed, she loved him more. She silently thanked Kara for her instructions. "Thank you," she bent and whispered to Iggie. "Thank you for choosing me."

Then Milla watched the duke, his face illuminated in the glare of the flames. He was grinning as he waited, eyes aglow.

The egg began to move, shaking slightly in his hands. A very faint *tap* came from inside it, fainter than the others had been. A tiny piece of shell fell away, leaving a thin white membrane still in place. Then the egg fell silent. Moments passed.

"Is it stuck?" Milla asked. Iggie woke and looked up, then stiffened. She felt his claws grip tighter.

Mraa! the dragon said, as if he were trying to warn her.

"What's wrong with it?" the duke demanded. He got to his feet, looking panicked. "It's got to get out, it needs air." He crossed to the table, lifted the egg, and broke it against the surface of polished wood.

"No!" Milla, Vigo, and Tarya all called out together, feeling their dragons flinch.

It was too late. The egg shattered with a damp crunch.

The duke pulled it apart, flicking away pieces of shell with his fingers. He lifted up a limp body streaked with blood. It was dark russet gold, like damp beech leaves. The dragon didn't move.

It couldn't be dead! Not when the others were all safely hatched? Milla clung to disbelief to keep her afloat, but she felt herself sinking.

Olvar looked down at it for one long moment, and Milla watched the hope turn to despair and then anger in his face. The duke slung the body down onto the yellow cushion and stormed from the room before anyone could speak.

Serina hurried after him. A moment later they heard a loud bellow, and the sound of something heavy being hurled across the room through the archway.

Milla heard the duke's fury and curled her arms over her hatchling. Vigo and Tarya mirrored her, shuffling their chairs closer to the fire.

Nestan and Finn stood apart, muttering in low voices, their eyes on the door.

Isak walked over to the four-leaf table and gently picked up the lifeless dragon. He joined the other three by the fire and sank to his knees. He draped the small orange body across his lap and started stroking it lightly, one finger after another. The light of the dancing flames made its scales gleam like those of a goldfish, Milla saw, just as they turned Isak's glasses to small suns.

Isak began to sing to it, a heartbreaking lament, sweet and sad and soothing, all at once. His voice was hoarse and gentle, and he broke off to cough now and again.

Milla's eyes filled with tears for the life that hadn't had a chance to begin, for all that beauty and potential, now lost. She stroked Iggie in sympathy.

Iggie seemed to stir then. He uncurled himself and tumbled down from her shoulder. She caught him on her knees and he craned forward, chirruping excitedly.

"What? What is it?" Milla whispered. "Are you sad, too?"

But he didn't seem sad. He turned his head back to her and forward again, gesturing to the orange dragon. Iggie hopped on the spot, impatient.

"You want to go nearer? Isak, I think he's telling me . . . Can I show him?" she asked, edging closer, with new hope kindling in her heart.

Without stopping his song, Isak nodded and made space

129

next to him. Milla knelt down and lifted Iggie so he could see the golden hatchling's body.

Iggie lifted his head and called, a soft whistling noise that echoed the notes of Isak's song.

Just then, Isak's hands stopped moving. He raised them and froze.

"She . . . she *moved*. I felt her!" He bent lower. "Come on, little one, come on!"

Iggie stretched so far forward that Milla was worried he'd fall. He kept up a constant song.

The other two dragons, still recovering from hatching, also lifted their heads and watched intently.

Milla stared at the fourth dragon, willing it to be true. One of its feet twitched. Then the tail flapped once, like a fish out of water. Finally, the head lifted and one green eye opened.

Isak bent his head and murmured soft words to the dragon.

The dragon stared hard at him, listening.

The servant holding the platter of chicken moved forward, offering meat.

Isak took a piece and put it in his own mouth, chewing it hard. When it was soft, he took it out and passed it carefully to the dragon on his knee. Without getting up, she accepted the food and swallowed it down, then closed her eyes again, resting.

Isak sang again, changing the song from sad to hopeful, adding energy and life.

The dragon opened her eyes, and this time she managed to stand.

"Bright star, Belara, brave one," Isak named her, praising his dragon.

She spread her wings and flapped once, accepting this name, accepting him.

Milla was smiling so hard her cheeks hurt. She stared from Vigo to Isak to Tarya. She felt giddy, breathless, intoxicated. She checked back at the duke's closed door.

Four dragons had hatched, and not one had chosen Olvar. She couldn't guess what he would do next.

Part Three

Part Three

CHAPTER EIGHTEEN

F our dragons had hatched on the night of the full moon. They'd chosen four people to bond with.

Hardly able to believe it, Milla stared at her dragon, drinking him in. Her fingers traced his little blue body, learning every detail: his tiny claws, the smooth, cool flanks, the ridges along his tail, the rounded chest that felt warmer than the rest of him.

"So pleased to meet you, Iggie!" she said. "At last. All that time, it was you in the egg, and I didn't even know. But I dreamt of you." She knew it now. "Did you dream of me, too?"

Iggie crawled up her chest to listen. He opened his green eyes wide.

"I always liked the blue one best." Now it felt as if she'd always known him. She couldn't remember what life had been like, before Iggie.

He raised his head and croaked softly.

"Did you hear me, inside your egg?" Milla asked, bending her face to him. "Did you recognize your song?"

He reached up and touched his nose to hers, light as a moth.

Something burned between them, a fierce pure blaze of love that grew with every heartbeat. It grew and grew till it was the biggest thing in the room, in the island, in the whole world. A new sun, warming her bones.

"Wait till we get home!" Milla said. "I can't wait to show you to Josi. And what will Rosa and Thom say when they see you? You'll give them something to talk about!" She pictured their life together. "You can sit on my shoulder while I work. We'll be a team . . ." Everything would be better, now that Iggie was here.

Iggie listened to her, drinking in her words. Then he crawled back to his first roosting place in her collarbone, his body wrapped around her neck. Milla held him carefully in position. What if he got cold or sick? He seemed so fragile. So small. Worry spread like a black cloud across the sun.

Tarya, Isak, and Vigo sat in a circle around the fireplace, talking to their dragons. She read the same mixture of joy and fear in their faces.

Tarya caught her eye. "What just happened? Oh, Milla!" She jumped up and came over to hug Milla, one-armed, while the other hand held her red dragon against her chest.

"Make space for me!" Isak said, coming to join in with Belara on his shoulder.

Vigo hung back awkwardly.

"Come on! What are you waiting for?" Tarya called to him.

The four of them made a circle, hugging and laughing, while their dragons called raspily to one another, sounding like flint on steel.

Eventually, they sat back down, letting the dragons clamber at their feet, bolder now.

"So, what do we do? I mean, it feels like Belara chose me. But will he let me keep her?" Isak said, looking at the door Olvar had stormed through.

"Of course Belara chose you: she's yours and you're hers." Milla was grateful he'd asked that question. If the duke chose to take a dragon, how could they resist him? They had each other. He had an army.

"I'll fight anyone who tries to take Heral from me," Tarya said fiercely.

Milla looked at the other three. It was different for them: they were used to having all they wanted, giving orders, being obeyed. "These dragons chose us, and everyone here witnessed it." She tried to recall exactly what Kara had told her. "So the duke can't take Iggie from me, not without hurting him. He wouldn't hurt a dragon, would he?"

She chose not to mention Kara, not yet. Milla's bruised arms reminded her how the guards treated prisoners. First she needed to listen and learn, before she dragged Kara into danger.

"My father must see that," Vigo said. "He didn't take Iggie from you at the start."

"That was when he still had three chances left," Milla said, hoping he was right. She was warming to Vigo, but she still felt a little shy in front of him.

"We won't let him, Milla," Tarya said. "These dragons are ours."

"How do we know what they need? It's such a responsibility." Isak looked down at Belara, pushing his glasses up nervously. Then he took the glass vial from his shirt pocket and swallowed the last of his medicine.

"I think they'll tell us!" Tarya watched Heral ripping into an enormous piece of chicken.

"But there's so much we don't know," Isak said. "We don't even know why they are the last dragons. What went wrong before? We have to find out!" He looked at each of them in turn, growing more urgent: "Don't you see? We have to find out, or how do we stop it happening again? If we don't get it right, they might leave us. Or they might die."

There was a pause while that sank in.

"People are always talking about it, what happened to the old Arcosi and the last dragons—how it couldn't have been a fire or an earthquake, 'cos everything was left so perfectly. How it wasn't a famine, 'cos they left food behind, how it wasn't a plague, 'cos it didn't spread to Sartola . . ." Tarya sped through the options.

"I don't know what people are always talking about: I never hear them," Vigo said quietly.

"My friend Rosa spoke of a mad king. Rufus? What do you know of him?" Milla asked. "He was the one who fought against Sartola . . ."

"I know about that war, all right. Every Sartolan does. My mother made sure I learned the history of her country."

Tarya turned to Vigo, and Milla could see how hard she

was trying to be polite and patient with him. Things had changed between them. After the hatching tonight, they were on the same side, all four of them. "And you live in the palace. So you must also know something about the people who lived here once?"

Vigo shook his head. "I know Sartolan history, but no one knows what happened here."

"All this stuff?" Tarya gestured around them.

Milla looked at the elegant room, the high glass windows, the carved ceiling with its gold leaf. She didn't belong here. She barely dared to touch anything lest she break it. She kept waiting for someone to tell her to leave, or to clear up the mess of plates at their feet.

"I mean, it's theirs, right?" Tarya was saying. "It belonged to the ancient people. The Arcosi, the last dragonriders? The Norlanders had nothing when they arrived here, none of it survived the voyage. So there must be evidence somewhere?"

"We need to find it, for their sakes." Isak agreed with his sister. "What if it was something to do with the dragons? Maybe they got sick? Maybe the dragons killed the people?"

"They wouldn't do that!" Tarya said. "Maybe it was the other way around!"

"I'm just saying, we have to keep an open mind. But we need more to go on. There must be pictures, maps, scrolls somewhere, if they left everything behind?"

Milla had kept quiet, till now. But here was a task. She thrived on those. "Does your father have a study? Where does he keep his papers?" she asked Vigo.

"Not that I know . . . Oh, wait." He looked thoughtful.

"He always keeps the northern turret room locked. No one else is allowed in there."

"Shall we look?" Milla asked.

"I said it's locked."

"I'm, er, good with locks," Milla said, feeling the heat rise to her cheeks. Had she really just suggested breaking into the duke's private rooms?

"We can't do that!" Isak said.

"Can't we? We have a duty to our dragons. I'll do anything for Heral," Tarya said stubbornly. "Look, it's getting light. We should go now before everyone wakes."

"Let's just look, no harm in that," Vigo agreed. "I'll answer to my father."

Tarya looked at him quickly, her expression unguarded. Then she gave Vigo a dazzling grin.

Vigo blushed and muttered, "He can't think any worse of me than he does already."

Milla was curious: that was the second time he'd spoken of his father that way.

"Come on, I'll show you the way," Vigo told them.

A few moments later, they were standing in front of the turret room door: wooden, solid, arched at the top. Milla ran her hands over its polished surface and tried the iron handle. Locked.

"Tarya," she said, bending down to examine the lock, "can you pass me two of your hairpins?"

She draped Iggie around the back of her neck so both her hands were free, bent one of the pins double, twisted the end of the other, and gently poked them both into the lock. It was

140

a trick Josi had taught her, and now she realized she'd never thought to ask why.

"I really don't think we should . . ." Isak began.

"What are you doing?" Vigo asked. "And can you teach me?"

"Shhh! I need to concentrate, Your Grace," Milla said, closing her eyes so she could feel for the inner workings of the lock.

"I think this takes us beyond Grace," he said. "Call me Vigo."

Milla's fingers grew damp with effort, and she tried hard not to think about what would happen if the duke found her now. With a light click, the last pin of the lock shifted. She turned the handle and opened the door.

CHAPTER NINETEEN

The heavy door swung inward to reveal an entirely round room, generously wide, with narrow windows letting in faint shafts of light all the way up the turret. Milla tilted her head to see the top, making Iggie mew sleepily from his position around her neck. It was lined with curving shelves, reaching right up above their heads, ending in ornate beams at the top of the tower, carved with dragons, birds, and fishes.

They all stood there, gaping.

"You guessed right," Milla told Vigo.

"I don't believe it!" he said, staring. "I never knew this was here . . ."

Milla spotted strange wooden ladders built on four legs, to let the reader climb high and reach down scrolls or books from the upper shelves. She went across to the nearest one and lifted down a book. Leather-bound and heavy, it fell open to reveal fine handwritten script, with beautiful flame-like illustrations framing each page.

"Oh! There's dragons in this one, look!" She held it open for the others to see. She moved her finger slowly across the page, sounding out the words in an old-fashioned version of Sartolan. "This must be the language of the ancient Arcosi— the ones who lived here once." She paused, looking at this still, bright room. What secrets had they left behind? "Remedies for . . . a spring chill. Oh! It's about healing. That's good, we might need that."

The others copied her, each moving to a different shelf and taking down books to read about dragons, as the sun rose and the room grew light.

Milla lifted down a new book, and a little scrap of paper fell out. She laid down the book and picked it up carefully. It was smaller than a page: no more than a fragment, with words written across it in a curling, looping hand. "Hey, listen to this one. I think it's a poem."

And she read:

The dragons will return one last time
When the trade winds blow from the east.
Walls must fall, peace must reign.
Or the nest be forever lost.
Daughter of the storm, three times reborn
Who bears the sign of the sea.
When four seasons wane, for this bright dawn,
She will be given the key.

Milla felt a shiver down her spine.

"It sounds like a prophecy, not a poem," Vigo said slowly. "Can you read it again?"

Milla did.

"Do you think it's about our dragons?" Tarya laughed out loud. "Hear that, Heral? You're so important, they foretold you."

"I hope not. It sounds a bit ominous," Milla said. "That stuff about the nest being lost forever . . ." She squinted down at Iggie, checking his breathing.

"Don't worry, it's just a poem," Isak said. "And if you're worried about prophecies, peace looks to be reigning just fine on Arcosi, so there's nothing to fear." And he went back to the scroll he was reading.

Milla met Vigo's eyes. He shrugged and smiled and returned to his book.

When the others weren't looking, she folded the paper and tucked it into her waistband. It sounded important to her. She vowed to memorize it later and puzzle it out, however long it took.

"If it's about danger to you," she whispered to Iggie, "then I want to know so I can protect you."

He didn't wake up, so she settled down to the next book.

They were all concentrating so hard they didn't hear Duke Olvar walk in, followed by Nestan and Finn.

"Here they are—we found them!" Olvar called over his shoulder. "What are you doing?" he asked them. "And how did you get in?"

Milla jumped in fright and dropped the book she was

holding. It landed on the floor with a loud slam. With one hand over Iggie's sleeping body, still draped around her neck, she backed away from the duke.

Without speaking, the four of them assembled into one united group: Milla flanked by the twins and Vigo at the front, with his green dragon, Petra, on his shoulder.

"We need to know how to care for the dragons. You can't blame us for that!" Vigo raised his voice to his father. "Why didn't you tell me this was here? That's so typical, keeping the best hidden away, just for you . . ."

"There's so much we have to learn about them, Your Grace," Isak intervened diplomatically, tucking Belara under his jacket, out of sight. "This archive is superb." He sounded different, all flattering and eager. "It must cover all aspects of dragonlore!"

Milla watched Isak trying to placate the duke, puzzled. Then she realized: Isak loved books. Isak in a library was like a hungry child in a bakery.

"That's right. It does," the duke told Isak. Then he picked up the book Milla had dropped and put it back on the shelf, patting the leather spine gently.

"Of course I don't blame you, Vigo." The duke came closer. Perhaps he hadn't slept either. His face looked gray in the faint dawn light. "Of course you must learn about them. In fact, I was going to suggest the same thing." He smiled, but it didn't reach his eyes.

Isak looked like he'd been offered a feast.

Milla listened hard, waiting for his meaning to become clear.

"You are all most welcome here in my palace," Duke Olvar went on. "Dragons need space, heat, food—where else would they live? The dragonhall was built for the purpose. And you've found the archive I was going to show you . . ."

"We can stay here? Thank you, Your Grace," Isak said.

Milla saw Nestan and Richal Finn exchange a glance at the duke's words.

Milla was struggling to keep up. "But . . . m-m-my job . . . my home . . . What will happen—?" she stuttered. Speaking to the duke made her feel clumsy and stupid.

"Everything has changed. You have a new job now." Duke Olvar reached past Vigo, toward Milla. "And a new home."

She didn't dare move. With one hand, she cupped Iggie's head, while the other supported his tail.

"Whatever anyone else might think . . ." he tried again. "That is, *this dragon* . . ." He reached out a finger and touched Iggie's back.

She licked her dry lips. "Iggie, Your Grace."

She wasn't keen on that hungry look in the duke's eyes, but she stood her ground, even though her skin itched at his proximity. Of all the things that had happened since last night, this felt the most unreal. She was standing here, talking to the duke himself about what her dragon needed.

"Iggie, then. He chose you." He uttered each word slowly and clearly, as if she were a very young child. "Do you want him to have the best care?"

"Of course, Your Grace," she whispered.

"Then he needs to stay here. Where else can the dragons be hidden, for their own protection?"

"*Hidden?* But—" Milla began, watching her dreams of introducing Iggie to Josi, Thom, and Rosa fade like sea mist. Instead, she would live here at the palace, among all this luxury. "I mean, thank you," she breathed.

"It's clear that the dragons must stay here," Olvar said. "The dragons need you. You stay here, too."

"Is it? Clear to whom, Olvar?" Nestan spoke up. He left Richal Finn and walked over to Milla and the twins, his cane tapping lightly on the polished floor. "We thank you for your generous offer of hospitality, but these are my children, and they are free citizens of Arcosi, I think."

"Excuse me, Your Grace," Tarya asked, with a quick look at her father. "Are you inviting us to stay? Or are you saying we can't leave?"

Nestan gently laid one hand on her shoulder, next to Heral's red back, lending his support to his daughter's words.

Clearly unused to being questioned, Duke Olvar glared at Tarya. He cleared his throat, with a deep, guttural cough. "As I said, overnight, everything has changed, whether we like it or not. And we must change, too, if we are to protect these precious dragons that have been given into our care."

"*Given?*" Tarya cried, then realized who she was speaking to. "I'm sorry, Your Grace, but didn't my father tell you? Someone died for these eggs. Someone gave their life to keep them safe."

"And that happened very conveniently on the property that you're so eager to return to, Nestan," the duke said, smooth as silk now. "Maybe you have other plans for the dragons? Maybe you always did?" He took a step toward Nestan, then another, so they were facing each other and the tension crackled between them. "Did anyone actually see this mysterious victim?"

Milla blinked. Instead of watching the duke and Nestan standing head-to-head, she was lost in her memories, seeing the cloaked man slumping forward in a pool of blood.

"Or perhaps you bought these eggs on one of your trading trips and forgot to mention it?" the duke suggested.

Milla dipped her chin over Iggie's head, as if she could protect him from the words tossed back and forth.

"Of course not. Did I not bring them straight to you?" Nestan said curtly, matching Duke Olvar's stare. "Have I ever given you reason to doubt my loyalty?"

Olvar's gaze shifted to Nestan's left leg before he could help it, and he flushed.

Nestan's injury was a constant reminder to the world of his loyalty to Duke Olvar, and the high cost of that loyalty.

"Don't ask me why the man chose to deliver the eggs to us," Nestan went on. "No doubt he was expecting to find the original inhabitants in my house. And we *do* have a witness. Isn't that right, Milla?"

She jumped.

"Is that true?" Richal Finn's head snapped up and he stared at her in surprise. She looked down, cheeks warm, praying no one mentioned the rest of the story. The duke wouldn't like the part about hiding the eggs.

"Well, then perhaps we should be thanking you, for finding the eggs and returning them to their true home. Where they belong. Where they will stay." Olvar's tone turned steely.

"Very well," Nestan told Olvar, "but I am trusting you to protect them. All of them: all four children, and all four dragons. If *anything* happens . . . to *any* of them"—he flicked a quick glance at Milla—"I will hold you responsible."

"Nestan, old friend." Olvar's tone changed entirely, as if they hadn't just been growling at each other. He stepped in to shake his hand. "We're family now. You don't even need to ask."

Milla whispered to Iggie, "Hear that, my love? We're staying." Her fingertips lightly stroked his scales, as she looked up at the turret roof of the library, so high above them, at the shafts of golden light slanting down. She felt like a princess in a fairy tale, waking up to a new life. Somewhere deep down, there was a niggle of unease, like a thorn in the sole of her shoe. Like a pea under her mattress. She chose to ignore it. This is where the dragons belonged. Surely she could learn to belong here, too?

For Iggie's sake, she had to try.

CHAPTER TWENTY

Milla was dragged from her dream like a fish hooked from the sea. She surfaced, gasping.

"Ouch!"

She'd been dreaming of sitting in Josi's kitchen, drinking cinnamon-spiced coffee, sweet and bitter at the same time. The dream faded, leaving a faint aftertaste of homesickness.

Iggie was sitting on her chest, needling her skin with his claws, like a cat. He blinked his green eyes to greet her.

"Iggie!" she murmured in delight, half-convinced she was still dreaming.

Her dragon was perfect. His scales gleamed. Each one was squarish, outlined in darker blue flowing down his back like a beautiful tessellated mosaic. His wings were smooth dark sapphire, folded away like bundled silk. He clawed her again, gently.

"I'm awake! Stop it." She peered up, and he leaned over to drag half a carcass of roast chicken a little nearer.

"Oh, thanks, Ig. Did you bring me breakfast?" She burst out laughing. "You're getting so strong: it's nearly as big as you!"

He flicked his tail from side to side and hissed at her, proudly.

Her heart swelled with love at the sight of him. Seeing him, touching him, being with him: it made everything feel right. She felt stronger and happier than she had ever been, as if there was a kind of power that spread from Iggie to her and back again.

"Aren't you hungry? You have this. I think I prefer bread." She sat up, shredded the meat and fed it to him, smiling as he growled and shook little pieces before he swallowed them. "Look at you, getting big and sleek. Am I feeding you too much? How would I know—you're not going to tell me, are you, greedy dragon?"

He just pawed her hand for more meat.

She wished she knew more. She felt drawn to find dragon-lore, like a compass needle seeking north. She had been yearning to see Kara again, to say thank you. She couldn't wait to introduce her to Iggie and see what she would say.

Iggie finished eating and sneezed, breaking into her thoughts. He jumped down from her bunk, already nimble and astonishingly fast.

They'd moved into the dragonhall a week ago, once it was clear that baby dragons would smash anything that wasn't fastened down. Milla was adjusting to the comforts of her life here quicker than she could have imagined. She drew back the curtains of her bunk and hopped out after him.

In the center of the dragonhall, like the hub of a wheel, there was a huge cylindrical brick oven that burned night and day, with a perch for the dragons spiraling around it. The high ceiling was inlaid with colored tiles.

There were two entrances: the main double doors standing open to let sunlight in, and the secret back door concealed behind a wall hanging. Milla had found it on the day they moved in, but she didn't tell anyone. That would have meant confessing that she'd seen Kara use it to escape on the night of the duke's ball. For her sake, she kept it quiet. But how did Kara know of the secret door?

"Morning, Milla." Isak and Vigo were drinking coffee: the smell must have crept into her dream.

"Morning." Milla flashed a wide grin toward them and helped herself from a basket of fresh rolls. Still warm, and she hadn't even had to knead the dough herself. Or chop the wood. Or build the fire. She bit into the fresh bread, gratefully.

Tarya came out to join them, yawning.

"What's wrong?" Milla asked as soon as she saw her face. For days, Tarya had seemed restless, like a tethered beast testing the limits of its chain. "Is it Heral?"

But Heral was peacefully snoozing, his red snout resting on Petra's green back.

"Heral's fine. I'm fine. I don't mean to sound ungrateful." Tarya glanced quickly at Vigo. "All this is so wonderful."

Milla couldn't believe the speed with which the duke had organized everything: builders, carpenters, tailors. All sworn to secrecy and paid double to be sure. She smoothed her blue silk nightclothes with her free hand: still marveling at their quality.

"It's just . . ." Tarya's voice faded out. She put her head in her hands, scratching through her curly mass of golden hair. Living indoors, her tanned skin had faded to a pale cream, and she had violet shadows under her eyes from waking in the night to feed Heral.

"Do you miss your dad?" Milla asked Tarya gently, giving her a quick sideways hug. "I miss Josi. I was just dreaming of her."

"Yes, that must be it. I'm fine," Tarya said stiffly. "Don't listen to me." She helped herself absently to a bread roll and started pulling it apart.

Milla watched as Iggie climbed onto the roost and wrapped his blue neck around Belara's gold one.

Prrt? he greeted Belara, ears pricked in welcome.

"Hey, Iggie," Isak said. "Look at them. They're friends, aren't they?"

Milla spoke with her mouth full. "Uh-huh. I think Belara is his favorite."

"Well, your Ig has very good taste," Isak told her.

Milla and Isak chatted easily about their dragons' latest tricks. Milla was glad to see she could still make him laugh with her impression of Iggie stalking pieces of chicken.

Isak opened his arms, like wings, coming to swoop after her.

Milla pounced on him, mimicking Iggie, and they fell in the sawdust, giggling.

Just then, a dark shadow fell across the floor between the open doors of the dragonhall.

"Good morning." Duke Olvar's voice was loud and disapproving.

"Your Grace!" Isak stopped laughing, rolled to his feet, seized his dragon from her perch, and went over to greet the duke, with Belara in his arms.

If he had a tail, he'd be wagging it, like a puppy trying to please a new master, Milla thought. She scrambled up, too, brushing the sawdust from her nightclothes.

"How is she today?" the duke was asking Isak.

"She's fine. See?" Isak lifted Belara up. The golden dragon had long, elegant ears and her green eyes were more almond-shaped than Iggie's. Now she twisted her head away from the duke as if he smelled bad.

Milla bit her lip so she wouldn't laugh.

"How many times did you feed her last night?" the duke asked.

"Three times, Your Grace. Her appetite increases every day . . ." Isak and Duke Olvar discussed every detail of Belara's diet, while the others waited.

"Well done, Isak," Olvar said eventually, laying an approving hand on his shoulder.

Isak looked delighted, but Belara started crawling over Isak's shoulder, determined to escape the duke's inspection.

Tarya snorted. Then she met Vigo's eyes, and the two of them started shaking with stifled laughter.

The duke noticed and spun around, scowling.

"Hear me, all of you. This is a serious business, no

laughing matter." Olvar's glance moved around the hall, lingering over each dragon. "These dragons are our only concern. Put them first. Forget all else. You aren't here for your amusement." He glared at Milla. "You are here for the dragons. And you have work to do."

They all froze where they stood, like guilty children caught raiding the honey jar.

The duke didn't understand. Milla didn't need to be told to care for Iggie: it came as naturally as breathing. She bent down to stroke his bright blue head with one finger. This love felt new and so powerful, it scared her. Rising up, with deep certainty, were feelings stronger than anything she had known before. She would fight for him. She would kill to defend him. Already she knew, without doubt, that she would die for him.

"We know, Your Grace," Isak said. "We'll get straight back to the library, as soon as the dragons have eaten—"

"Wait a moment," Vigo objected. "Why do you get to tell us what's best for our dragons?"

Milla held her breath as Vigo challenged his father, but Tarya was watching him with something like admiration in her gaze.

"Aren't they worth it?" Duke Olvar snapped. "Are you so reckless and ungrateful you'd risk your dragon's life? What if Petra falls ill? How will you know what to do?"

"Of course they're worth it. Of course we'll keep reading." Vigo raised his voice. "But we're not lazing around out here. We're caring for them. We're feeding them. We're playing with them—don't they need that, too?" he finished.

"Did you find a scroll saying that?" Olvar asked, looking down his nose at his son.

"What if the scrolls don't have all the answers?" Vigo retorted. "What if you trusted us to know what our dragons need?"

"I suppose they need you to roll around in the sawdust, too?" Olvar snapped. "Ignoring them?"

That wasn't fair! Milla hadn't been ignoring Iggie—she'd just fed him!

"Get dressed and get to work." The duke turned and walked out of the dragonhall.

There was a long silence.

Tarya put a hand on Vigo's arm, making him jump. She smiled at him reassuringly, but he was still frowning at his father's interruption.

"It's only because he cares about the dragons," Isak said eventually.

"I know, I'm sorry," Milla sighed. The thought of the library made her feel daunted. "I'll do my part. It's just"—she felt ashamed as she confessed—"I can't read as fast as you."

"It is slow going," Isak said. "Too slow."

"How can you say that? You're the fastest!" Tarya told her twin, with an edge that made Milla wonder if she minded not being the best, for once.

"Still," Isak said, "it's going to take us years to get through all those books. We should get back to it."

Milla looked at the dragons, drowsing now on the perch in the warmth of the stove. Kara had been so clear in her advice about the eggs, perhaps she would know more about dragons than a dusty old book? Was she still at the Yellow House, or had she fled the island already? Talking to Kara could be just the shortcut they needed.

Even if she was still hiding with Josi, there still remained one problem: how could she arrange to see Kara without leading the duke's soldiers straight there?

"We should focus. It's the big questions we need to start with." Vigo handed Tarya a cup of coffee, getting a weary half smile in thanks. He listed them on his fingers. "Where did they come from? What happened to their parents? What do they need to survive?"

"Yes, we need to narrow it down. If only there was someone who could tell us," Isak said. "At least show us where to look."

Kara would know. Kara could tell them. Milla glanced at her three friends—at the four dragons. She could keep faith with her friends and with Kara at the same time, if she navigated carefully around her promise.

"There might be someone," Milla began. "Do you remember the old woman who spoke at the duke's ball?" She gave them a trimmed-down version of meeting Kara on hatching night. She left out her exact words, and the part about taking Kara to Josi.

"The duke is looking for her! Let's tell him. He can send his men, bring her straight here!" Isak burst out.

Milla stared at him. As a Norlander, Isak didn't understand how the duke's soldiers treated other people on Arcosi.

"Er, why don't I speak to her first?" She tried not to criticize the duke in front of Isak. "She hasn't done anything wrong."

"She wrecked the duke's ball—that's when she told us the dragons were returning, that night," Tarya recalled in a rush. "Wait, did *she* bring them? Was she with that man who was killed?"

"Will someone tell me what's going on?" Vigo sounded utterly confused.

Milla took a deep breath and told him everything she knew about the murdered man bringing the eggs to the Yellow House. "The rest, I'm just guessing, same as you. I think Kara must have been traveling with him. I haven't even told her yet that he's dead. There wasn't time."

"So where is she now?" Isak asked. "Will she want the dragons back?"

Milla was facing Vigo. He looked directly at her and gave a very slight warning shake of his head.

"I'm not sure where she is," she bluffed, heeding the warning for Kara's sake. "Let me go look for her. I'll see what she knows. But don't worry: the dragons are ours."

"No! You can't trust her," Isak said. "We need to bring her straight to the duke."

"What is it with you and the duke?" Tarya demanded. "You've been cozying up to him all week. No, ever since his ball!"

"Why shouldn't I?" Isak snapped at his sister. "The duke's listened to me more this week than our father has all year!"

"That's not true," Tarya said.

"You can't see it, because you're our father's favorite. I'm just his disappointing son."

Tarya jerked back with tears in her eyes. It hurt, Milla

saw, because there was a grain of truth in it. Tarya was more like Nestan, and they did talk more.

"Stop it. He loves you both!" Milla said. "More than anything."

Taking a breath now, Isak mastered himself. "Anyway, why shouldn't we trust Duke Olvar? Look at everything he's done for us."

Milla had been puzzling over that. Why was the duke being so generous to them all? Perhaps he was just waiting for the right moment to steal a dragon. She was just a servant girl; surely he'd come for Iggie first?

As if Isak could read her mind, he added, "He's already given me his word that he won't try to take the dragons from us . . ."

"And why is that?" Vigo said tightly. "He won't? Or he can't?"

"He can't!" Tarya told them urgently. "I was reading about this, late last night. That's why I'm so tired. A dragon will pine to death if you take it from its person," she said. "They only rebond in rare cases, when their original person dies. Even then, they might not. You make sure you tell the duke that, Isak. Stop him getting any ideas."

Shocked silence fell.

Milla leaned down and scooped sleeping Iggie from the perch, cuddling him close to her chest. "Don't you worry, Iggie. Nobody's going to take you from me, I promise."

More than that, she had to stay safe. His life might depend on it.

Iggie raised his head sleepily and blinked. Sensing her

mood, he rubbed his cool scaly head along Milla's chin, crooning softly.

"Iggie, my Ig," she told him fiercely. "You're mine. No one else is having you!"

There was a long pause while the four of them spoke only to their dragons.

"Fair enough, then; go and see your mysterious woman," Isak said at last. "But make sure she tells us everything! What was she doing with the eggs? Why bring them now? And what did she mean about the old Arcosi returning—are they about to invade?"

"Don't forget: we owe all this to her," Milla reminded Isak. "I'm not going to interrogate her—we should be thanking her. But if she's well enough, I'll ask her what happened to the last dragons, and what we need to know now."

"I'll come with you," Tarya said, standing up.

"No, let me go," Milla insisted. "I'll take Iggie, but I need you three to cover for me here. You heard the duke," she added. "Please?"

The twins exchanged a long glance without speaking. Sometimes they were so in tune it left everyone else shut out. Something passed between them: A question. An apology.

"Fine," Tarya sighed eventually. "And if you pass our house, tell Dad to come and see us tomorrow? He is interested in us both, Isak, whatever you might think."

"We'll cover for you," Vigo said. "But you'll have to be quick, before my father notices."

"Come on." Tarya took Milla's hand. "I'll help you get ready."

They each had a little dressing room by their bunks, and sets of new clothes in the colors of their dragon. Tarya helped Milla, buttoning up a long blue cotton dress that fitted perfectly.

"Be careful out there," she said, doubling Milla's blue scarf to make a secure pocket for Iggie and tying it at her back. "You will come back, won't you?"

"Of course I will!" Milla exclaimed. She turned to face her friend. "We'd never leave you, would we, Ig?"

"Good." Tarya hugged her carefully so she wouldn't squash Iggie. "It's just, well, you have Iggie. Josi. You have your other friends."

"Stop it! Of course we'll return to you. You and Isak are my family." But Milla wondered if Isak still felt the same. He seemed to be drifting away from them both since the eggs had hatched. Drifting closer to Duke Olvar.

CHAPTER TWENTY-ONE

M illa's new clothes made things easier: now she passed for a person of consequence. Today, the palace gates were opened without hesitation.

"I won't be long," she told the guards at the gate airily, as if she'd been born to a life of giving orders.

"See you soon, my lady." The guard actually tipped his hat to her, keeping his eyes respectfully averted.

Her fine clothes also allowed her to conceal Iggie, tucked under her wide silk scarf and covered with a velvet cloak in a darker royal blue. He was completely hidden among the folds of fabric. She kept one hand cupped over him, feeling the tiny flicker of his pulse against her chest.

As she walked down the main road, cradling Iggie's sleeping back, her lips curved in a smile. The streets of Arcosi had never looked so beautiful: stonework gleaming in the cool amber sun. The autumn wind tugged lightly at her curls, and sent crinkled russet leaves skittering around the cobblestones. Right then it felt to Milla as if anything were possible.

When she reached the Yellow House, Richal Finn was on gate duty and she called out a greeting.

But Finn only glared at her and didn't open the gate. "What are you doing here?" He almost sounded angry. "Come to gloat?"

"Visiting Josi." It wasn't the welcome she'd expected. "Don't panic. We aren't prisoners up there, you know." Her good mood vanished.

"Does the duke know?" Finn hissed.

"If he finds out, I'll know who told him," Milla snapped, hurt. "Are you going to let me in?"

"Watch yourself, Milla," Richal Finn called as the gates swung open and she walked into the courtyard.

Lanys emerged from the kitchen with a basket on one hip. Her nose was peeling, pink and sore. She halted and glanced sharply at Milla's new clothes.

"Morning, Lanys." Milla stayed polite, but she turned her body away instinctively, folding her arms across her chest to hide Iggie.

Lanys pushed past her, too furious to speak, shoving Milla hard with one shoulder.

Iggie woke with a surprised *mraaa?*, sensing a threat to them.

"Shhhh, it's all right, Ig," Milla whispered, watching Lanys struggle through the gate with her basket, feeling a surprising rush of compassion. She wouldn't change places with her now, not for all the gold in the world.

Pausing in the kitchen doorway, she felt another dizzying shift, like the time she'd climbed the mast of the *Dolphin* with Thom, looking down at her familiar city from a whole new perspective.

She breathed in the familiar smells of home: roasting meat, rising dough, the orange zest that Josi was grating, right there at the workbench.

"I said, not till you've finished—" Josi shouted without turning.

"It's me," Milla said, in a small voice, suddenly doubtful of her welcome.

"Oh!" Josi spun around, so fast that Milla found herself wrapped in a hug before she could warn her about Iggie.

"Careful!" she mumbled into Josi's chest. "Don't squash him . . ." Pulling back, she caught a quick glimpse of Josi's brown eyes glittering with emotion.

"You didn't bring the—" Josi stopped, unable to say the word. So Nestan had told her about the eggs hatching.

Laughing with delight, Milla nodded. "Yes!" She patted the scarf. "Do you want to see him?"

"Wait!" Josi crossed to the kitchen door, closed it, and bolted it. "Now!"

"Where's Kara?" Milla asked. "Is she still safe?"

"Of course," Josi snapped. "What do you think?"

"I didn't mean . . . Where?"

Josi nodded at the last storeroom door opening off the kitchen.

"Who else knows?"

"The master."

Milla took this in. Of course Josi and Nestan would share secrets if they were a couple. She wondered who else knew about their relationship.

"Come on, see for yourself." Josi opened the door, letting light pour into a small whitewashed room. The back wall was filled with shelves, stacked with preserves, jars of oil, waxy cheeses. There was a pallet bed against the long wall, covered in a thick woolen blanket.

Kara was lying motionless under the blanket, curled on her side.

"Morning," Milla called softly in Sartolan. "It's Milla, come to see you. Are you all right?"

Silence.

She spun around to check with Josi, standing behind her with her arms folded, her face unreadable.

Milla looked back at Kara, now that her eyes were adjusting to the dimmer light, and noticed the old woman's cheeks were shining with tears.

"Kara, what's wrong? What's happened?" She bent and touched her shoulder, feeling the tremors that shook her body. "Is it about the dragons?" Her hand flew to Iggie's sleeping form under the scarf.

Kara only curled up tighter and turned to face the wall.

"Josiah," she managed to say. "He's dead." And then she lost herself in a fresh wave of sobbing.

"How long has she been like this?" Milla twisted around to ask Josi.

"Since she found out, last week . . . Let me help. Come here." With one arm around Kara's shoulders, Josi helped her sit and tenderly tucked the blanket around her knees.

Milla bent down and asked, "Kara, are you all right?"

Kara wiped her face on her sleeve. "No. My Josiah was murdered. Protecting the eggs."

Milla bit her lip. She dared not confess she was there, that she could have stopped it.

"All our lives, we've guarded them, and he was killed here on Arcosi. At the very last step." Kara closed her eyes.

Milla and Josi exchanged a worried glance.

"So tell me: was it worth it?" Kara asked now, staring up at Milla with some of the defiant spark she'd shown at the duke's ball. "Did you reach them in time?"

That was when Iggie stirred underneath the silk scarf. Milla lifted him out carefully in her cupped hands, though he was almost too big to hold in them. "There's someone I want you to meet. Iggie, meet Josi and Kara."

Milla opened her hands.

Josi gasped.

Kara jerked upright sharply, her cheeks burning fever-bright.

Prrt? Iggie asked, lifting his head. In the faint light, his scales gleamed lapis lazuli.

"Oh, Milla," Josi said, "he's beautiful!"

Milla gulped, unable to trust herself to speak right then.

"You did it!" Kara's eyes were huge black pools, glistening with tears. She lowered her head toward him, stiffly, and

166

waited. Iggie stretched up, sniffing, and then touched his nose to Kara's.

"Oh! He's like Cato come again," Kara breathed. "May I?" she held out her hands, making her gold bracelets jangle and revealing her tattoo.

Iggie chirruped and stepped from Milla's hands to Kara's, balancing his weight between her wrinkled palms and unfolding his wings. He flapped eagerly. *Aark?*

Milla felt a pang of jealousy to see Iggie's excitement at meeting other people. Wasn't she enough for him anymore? But she was being ridiculous: if it wasn't for Kara, she wouldn't even have her dragon.

"That I should see the day," Kara whispered with emotion. "The others? All safely hatched and bonded?" She passed Iggie to Josi, waiting patiently for her turn to greet him.

"Hello, little one." Josi's deep voice was hoarse with emotion. Just as before, Iggie stretched up and greeted Josi, nose to nose, with a quiet *prrrt.*

Milla nodded, blinking hard. "Thank you, Kara, for making me rush to him that night."

"Dragons. Home. On Arcosi." Kara let tears roll freely down her cheeks, smiling at Iggie on Josi's lap. "Here, in the city, not trapped in the palace . . . Oh, you did well, daughter. Look at him."

Iggie was nuzzling the heel of Josi's palm with his head, making a crooning noise. He liked her!

"But what do you mean, *trapped?*" Milla asked. "The others are still in the palace. Shouldn't they be there?" Here was her chance to learn. "Please, tell me what I need to do to keep him safe. You said you spent your life guarding the eggs. Well, I want to spend my life guarding him, but there's so much I don't know."

"What do you know?" Kara's voice was faint, but she was listening.

"They need meat and water, warmth, bonded love—we've learned that much. But what else?"

"You're giving him plenty of spring water?" Kara asked. "That's the most important thing."

"Of course! They drink all the time. So will you tell me: what happened before? What happened to the last dragons?"

Kara looked utterly drained, and Milla felt a pang of guilt for pressing her.

"Aren't they doing well?" Josi asked. "He looks strong, this little one, and I know that Milla is."

Milla felt a warm surge of gratitude at that, watching Josi and Iggie get acquainted.

"You'll need that in the days to come . . ." Kara faltered.

"What do you mean? What is to come?" Milla prompted her.

"The dragons belong . . . to the city." Kara spoke in short bursts now and seemed near the end of her strength. "Not the palace. That's the mistake. That almost finished them."

"But what else can we do now? I'm sorry, I don't mean to push you. Rest a moment?"

"No, it's all right. This is why we returned. You need to know the story of Karys Stormrider and the last dragons of Arcosi. So you don't make the same mistakes again."

168

CHAPTER TWENTY-TWO

Kara sat up straight to tell her story, her gestures graceful, her bracelets clinking lightly as she spoke.

"The dragons used to hatch in the city marketplace. Every child of Arcosi would attend. Anyone could be chosen: a fisherman's daughter, a merchant's son, the baker's apprentice. But the royal family didn't like that." Kara's voice found some strength in retelling this tale, turning musical and deep: "Over time, they changed the rules to serve them better. Soon, hatching happened at the palace. Only the royal family could attend."

Milla felt guilty. That had happened for her and Iggie. What were the odds he'd have chosen her if the whole city had been there?

"It isn't good for them. That's what you need to remember." Kara took Milla's hand and pressed it as she spoke these words. "Fewer and fewer eggs came. In the end, there were only three dragons left. And three dragonriders."

"Dragonriders!" Those mythical figures, painted on the dragonhall walls. "Who were they, the last dragonriders? What happened to them?"

"There was Rufus Goldeneye and his dragon, Juna; his sister, Karys Stormrider, and her dragon, Cato; their cousin Silvano Cloudglider and his dragon, Aelia." She paused a moment to catch her breath.

Karys Stormrider. The name seemed to resonate in the air between them. "Go on," Milla whispered.

"Rufus was the result of his family's many mistakes. Firstborn child, spoiled utterly. He'd always had everything he wanted. Every whim. Every wish. So when he couldn't control events, his mind grew . . . *altered.*"

"Altered, how?"

Kara coughed then, a hollow, rattling cough that shook her whole rib cage.

"Let me bring you something for that," Josi said, passing Iggie over gently. "Here, take your dragon, Milla." She warned, "We don't have long. I'll need to open that door before anyone notices," and she went out of the storeroom into the main kitchen.

Kara picked up the tale, slower now. "Difficult years came, as they often do. Harvests failed. The island flooded. Ships were lost. The people of Arcosi grew hungry. They grew desperate. Rufus convinced Karys they should carry out one swift raid on the old enemy, Sartola. She agreed, for her people's sake."

"What did they do?" Milla asked, horrified at the idea of

using Iggie to fight. She held him in her lap now. His round green eyes were sleepy, but he was listening, too.

"The dragonriders of Arcosi waged war on Sartola. They burned it. They raided its treasury. Karys was injured, so she didn't see the worst."

Milla closed her eyes, trying to banish the images that sprang up, unbidden: choking smoke, burning buildings. After a moment, she asked, "So they got their gold. Was Rufus satisfied?"

Kara let out a short, barking cough. "Oh, no." She looked up as Josi came back in, carrying a tray of steaming mugs. "Thank you. No, that traitor was not satisfied. His dragon fell ill. Rufus kept all the Sartolan gold for himself. He didn't even pay his troops. He convinced himself that Juna needed more gold. This time he took it from his own people, imposing higher and higher taxes. They had nothing left to give."

"Is that why they left?" Milla asked, remembering the deserted villas of the shadow strip.

"They chose exile, those who could: the lucky ones. The unlucky ones had no choice. When Karys recovered from her injuries, she found the city of Arcosi almost empty. A ghost city, given to rats and scavenging dogs. By the time she realized what her brother had done, it was too late."

"What do you mean? What had he done?" Milla whispered.

Kara sat up a little straighter, as if it cost her to speak these words. "He sold his own people. For the gold. For his dragon."

"No!" Milla lifted Iggie close to her heart.

"Karys stopped it. Oh, yes. She and Cato, they burned the ships, there in the docks, before they could load another cargo . . ." She broke off, making a strange noise. "But Juna died anyway. So it was all for nothing, all that suffering, all those deaths." She was laughing: a bitter, mirthless sound.

"Rufus was wrong. It's a myth. Dragons don't need gold." She bent forward and spoke urgently to Milla, pulling her close, so she heard every word. "Dragons need their people. Haven't you felt it? How he draws energy from you and you from him? It's the same with everyone he meets. Dragons need contact with their people: they belong to them."

"But . . . but . . ." Milla gulped, feeling her cheeks burning.

"What, child?"

"Doesn't he belong to me?" she asked faintly.

"You're his chosen person, his bonded, his rider, one day. Of course! How can you doubt it? But you've seen the basking nests, built into the marketplace? That's where they belong: in the heart of the city. Without their freedom and their people, they sicken and die. That is what Rufus never understood. He did the worst thing possible. The people of Arcosi were gone: fled, sold, broken."

"You said there were three dragons. And Juna died. So there were two left. What happened to them?" Milla waited, desperate to know. This was Iggie's story, too: it must be. She leaned down and touched her lips to the top of his head. What was the link between him and these dragons?

"After Juna died, Rufus grew more deranged in his grief.

172

Most of his servants fled, all but the most loyal. Even Karys grew afraid of him and started planning her escape.

"One night, Rufus laced their evening meal with poison: just enough to send Karys and her cousin Silvano into a deep sleep. They awoke in the dragonhall to find themselves in chains."

"Why?" Milla gasped in horror. She reached for the mug of steaming liquid in front of her and took a sip. It tasted sweet and strong, like raisins and honey and cloves.

"Rufus wanted to bond with another dragon. He tried with Aelia, thinking it might be easier with a female, like Juna."

"But you said Aelia was Silvano's dragon?" Milla asked in sudden fear.

"Yes, that's right."

"I thought the bond was for life?" She put her mug down, feeling sick.

"It is," Kara said, looking grim.

"I don't understand," Milla murmured, afraid that she did.

"Rufus murdered his cousin Silvano so he could try to bond with his dragon. And Karys witnessed it all, unable to move."

"No . . . In the dragonhall? Where I live now?" She couldn't believe that warm, safe haven had seen such horrors. She lifted Iggie close with both hands, needing to feel the warm pulse under his throat, his aliveness.

Just then, there was a pounding on the main kitchen door, and Lanys's voice, calling, "Josi? Where are you?"

Iggie stood tall, barking his danger call: *Mraaa! Mraa!*

"Shhhh!" Milla hushed him. "Be quiet now."

Josi jumped up, startled. "That's Lanys, back from market already. Stay in here while I see her. She mustn't find Kara." She left the room.

Milla took a few moments to settle Iggie, showing him they weren't in danger.

Kara seemed exhausted by the story. She lay down again on the pallet bed, pulling the blanket up to her neck.

"Milla?" she asked. Her voice was so soft, Milla had to kneel by her head to catch it all. "All the dragon-bonded need to know what happened. Learn from these mistakes; don't repeat them. When they've grown up, don't hide the dragons away. Their lives depend on it. When we lost the dragons, we lost ourselves and our home."

Mraa! Iggie said, one last time.

A few moments later, Josi was back, sounding agitated. "You better leave now, Milla. Here, let me retie your scarf." She bustled her to her feet, tying the fabric while Milla held Iggie safely in position. "Have you heard the news from the lower town?" Josi asked softly so only Milla could hear.

"No, what?" Milla's thoughts raced straight to Rosa and Thom.

"Explosion in the marketplace last night. Firepowder. Some Norlander stalls destroyed."

"What?" Milla gasped. "Is Rosa all right? And Thom?" Milla wanted to run down and find her friends right now. "I need to go . . ."

"No, don't even think about it," Josi told her sternly.

"Back to the palace. Get that dragon home safe. I'll check on your friends. I'll let you know."

"Take a note to them, from me?"

Then they were hurrying, whispering farewells, hiding Iggie, hiding Kara, and bundling Milla back into the bright daylight.

The streets of Arcosi didn't look so golden now. The sun had gone in, and there were new shadows everywhere as Milla rushed back to the palace with her dragon. The puzzling words from the old fragment of parchment echoed in her mind, in time with her hurrying footsteps:

The dragons will return one last time
When the trade winds blow from the east.
Walls must fall, peace must reign.
Or the nest be forever lost.
Daughter of the storm, three times reborn
Who bears the sign of the sea.
When four seasons wane, for this bright dawn,
She will be given the key.

But she was no closer to understanding what they meant.

CHAPTER TWENTY-THREE

Milla walked toward the dragonhall, mulling over Kara's story, trying to banish the image of Silvano's murder within its walls. Just as she reached the door, she heard voices inside. Duke Olvar and Isak were talking, as Isak settled Belara to sleep on the dragonperch.

Milla didn't want to face Olvar's scrutiny, not with the horror of Kara's words still fresh in her mind. From old habit, she flattened herself against the outer wall of the dragonhall and listened.

"The translation you showed me is interesting," the duke was saying to Isak. "About maturity and the egg cycle. Not as long as you might think before the first brood is possible."

"A brood?" Isak interrupted, sounding surprised. "You mean, when they lay eggs? Of course I hadn't thought of that for Belara. Not yet. Bel, do you hear that? You will be a mother one day."

"She will. And not long either . . ." The duke had most definitely thought of that. "And it must be right here, near the spring water of Arcosi—that's why this island is the only place in the world that can raise dragons. Did you know that?"

Something clicked into place, like the pins of a lock. This was why Duke Olvar was being so generous. It was why he could bear to see the dragons every day and know none of them chose him. He was placing all his hopes on the next generation. If he controlled the island, he controlled its spring water, and therefore he controlled any future dragons, too.

Milla shivered hard and fled into the grounds, taking a corner so fast that she almost collided with Duchess Serina coming the opposite way.

"Are you all right, Milla?" Serina spoke Norlandish with a faint Sartolan accent. Her long crimson gown brushed the paved path as she walked. She wore a lily tucked behind her ear, and her knot of black hair was so neat and gleaming that Milla felt instantly disheveled.

"Fine, thank you, Your Grace!" She glanced down to check that Iggie was fully concealed, aware of the heat in her cheeks. "I, er, I like to walk . . . To clear my head."

Serina reached out and took Milla's free hand. Hers was very soft. She switched to speaking Sartolan. "I know you've got Iggie in there. I know you went out today."

Milla squeaked in alarm, "I was just . . ." She cast around for explanations, but for once, her well of stories seemed to have run dry.

"Shh, don't worry, you won't hear a lecture from me."

Her brown eyes told Milla she could trust her. "The duke's another matter: step lightly around him. He has good intentions, but he can be quick to judge." In her lilting voice, it didn't even sound like criticism, just stating what she knew.

So how do you bear it? Milla wanted to ask, intrigued by this sudden frankness.

"But now, let me show you something." Serina linked arms with Milla. "This way. It might interest a girl like you."

Milla swatted away the questions that buzzed around her mind. She was due back in the dragonhall: the others would be waiting. But this was an honor—you didn't say no to a duchess. Something in Serina's calm manner was mesmerizing, and Milla let herself be gently tugged away.

The duchess led Milla to a walled garden at the far northern edge of the palace grounds. Inside, the air was warmer, protected from the winds. Insects still flitted from leaf to leaf, and a blackbird was singing somewhere.

"Over here." She walked to the farthest corner, away from the palace.

Milla followed Serina, still half expecting a scolding.

Serina ran her hands along the outer wall, pulling aside the draping ivy like curtains to reveal a small wooden door with an iron handle. The duchess unlatched it and pushed it open, just enough so Milla could make out the steep stone steps that clung to the wall on the other side and twisted down, out of sight.

"Where does it go?" Milla kept her voice a whisper, even though they were alone out here.

"I think they call it the shadow strip in Norlandish. Is that right? From there, you can go down into the city. So I've named this the shadow gate. It suits me well that people avoid the area. As I see it, the shadows are our friends: they offer concealment and protection, don't they?"

It was like a secret passage to freedom. She could get home to the Yellow House without anyone knowing. Milla stared at the duchess. It was as if she'd read her mind and given her what she needed most.

"Milla, you must be careful. Only a few know of this door, and I mean to keep it that way."

"Why are you showing me?" Milla said, and then quickly, "I mean, thank you!" She added this fact to her hoard of knowledge about the island. "You can trust me with it. I'll keep your secret."

"I know you will," Serina told her. "When I'm needed with my healers in the lower town—births, deaths, sudden sickness—I need to move fast. I can't wait for permission, or for guards to open gates."

"So the duke . . . ?"

"He doesn't know," Serina said, serious now. "There's something you should understand about him if you're to have a smooth time as our guest."

"Yes, Your Grace?"

"Olvar needs to feel in control. Once in his life, he suffered a great shock, so terrible he never really recovered. Have you heard this story?" she asked.

Milla shook her head.

"Well, maybe that's how he likes it now. But I'll tell you so you understand. He was never meant to be duke, you know."

"So who was?" Milla stood very still, aware of leaves rustling and the scent of lavender on the breeze.

"Ragnar, his older brother and his hero. Ragnar fitted the image of the perfect Norlander. He was brave, handsome, and he lived for the sea, just like their parents. That was how they died, in the end, all three together, and more besides. Lost on the voyage back from visiting the homelands."

"I never knew. How old was Olvar?"

"He was fourteen then."

Milla tried to picture the duke as a young boy who'd just lost everything. Maybe he wasn't so different from her after all.

"His father's advisers ruled with him till he was older," Serina said. "When my father attacked this island, Olvar led its defense." She paused. "Afterward, we were married as part of the peace treaty. Arcosi and Sartola have been peaceful neighbors ever since."

"That attack, is that why he hates us?" Milla blurted out. "All of us who aren't Norlander."

"He doesn't hate us." Serina smiled at Milla's raised eyebrows. "He promised his father he would protect the Norlander people. That instinct is so deep-rooted, he didn't notice when protecting his people became something else entirely." Her gaze shifted away from Milla then, and she seemed lost in thought.

"But what about all his soldiers?" Milla persisted. "If it's all so peaceful and *protective*, why does he keep them?"

Serina shrugged one elegant shoulder. "As I said, he likes to be in control. He likes things predictable. Orderly. And the army gives work to half the island, doesn't it? Who clears the storm drains? Rebuilds the walls?"

That was true enough. Milla frowned, unsatisfied.

"I'm not saying I agree! I like to bypass the guards, as you see. And now you can, too."

Then Serina gave her a quick, light hug, taking care not to press against the sleeping Iggie.

"I know it's not easy for you, adjusting to life here, when you belong in the city." The duchess's eyes glowed warm amber in the sunshine. "I know how it feels to be an outsider in this palace, but believe me, it gets easier."

Milla began to see why Serina was such a good healer. "Thank you."

"I noticed you've lost a necklace," she said next, surprising her.

"How?" Milla stared. But her fingers jumped to the empty spot at her neck, where a little circle of her skin was paler than the rest, answering her own question.

"So I wonder if you'd like this one?" Serina brought out a silver chain from her pocket. It had a delicate pendant of a leaping fish dangling from it and it matched the one the duchess wore.

"The symbol of Sartola," she told her. "It won't be as special as your old one, but it's yours, if you'd like it?"

"It's lovely," Milla stuttered, "b-b-but shouldn't you give that to Tarya, not me?"

"I gave Tarya another gift. This was my daughter's. Well, it would have been." Serina paused, then went on. "I imagine if my daughter had lived, she might've looked a little bit like you."

Silence spread between them, silken and soft and sad, broken only by the birdsong.

Milla turned around at Serina's gesture and lifted her hair. "Th-thank you, Your Grace."

"Isabella lived only six short weeks." Serina's voice sounded husky and soft with emotion, as she fastened the clasp. "But she would be about your age now."

Milla had no words for that, so she hugged Serina tightly instead.

"Thank you, my dear." Serina whisked a tear away from her eyes with a quick flick of her long fingers. "Now, let's go back before anyone notices. If you're ever challenged, you can say I asked you to gather herbs. These ones are good for the dragons, I believe." She leaned down, plucked a few sprigs of sage and rosemary, and passed them to Milla.

The scent clung to Milla's fingers for the rest of the day.

CHAPTER TWENTY-FOUR

So? What did Kara say?" Tarya demanded as soon as they were alone. She was buzzing with unspent energy, her hair a wild halo around her face. Heral clung to her shoulders, tense and alert, his spiny red tail whipping from side to side.

"Wait! Let me get the door closed." Vigo slid the large dragonhall door into place and came to join them on the low seats near the stove, with Petra at his heels.

Milla noticed Vigo's caution and it unsettled her.

"She wasn't well. We only spoke a little." Milla tried to recall Kara's exact words. "But one thing is clear: the dragons don't belong here in the palace." She untied her cloak and scarf and let Iggie loose on the sawdust. He stretched and rolled on his back, then pounced at Belara playfully.

"Oh, really?" Isak said. He was copying the duke's drawling intonation. "How very convenient for her. I suppose they belong exactly where she is?"

"No!" Milla felt instantly defensive of Kara. "She said

183

they should be in the city, with the people, not trapped in the palace."

"They're not exactly trapped," Tarya said. "Or only as much as we all are." She spoke those words with feeling. Her left heel was drumming anxiously on the floor.

"She's bound to say that, isn't she? If they're in here and she's out there." Isak sounded scornful, draping his fingers for Belara to paw at. "Can you imagine the riot if we took the dragons down to the marketplace? They'd be crushed. Aren't we taking good care of them?" He tugged at Belara's gold ears now, and she closed her eyes in bliss.

"I thought you wanted to know how to care for the dragons? How not to repeat old mistakes? Their lives depend on it," she said, her heart sinking. How was she going to get them to listen to her?

"We do want to know," Vigo said. "We've been reading all day in search of this kind of information. Go on, Milla."

"Look, this is the person who spent her whole life guarding the eggs. Her friend Josiah was killed for them. We need to listen to Kara."

"We will listen, if it makes sense," Isak said. "But you have to admit the dragons are safest here. Duke Olvar said they have to be here, something about the water?"

"But they almost died out last time, living here!" Milla hated the way he was looking at her. "When they're grown, they belong in the city: that's what she said. And there are wells of spring water all over the island." She had never felt at home in the palace, and now she knew: she wasn't supposed to! Nor was Iggie.

"Come on, then, Milla, tell us," Tarya said, serious now. "We're listening."

So Milla repeated Kara's story. When she got to the part about Rufus killing Silvano, she called Iggie to her using the five-note tune and kept her hands moving across his scales as she spoke.

In the silence that followed, Milla noticed Vigo had slumped forward, his head resting on his arms, while Petra nuzzled at his chest, trying to reach his face.

"Oh, Vigo, I'm sorry." Milla had not considered how the story would sound to someone of Sartolan heritage.

"It's all right," Vigo said, sitting up very slowly. His eyes looked bloodshot, washed green like sea glass. "I mean, it's not, but I've heard this before. I know it happened." He shrugged, as if this didn't hurt. "Every Sartolan schoolchild hears it: how the dragonriders of Arcosi destroyed our city in the great burning war. And afterward, they vanished from the face of the earth, like a mysterious punishment. My great-grandfather died in that war—that's why my grandad attacked Arcosi, you know, as revenge."

"But your dad stopped that one," Tarya said.

"Yeah, and my mom had to marry him after the war."

Milla watched Vigo's face, realizing now this was the stuff of his life, not just a history book. He had the opposite problem to hers—he knew exactly where he came from. She went over and gave his shoulder a squeeze. "Look, we're all tired, let's leave it for today."

Milla moved to the perch and lifted Iggie onto it with difficulty: he was almost too big for her to hold now. "Here,

Iggie. Time to sleep, my dear. I'll be over there." He squirmed and wriggled under her fingers.

Aark! He twisted from her grasp.

"Ig! I know." She patted his back and slowly, slowly, pulled her hands away. "It's been a busy day. But you need to sleep. Really. And so do I." She wanted to be alone and run through Kara's story again in her mind. "Look, I'll just be here, all right? Night!" She turned her back and started heading for her bunk.

"Argh!" Iggie landed very suddenly on her left shoulder, claws digging into her flesh. *"Ow!* What did you do that for?" She lifted him off, cradling him and asking, "Did you just jump all that way?"

Iggie was very pleased with himself, wriggling with pride and batting her face with his nose. *Aark! Aark!* She could feel excitement flowing off him in waves.

The others were all staring in shock.

"He didn't jump, Milla," Tarya said. "He flew to you!"

"Can he do it again?" Vigo rushed to the dragonperch, glad to be distracted. "Petra, do you want to try?"

The other three dragons were eager and jittery, climbing up and down the perch. But when Vigo reached up to lift Petra higher, she opened her mouth and a flurry of sparks emerged, scalding Vigo and making him jump back in shock.

"Dragonsblood!" he swore, running to plunge his hand in the dragon's water trough. "Flame and flight, all at once? Really? I think you're ahead of yourselves. This isn't meant to happen till next month, I thought?"

Petra exhaled a long orange flame in reply.

All the others clapped, while Milla watched uneasily. She should be celebrating Iggie's new skill. Instead, she flopped down on the floor, Iggie in her arms.

He could tell she was unhappy. Subdued now, he reached up and rested his blue head on her collarbone. When he *craaak*ed quietly to her, she could feel the heat building in his chest. He was built for making fire, for burning things.

"Milla?" Tarya said. "What's wrong?"

"It's just . . . seeing them flame today." She struggled to put her disquiet into words. "After what we heard about Sartola burning. It makes it all more real: what happened back then."

"We're not going to take them to war!" Isak said.

"No, but look at them." She studied Iggie, the most beautiful thing in her world, with a sense of trepidation. "They can fly. Make flame. One day, they'll be huge. They're going to be capable of . . . damage."

"So we train them," Vigo said firmly. "We train them when to stop."

"We have to," Tarya agreed, stroking Heral's ruby scales.

"For their sakes," Milla said, "and everyone else's."

Part Four

CHAPTER TWENTY-FIVE

Kara's story circled Milla's mind like a distracting fly just out of reach, but she told herself the dragons were safest at the palace while they were still growing. Training Iggie ate up all her time now.

Tarya and Vigo were used to gentling horses, so they showed Milla and Isak how to teach the hatchlings: slowly, with great patience and many rewards.

"Fire!" was the signal to flame, with an arm pointing forward.

"Fly!" told the dragon to launch into flight, with an arm pointing straight up, while "Land!" had the opposite direction.

"Hold!" was the signal to stop flaming, along with a clenched fist.

It took weeks.

Kara said Iggie belonged in the city, but Milla didn't dare take him down there again. It was too dangerous, unless she wanted to set the whole island alight. Iggie wasn't so good at stopping his fire. He was too overexcited by his new skills, flying in circles and sending little jets of flame up into the air at the same time.

She felt bad for not visiting Josi and Kara, but at least they knew what kept her away. She didn't dare mention Iggie in her notes to Thom and Rosa. She'd written to say she had accompanied Tarya to her new home. Now her friends must think she'd abandoned them for a fancy new job in the palace. As soon as Iggie was a little older, she'd be able to leave him and visit them. But right now, he had to come first.

"Yes, you are a clever dragon. But seriously, Ig. *Hold!*" She ducked to avoid his flame. "You nearly singed me!" She sighed. "I wonder how many times they had to rebuild this dragonhall after it was burned down by enthusiastic baby dragons?"

"Those ceiling tiles will never burn: they knew what they were doing when they built this thing," Isak called.

"Did you get burned, Milla?" Vigo asked, offering her a jug. "Water?"

"No, I'm fine, thank you." Milla was touched by his concern. They paused by the water trough to let Iggie and Petra drink.

"I've been thinking about Kara's words." Vigo raised the subject quietly, while Isak and Tarya were out of earshot on the other side of the hall.

Milla looked up at him in surprise. Why was he whispering? Then she guessed: telling Isak something was like telling the duke, and Vigo didn't want his father hearing this.

192

"I'm sure it's true," he was saying. "Sartolans have their own stories, you know. About the old days, the golden age of Arcosi, and their dragonriders. When the dragons belonged to the city."

"The way Kara spoke, it's more than belonging. It's what the dragons need."

"We could do it. Take the dragons to the city. Make another golden age. Only this time, Sartola won't be the enemy." Vigo was talking quickly now, keeping his eyes on Isak on the other side of the hall. "Do you remember that prophecy you found? Didn't it say something about tearing down walls to make peace? We can do it. We have to."

"What about your father?" Milla asked. "He'll never let us. He wants to keep the dragons secret."

"We only have to wait. You can see how fast the dragons are growing. One of these days, he won't have any choice. He's been controlling me all my life." His green dragon finished drinking and came over to press herself against Vigo's long legs. "You'll soon put a stop to that, won't you, Petra?" Petra lifted her long, lithe neck, showing the creamy-pale scales of her throat. She growled in agreement, sending tiny sparks flying.

"Are you with me, Milla? Are you ready to try Kara's way, when the time comes?" Vigo asked urgently.

"It's not just about proving your father wrong?"

"No, it's about doing the right thing—for the city and the dragons!"

Heral and Belara were flying toward them, with Tarya and Isak close behind.

"Yes, then I agree," Milla said, seeing how determined he was. "But we have to talk to Kara, plan it right."

Vigo nodded.

"Maybe this is the kind of stuff their moms should teach them? How to preen, how to hunt, how to flame, fly, and *stop!* I mean, *hold*, Belara!" Isak panted, passing them in pursuit of his little gold dragon, holding his eyeglasses in place with one finger. Serina had made Isak more of his medicine, but he didn't seem to need it as much these days.

In fact, Milla realized, none of them had been ill since the dragons hatched.

"I don't know. They seem to be doing pretty well on their own!" Tarya replied to her brother, coming to a breathless halt as Heral turned a somersault up near the rafters. "Don't forget how much they've learned already."

"Come on, let's race them," Vigo suggested, with a wicked glint in his eye.

"Hey, you've been practicing! Not fair," Tarya protested.

"Scared to lose? Petra's faster than Heral any day!" Vigo challenged her.

"Never. Just watch us . . ." Tarya took the bait. "Heral? *Fly!*" She pointed up and raced out of the dragonhall with Heral, hotly pursued by Vigo and a green streak that was Petra.

"Just don't let them be seen from the city!" Isak called. "They're supposed to be hidden, remember? For their own protection."

Watching them race away, Milla saw the flaw in that line for the first time. By the time the dragons were big enough to fly over the city, they wouldn't need anyone's protection.

"Go on, Heral. You're winning!" But Tarya was so busy looking up that she tripped and fell facedown onto the muddied path. Heral hovered and flew back to check she was all right.

Vigo could've raced ahead and claimed victory, but he stopped instead and helped Tarya, dripping, to her feet.

She laughed, spitting mud.

"He should know better than that," Milla said, nudging Isak. "Look—Vigo's about to learn that chivalry won't get him anywhere with Tarya. She's ruthless, and I've got the scars to prove it."

She lay back in the sawdust to watch Iggie gliding in circles around the upper rafters of the dragonhall. His wide blue wings caught the light. She'd never seen anything so lovely as her dragon in flight. She wanted him to be free. She pictured Iggie flying over the sea. Hadn't she dreamt about that?

"Ha! Yeah, look," Isak said. "She's pulled him into the mud, and now she's running off . . . Now he's catching her! *Oh!*"

"What?" Milla sat up.

Isak was flushing slightly.

She peered past him to see what was going on outside.

Vigo had caught Tarya in his arms and was holding her very close. Their muddy faces were almost touching. They were both laughing now. Then Tarya reached up and kissed Vigo.

"Why shouldn't they?" Milla shrugged. "I'm pleased for her. So, do you want to race?"

Isak frowned and pulled away from her, getting to his feet. "I think we've got more important things to worry about, Milla. The dragons are an honor and a serious responsibility. I haven't got time for anything else. I'll be in the library."

Milla watched him walk away, thinking that he sounded more like Duke Olvar and less like Isak with every passing day.

Just as autumn gave way to winter, Milla dared to visit Kara again. She picked an evening when Isak was busy in the library with Duke Olvar and made Tarya promise to guard Iggie with her life.

She used the shadow gate for the first time, slipping through the deserted streets of the shadow strip. It was dark, but she used the Yellow House tower as a guide, lit up against the night sky like a beacon to show her the way. As she arrived, she heard Nestan chatting to the guards at the gate.

"Hold. Who goes there?" Then Nestan caught sight of her and roared with delight. "Milla! Come in, come in. Open the gates, quickly."

She had barely stepped through them when he lifted her off her feet in a massive hug, swinging her easily in his strong arms. "Dear child. Is everything all right?"

She wobbled when he put her down, slightly shocked by this enthusiastic welcome. Was he missing the twins so badly? He visited every week, but it wasn't the same. His house must feel empty without them. She noticed the extra white in his beard, and the new lines around those intense blue eyes.

"How are the twins today?" Nestan asked.

"They're doing well, sir," she said carefully, aware of the guards listening.

"Come along, Josi will want to see you." He led her across the courtyard, past the orange tree where she'd hidden on the day of the murder. He lowered his voice conspiratorially, unable to mention the dragons: "And your . . . little friends?"

"Fine, sir." Did he think they were being spied on? Milla looked around the empty courtyard, at the shadowy doorways to the main house. Surely they were safe here?

The kitchen door was closed when they arrived, and Milla waited as Nestan knocked out a particular rhythm with six beats.

Josi unlocked the door and peered out. Her face lit up when she saw Milla.

"Why do you keep this door locked now?" she asked, pushing through to greet Josi and Kara hidden behind her.

"It's the best way." Nestan locked the door behind them with a soft warning. "There may be a listener in my household."

"Sorry it's just me today, not Iggie," Milla told the three of them.

"Good to see you, child." Kara gave her a quick embrace. She was wearing a new dark red cloak that made her brown eyes gleam in the light of the kitchen oil lamps.

Surprised again by the warmth of this greeting, Milla hugged Kara in return.

Kara pulled away and caught sight of Milla's new chain. She said sharply, "Where did you get that necklace? What happened to yours?"

"I used my old necklace to bribe my way into the palace on hatching night. So Serina gave me this one. Why?"

"It's Sartolan: the sign of the sea."

"So? I don't mind. It's pretty, I like it, and the duchess has been very kind to me."

Kara looked disapproving, but she moved on. "And Iggie?"

"He's so big! Wait till you see him. He can nearly control his flame."

"Well done. Keeping working on that. Are you feeding him plenty of eggs and fish now, as well as chicken?"

"Eggs? I'll ask for some. Is there anything else he needs?"

Kara took her arm and led her to the kitchen table, listing all the things the dragons could eat now.

Sitting there with Nestan, Josi, and Kara, Skalla purring around her ankles, a wave of longing and homesickness washed over Milla, so strong that she had to grip the edge of the table till it passed. It felt strange to see them all, so easy together, like a family.

"Come on, then, tell us everything. Enough about what dragons eat! What have they been feeding *you*?" Josi prompted her, pouring them all a small measure of sweet Arcosi wine and slicing some bread and cheese.

"Mmm," Milla said, taking a huge bite. "This tastes like home. I promise you, Josi, their bread isn't as fluffy as yours; their cheese is never as creamy; and the palace cooks have no idea how to use spice. Rest assured: you are still the best cook on this island. Have you got any of your sweet pickle for this cheese?"

Josi dropped a kiss on the top of her head and went to fetch it.

Then Milla had to face a barrage of questions about the twins and the dragons and life at the palace.

Before Milla could answer, they all heard raised voices in the courtyard outside.

"Nestan!" a man shouted.

Kara stood at once, and Josi helped her into the storeroom that served as her chamber and hiding place.

Nestan swung a small table across the storeroom door and put a bowl of oranges on it. Josi unbolted the kitchen door, with a quick backward glance to check there was no trace of Kara's presence here.

"You're wanted at the gate, master," one of the guards called through. "Some fisherfolk from the lower town."

"Thom!" Milla called out in astonishment. "What are you doing here?" He was standing at the gate with his father, Simeon, being interrogated by Richal Finn.

"Nestan, I need your help, old friend," Simeon called.

Thom saw Milla and shouted through, "It's Rosa. She's been arrested."

CHAPTER TWENTY-SIX

W hat did she do?" Milla asked when Nestan had brought Thom and Simeon into his study. She recalled how angry Rosa had been all those months ago. Things must have become even worse for her friend in the time they'd been apart.

Thom was looking around the room, taking in the wood-paneled walls, Nestan's shelves full of maps and ledgers. He twisted his hat in his hands as he explained. "After that explosion, they raised the fees again, but only for the stalls on the Sartolan side. Rosa and her family, they can't afford to work there now."

"It was already too high," Milla said.

"They can never earn that back in a day," Simeon said. "It's just not fair. They'll have to leave Arcosi—and that's exactly what the duke wants. Bleed them dry till they leave Arcosi for the Norlanders alone." Simeon might be Norlander, but his wife, Livia, was of Sartolan descent and he felt the injustice keenly.

"So what did Rosa do?" Nestan asked. He and Simeon knew each other from childhood, though they hadn't worked together for years.

"She organized the marketfolk. They blocked access to the Norlander stalls, just for a morning, to let them see what it's like."

"Rosa didn't want to hurt anyone," Thom added quickly. "She just wanted to make a point."

"And the duke arrested them?" Milla couldn't help feeling proud as well as fearful.

"The soldiers took every single one," Simeon said. "No one can pay the release fee."

Thom said angrily, "Bet the Norlander marketfolk will be pleased—they've got no competition now."

"You did well to come to me," Nestan said to Simeon. "I'll pay the fees. Let's get them out."

"I'll come with you, too," Josi added.

Milla stared at them, awash with relief and gratitude. They barely knew Rosa, but they were ready to risk themselves for her and a group of strangers.

Josi wrapped a warm cloak around her shoulders, preparing to leave. She checked the folds of her waistband: Milla spotted a knife and a pair of skewers concealed there.

Nestan was giving orders. "Finn, I'll need my sword. And my plain oaken cane. Josi, bring that lantern."

Milla watched their hurried preparations. "Wait, I'm coming, too," she said.

"No. Too dangerous. What about everything you left at the palace?" Josi snapped a coded warning.

Thom flashed Milla a quick puzzled glance, but this wasn't the moment to tell him about the dragons.

Milla paused: what would Iggie think if he woke up and she wasn't there? Tarya would tend him, feed him, but it wasn't the same. She sent a prayer out into the night that he would understand: she couldn't abandon Rosa.

"Rosa is my friend," she said. "And I can get you there quicker than anyone. I know a shortcut to avoid patrols."

Nestan looked at her hard. "Very well. But be careful and do as I say."

"Sir," she said, "can you climb? So we can go the back way?" she suggested. "So we don't have to tell the guards."

"I might not be able to run, but I can certainly climb down my own garden wall." Nestan nodded, with new respect for her in his glance. "And you're right—the fewer who know, the better."

"Where are they keeping them?" Milla whispered as they reached the dockside, hiding in the shadow of the great seawall. The night air was cool, with that familiar salty mix of seaweed and rotting debris at the high-water line. She knew the area well, used to carrying messages down to Nestan's warehouses. Farther to the west lay a shallow beach where the children of Arcosi learned to swim.

"Over there." Thom pointed across the dark, deserted wharves. "That warehouse? The duke turned it into a prison.

It was built for storage. Now it stores criminals. Only it doesn't take much to be classed as one of them."

"Simeon, Thom?" Nestan said. "Stay out here and watch for trouble. Whistle at us if we need to get out."

"I'm coming," Milla insisted.

"Then so am I," Josi said.

"Well, then, let me do the talking. Pull your hoods low and follow me," Nestan said. He didn't have to spell it out: *Don't let them see that you're not Norlander.*

Milla watched how easy it was for Nestan to gain entrance: a hearty Norlander greeting, a bawdy joke, a hand-shake to slip coin from one palm to another. She hoped it would be as easy for them all to leave.

They walked in. It was a long single-story building, crudely adapted to its new purpose. In the small entrance lobby, three guards sat at a trestle table, playing cards. They wore black, like the palace guards, but their uniforms were tatty and stained. Even in the dim light of their storm lantern, Milla saw clearly what kind of place this was, with its damp walls and a sour stench of unwashed bodies rolling toward them.

She was filled with a raging fury against the duke. He had created this prison. It felt like a symbol of his whole rotten system. It didn't just protect Norlanders! It punished every-one else for not having the right ancestry. Rosa should not be in prison. It was only the unfairness of the duke's rules that led her to protest in the first place. And if the rules were wrong, wasn't it right to object?

Milla kept her temper with difficulty, but she hung back with Josi while Nestan strode up to the table.

He leaned casually on his walking cane. "Evening, gentlemen."

Milla peered from under her hood. Behind the guards, there was a gate with iron bars. The prison itself must be through there. She stared into the darkness beyond: keys glinted dully, hanging on a wall of hooks.

"What's this, then? Come to join our game?" the head guardsman said, glancing at Nestan over his hand of cards. His thick blond plait stuck out below his cap, and his face looked yellowish and greasy in the guttering light.

"We are here to secure the release of Rosa Demarco and her fellow guild members of the marketplace," Nestan said.

"Guild members! Hear that? Bit rich, for these Sartolan scum." The man looked down at his cards.

Milla felt her fury rising, but she remembered her promise to Nestan and managed to stay silent.

Nestan hit the table with the tip of his walking cane, making the guards jump. "I didn't ask for your opinion. Just do your job, or the duke will hear of it before the night is through."

The man stood, tugging at his belt, puffing his chest out. "It'll cost you," he said resentfully. He'd have drawn a blade on anyone else by now: Nestan's wealth and confidence protected him better than armor.

"Show me the calculations in full." Nestan met his gaze. "I'll have them checked, and if you've cheated me, the duke will hear of that, too."

The man sucked in his cheeks and reached down a large record book, muttering a word that might have been *cripple*. Taking his time, he slowly leafed to the correct page, making them wait. He painstakingly ran his finger along each line, jotting down prisoners' names and figures.

Nestan tapped his cane on the table loudly as he waited, choosing to ignore the insult.

Finally, the man named a sum so high that Milla gasped, "You can't pay that."

Josi put her hand on Milla's arm, telling her to keep quiet.

Nestan pulled out a leather purse and started counting coins.

Just then, Milla smelled something new—a familiar, acrid smell—not just the unwashed guards. She sniffed. "What's that?"

Nestan raised his head, on alert. "Smoke."

"Fire!" Another guard appeared behind the iron gate, fumbling with the lock. "Fire!" he yelled. "Get out of here. That idiot Jensen knocked his lantern over—didn't even bloody notice till it spread. *Fire!*" He swung the gate open and ran through. Coughing hard, with his sleeve held over his mouth, he pushed past Nestan, immediately followed by two more uniformed guards who looked no older than Milla.

The guard with the record book moved faster than Milla thought possible. "Get out!" Dropping cards, knocking over their stools, all three remaining guards dashed for the doorway, jostling Milla and Josi out of their way.

"Wait!" Nestan bellowed. "What about the prisoners?"

The last guard half turned as he reached the outer door. "I'm not risking my life for them."

Then the door slammed hard, and they were gone.

CHAPTER TWENTY-SEVEN

Quick!" Milla reacted first, throwing back her cloak. "Get the keys." The inner gate swung open, and she saw a whole row of them hanging there.

Nestan pushed through the gate. "Let's take them all. Come on, hurry!"

Milla grabbed at sets of keys, her fingers stupid and clumsy, ripping her skin on the raw metal hooks. She glimpsed a corridor stretching away, with cells opening off each side. It was darker in here, lit only by Nestan's lantern. A long bare room, divided by iron rails, men on one side, women on the other. No privacy. No better than a stable.

Smoke began creeping toward her. Prisoners were screaming. Bellowing for help, in pure terror.

Milla found a door, tried a key in the lock. It didn't fit. She was fumbling for the next, when a woman's hand shot out and grabbed her arm.

"Help us! Hurry!" she shrieked.

Milla dropped the keys. "I'm trying. Let go!" She pulled herself free and lost precious moments scrabbling for the keys. Which one had she already tried?

Josi was on her knees, picking a lock with the skewers she'd hidden in her waistband.

Tears were streaming down Milla's face as the smoke grew thicker. It was like hitting a wall, impossible to breathe through. She didn't dare look at the far end of the building, but she could hear the crackle of flames, and the heat was building.

The second key didn't fit. Nor the third.

Keep calm. Keep trying. Every instinct in her body told her to run.

The next key was stiff. It didn't move. She pressed with all her strength—click—the lock fell open.

Milla dropped that key in the straw and jumped back, as the desperate women flung the door open, almost crushing her fingers.

Other cells were open already, prisoners stampeding past her, and Josi was there, working on the next.

"Rosa! Rosa Demarco! Where are you?" Milla coughed out, moving to the next door, bent double.

No answer came.

Josi tugged at her arm. "Cover your face," she mumbled, showing Milla. "Like this."

Milla copied her, ripping fabric from her cloak lining, tying it across her nose and mouth. She kept working on the next lock, testing key after key, then swapping with Josi.

She heard awful howls of fear from the farthest, darkest end of the prison. Nestan was down there. She made out his outline against the livid brightness of the flames suddenly roaring up the wall.

Milla's vision started breaking up. There were only moments left before it was too late for them all.

"Milla!" It was Rosa's voice, shrill and scared, but alive. Here, in this cell.

Women's hands reached out, grabbing at Milla, yelling for help.

"Get back," Milla begged, fumbling with the keys, only two left to try. "I can't see."

There was a loud crash, as a burning beam fell from the roof. A figure staggered past, carrying the weight of another. She prayed one of them was Nestan.

The screams got louder.

Milla could feel the heat now, almost unbearable on the exposed skin around her eyes. She would not give up.

She closed her eyes, gasping against the fabric. Working by touch alone, the world shrunk to this breath. This key. This lock. She fitted the last one. Turned it. Then she collapsed on the floor, dimly aware of feet rushing past. She tried to crawl away, but she'd lost all sense of direction.

"Milla! Come on," Rosa's voice spoke in her ear. "Move!"

She managed to lift her head. For Iggie's sake, she had to live. Coughing, gasping, crawling, she followed Rosa out of the burning building, hoping the others had made the same decision. It was too late to check. It was too late for anything.

Milla's world went dark.

"Come on, stay with me." That was Josi, pleading hoarsely. "Milla?"

Milla opened her eyes. The night sky was full of tiny orange sparks, like fireflies. Someone was smoothing her face with a damp cloth.

"You're alive!"

Milla rolled onto her side, coughing, harder and harder, till she vomited. She lay there gasping and gulping down the cool sweet air that wasn't full of smoke.

"Easy, kitten, take it slow." Josi was there again, helping her sit.

Milla saw a scene of devastation. Josi must have pulled her away from the burning warehouse-prison. It was ablaze, sending plumes of smoke and fire shooting high into the night sky. She could see them reflected in the inky square of the harbor. There were bodies scattered across the dockside. Some were moving. A few were not.

"We can't stay here," Josi was saying. "We need to move before the soldiers get here and lock everyone up again. The records were destroyed in the fire. They'll arrest first, ask questions later."

Milla tried to speak, but her throat was swollen and it hurt so much she almost passed out again.

"Someone's coming." That was Nestan's voice.

He was alive. Her tears leaked, blurring the sky into smears of orange and black.

"It's all right," Josi told him, "it's not the soldiers, look . . ."

Milla knuckled the tears from her eyes, to see people spilling out onto the dockside, pulling carts, carrying mats, an old door. Ordinary people, men, women, children, working together, silhouetted against the fire. Wait! Serina was there, too. They worked fast, loading up the survivors and carrying them away to safety.

"Rosa?" Milla whispered hoarsely.

"Alive," Josi croaked. "With Thom and Simeon. Come, we must go before the soldiers get here."

Josi leaned down and took one of Milla's arms, Nestan on her other side. He'd lost his cane, but they all supported one another, and somehow managed to limp away from the dockside. In hoarse gasps, Milla directed them to the smugglers' steps. Every step took more stamina and strength than Milla thought she had. It felt like hours later when they finally fell through the gates of the Yellow House.

Milla went straight to the kitchen well and collapsed. Fumbling blindly for the pail, she dipped it deep in the stone basin and then poured sweet, cold water over her head.

"Here, let me," Josi said, smoothing back Milla's hair, smudging the smoke stains from her skin. When she'd finished, Josi sank back, exhausted, and huddled there, knees to chest, shivering hard. For the first time in her life, Milla saw that this strong woman was not invincible.

"You next." Milla coughed, though she was shaking with cold now, too. And she poured clean water over Josi's head in return.

Still coughing, still hoarse, they staggered, dripping, back to the warm kitchen and changed out of their smoky clothes.

Milla wanted nothing more than to lie down by the fire and sleep, but the thought of Iggie, alone, spurred her on.

"Here. Eat this," Josi said, handing her a bowl of cold soup. "Then let's get you back to the palace before they spot you're gone."

They wearily set out again, exchanging a silent hug of farewell just outside the shadow gate.

To avoid the sentry, Milla used the hidden door at the back of the dragonhall: the one that Kara had escaped through, all those months ago.

She slipped noiselessly inside. The others were all asleep: she could hear their deep calm breathing. She fell into her bunk. Iggie crawled in next to her, taking up most of the space now, and kindled gently to warm her up while she cried. As she hugged Iggie, the pain in her throat eased, as if he were taking it away.

Milla wept for Rosa, and the horror she'd endured. She wept with relief that all her friends had made it home. She wept for the people who hadn't. And she wept for her divided city, rotten at its core, where such things were even possible.

CHAPTER TWENTY-EIGHT

Three months later: Midwinter

Winter had arrived in Arcosi. Sleety rain fell and the wind howled around the dragonhall. The duke's curfew covered the whole island, including them. Everyone was stuck indoors, grumpy and restless. Even the dragons' play fighting took on real aggression.

"I'm bored," Vigo said.

Milla rolled her eyes. "You've got everything anyone could possibly want." She thought of her friends in the city. Since the fire, she had barely left the palace, though Nestan visited them and whispered the news to Milla.

Arcosi was tense and dangerous, ready to explode. Six people had died that night. Their funerals triggered riots: first, Norlander homes and businesses were looted; then Sartolan ones were burned in revenge. Some islanders of Sartolan descent chose to leave Arcosi. Rosa and her family refused to go. Banned from the marketplace, now they sold their goods door to door in the lower town, in all weathers.

Milla's tone turned bitter. "You have more food than you could eat. A warm dry home. *A dragon*." She didn't know why she was taking it out on Vigo—all these things applied to her, too. Maybe that was it: she felt guilty and it made her irritable.

"Is the little duke bored?" Isak readily joined in, teasing Vigo with an undercurrent of something darker. "Servants? Bring entertainment, this minute!"

There was a growing tension between Isak and Vigo. Was it because Tarya preferred Vigo to Isak these days? Or because the duke treated Isak more like his son than Vigo? Probably both, Milla realized.

Vigo's face fell. "I'm not *that* bad."

Nobody answered him.

Milla leaned on the wall of the dragonhall. Being confined in here made her gloomy and snappish. She kept thinking about Kara's story of Silvano's murder. Where had it happened? She looked around the warm, airy hall: for a heartbeat she saw hot, dark blood pooling on the floor. She shivered, hugging herself tightly, tugging her jacket closed.

She couldn't even enjoy these fine clothes anymore. How much money could she raise if she sold each one? This jacket? It could pay for Rosa's stock for a month. This silk tunic? It could cover Thom and Simeon's harbor tax. *How can I keep living here?* she asked herself every morning. If she and Iggie didn't leave, they were part of the system that kept her

213

friends suffering. *Just a little longer,* she told herself every day. As Vigo said, they just needed to wait and be patient. Just till spring, till Iggie was bigger and stronger. Then things would change, she would make sure of that.

What if spring was too late? The words of the poem circled in her mind:

The dragons will return one last time
When the trade winds blow from the east.
Walls must fall, peace must reign.
Or the nest be forever lost.

It was just a poem, she told herself. Iggie was fine, wasn't he?

Right now, the dragons were all preening on the dragon-perch, while their people lounged nearby. The perch had been rebuilt twice to keep up with their astonishing rate of growth.

All of them had been snacking in a lazy manner: the people had sugar cookies; the dragons had crunchy lamb bones. Iggie's flanks were lightly covered in claw marks. Their fights had turned more serious. These days, if the dragons were fighting, you stood well back.

As if he heard her worries, Iggie looked over, blinking slowly.

She smiled at him and he went back to preening his wings.

"Am I that bad?" Vigo asked at last.

"Nah, you're not usually that bad. Not anymore. You could almost pass for a person, not a prince," Tarya told him, leaning up to drop a kiss on his cheek. "And you're right, we need distraction before we all fall out. Who's got a story?"

"I heard something this morning," Isak said. "Someone blew up a Norlander warehouse. The duke's arrested a load of troublemakers."

Milla felt an icy finger up her spine. Did that include Rosa? She hadn't told any of them she'd been present at the prison fire, for Rosa's sake: no one spoke of the rescued, in case the duke's soldiers decided to rearrest them. Her friends knew she'd been with Josi that night, that was all.

Iggie glided from the perch and came to her, nosing at her side. She stroked his large blue head, grateful for his understanding. He was huge now, the size of a pony. He curled up, leaning his snout on her, and its weight was comforting.

"What troublemakers? What are you talking about?" Tarya sat up straight. "More riots?"

Heral raised his head, growling softly.

"Some Sartolan-born vandal, destroying Norlander property." Isak sounded dismissive.

"That's terrible!" Tarya cried.

"Did you hear any of their names, these *vandals*?" Milla asked. "Where were they taken?"

Iggie whined, and she wrapped her arms around his neck.

"Is our house all right?" asked Tarya. "Why would they do that? Destroy property?"

"Really, Tarya?" Something snapped inside Milla. "If you think for half a moment, even you could work it out."

The other three all stared back. Milla was never mean to Tarya.

"Milla! Do you . . . Are you saying you know these people? That you understand?"

"Are you saying you don't understand? Oh, wait, you two are Norlanders, and you're the duke's son. Of course you don't!" As soon as her words were out, Milla regretted them, seeing their faces slam closed. She braced against the wall and released Iggie, ready for a confrontation.

"Come on, then, Milla," Isak hit back, his sarcastic tone matching hers. "Enlighten us, with your superior knowledge of Arcosi life!" Belara had joined him now, and she was making a high, distressed noise in the back of her throat, her golden ears flat against her head.

Iggie growled softly, warning Isak.

Milla took a deep breath, resisting the urge to scream Rosa's story in Isak's face. Instead, she thought for a moment, then took the plate of sugar cookies that lay on the floor between them and counted them. "See this plate, here, this is Arcosi . . . And there's twelve cookies, right?"

They were watching her carefully, people and dragons.

Milla tipped all the cookies off the plate, then added two back on. "Here's the Norlanders, arriving on Arcosi, fifty years ago, finding a lovely empty island, and settling here. Right?"

"Right," Tarya said. "That's our grandparents, and dad was born here, just after."

Heral kept his eyes on her, alert and ready to fly to Tarya if she gave the word.

Milla added four more cookies onto the same half of the plate. "Oh, yes, the Norlanders bred and settled here."

"And here come the Sartolans." Milla added the rest of the cookies, slowly, one by one, onto the other half of the plate. "Over time, they settle here, too, coming just over the Sartolan Straits, to their nearest neighbor, because Sartola is still recovering from the war, and there's work here on Arcosi." She added a cookie. "There's space in the harbor for another boat." She added another. "There's room in the marketplace for Rosa's family's stall. Opportunities, if you work hard. Right?"

"Right."

"Half and half, more or less. Norlanders. Sartolans. Side by side. There should be enough room for everyone. But watch."

They watched as she spread the Norlander cookies all over the plate, pushing the Sartolan ones into a corner.

"Only who has the best houses?" She moved another Norlander cookie over so it occupied the Sartolan side. "The best jobs?" And another. "Best stalls?" And another. "Lowest fees, for everything? And the duke likes it that way because it favors his people, and he promised his dead father he would protect them at any price."

Isak scowled and looked ready to interrupt.

"Oh, and the people of Sartolan descent?" Milla went on, before Isak could speak. "You can fight it out over here, for the scraps . . ." She took the Sartolan cookies, all squashed into a quarter of the plate now, and jostled them up against each other.

"I'm not sure that's true, Milla," Tarya said, looking hurt.

"Oh, I haven't finished," Milla said. "What happens if a person of Sartolan descent dares to speak up in protest?"

The others were silent.

"Well, the duke's got rules about that . . . Don't start having ideas above your station! Here come the soldiers—they'll take you away to prison." She lifted up one of the Sartolan cookies. "And Duke Olvar sets the release fee so high because he clearly isn't rich enough. And if you don't have enough money to pay it? Bye-bye!" She shoved the cookie in her mouth and crunched it up, scattering crumbs down her blue tunic.

Tarya's cheeks were flushed. "So, what are you saying? That it's acceptable for people to go around blowing things up?"

Iggie barked, *Mraa!*

"That it's all right to do this?" Tarya struck the plate from below. It flew from Milla's hands, sending cookies and crumbs everywhere, and shattered into pieces.

They glared at each other across the mess.

Iggie and Belara jumped back, thrashing their tails, confused and upset by this new behavior.

"I think we all need to calm down," Vigo said. He'd been stroking Petra the whole time, soothing her. "It's a bit more complicated than cookies."

Milla ignored him. "I'm not saying it's *right* to go out rioting! I'm saying it's *understandable*. I'm saying things have got to change. If you'd spent your whole life fighting twice as hard for half the gain, wouldn't you be angry?"

"You do seem very angry, Milla," Isak said, ignoring Belara's attempts to climb onto his knee, even though she was far too big for that these days. "Who knew? When a Norlander family took you in and gave you work?"

218

"Oh, I'm sorry, did I forget to be grateful for my crumbs?" she yelled at him. "Anyway, it's not about me. You know what it's really about?"

"I think you're going to tell us," Isak said.

"It's about whether Norlanders and Sartolans, or anyone else, deserve to be treated the same." Images flashed through her mind's eye: all the times she'd watched Norlanders cutting lines, breezing through checkpoints, taking the best moorings in the harbor, the best stalls in the marketplace. And all without realizing. "What do you think, Isak? Are you better simply because your ancestors are Norlanders?"

He didn't answer.

"And if you think you are"—she struggled a little here, aware that tears were rising behind her anger—"at least have the courage to say so. Don't pretend it's the same for everyone else. And don't pretend to be surprised when people get around to showing their anger."

Iggie stretched his large blue head down over her shoulder. She patted his long nose and rested her cheek against his, trying to calm her breathing.

"Of course we're not better because we're Norlander," Tarya intervened. "I've never said that, or treated anyone differently because of their family. Right, Isak?" She nudged her brother hard.

"What would you have done, then?" Isak said, more quietly. "Remembering none of us chose the family we were born into?"

"What do you mean?" Milla tried to hear him out.

"Say you're a Norlander, like the duke. Like our father.

You find refuge on an empty island, you make it yours. You build a home. You protect your own. Just like anyone would do in their own home. Would you let a random stranger who'd just walked in start telling you what to do?"

"Oh, so it's about who was there first?" Milla said. "I'm just making sure I understand." She matched his tone now, making hers soft and quiet, too. Iggie sensed the tension and raised his head. She could sense him glaring at Isak for upsetting his person. At least someone was on her side.

"Why not?" Isak said.

"That's a very dangerous game for a Norlander to play." Milla had lost control, but she was too angry to care. The words kept tumbling from her lips. "This island isn't yours by right. Fifty years isn't that long. What if someone comes to Arcosi and says they were born right here; are you going to get up and walk out, and give it all back to them?"

"Oh, is this your mysterious Kara who knows everything? Born here, was she? Of course she was!" Isak laughed. "Why didn't I think of that one? You're so gullible."

"I knew it! Your argument doesn't work, even for you!" Milla cried at Isak. "You'll never give up your privilege. You've got too used to hanging out with the duke!"

"And you've got too used to hanging out at the docks." He leaned in close, with a sneer. "Maybe that's where you belong!"

Milla pushed Isak away, hard. She heard the light crunch as his eyeglasses broke.

"I'm sorry! Isak, I didn't mean to." She was filled with instant remorse.

"Yes, you did," Isak said. "You've made it very clear where your loyalties lie, Milla." His face was flushed bright red, and he looked vulnerable and younger without his glasses on. "And your blind spots." And he stood up carefully, collecting the fragments of glass from his shirt, and left the dragonhall. Belara followed him miserably, with her tail between her hind legs.

Milla looked at Tarya and Vigo and burst into tears.

"Oh, Milla." Tarya rushed to her and put her arms around her tightly.

Milla could feel Tarya's tears trickling down the back of her neck; Vigo's hand on her shoulder. For a long time, they didn't speak. Words were messy, hurtful things, and Milla didn't trust herself to find the right ones anymore.

Eventually, they sat down, each resting against their dragon. Touching their dragons calmed them all down.

"Why didn't you tell me how bad it was?" Tarya said eventually.

Milla sniffed. "Not that easy. As you see. People get defensive."

She saw Tarya reach for Vigo's hand.

Vigo cleared his throat. "I had this tutor once. A Silk Islander. He was the best, till Dad made him leave. Anyway, he used to say we aren't born knowing things: that's what life's for."

"And?" Milla wiped her face, grateful for Iggie's presence,

for his long blue back that curled around her, making her feel safe.

"If Tarya didn't know how it was for you, maybe it's not her fault—"

"It's not my fault either!"

"No, it's not." Vigo was very calm and serious, and Tarya was gripping his hand tightly. "So that's why you have to tell each other how it is for you."

Milla hesitated, still smarting from Isak's tone.

"Listen to me," Vigo went on. "If we are going to change things on this island, we have to be honest. We have to listen. And not take offense. Starting with us, right here, right now."

"Will you, Milla?" Tarya burst out. "Be honest with me! But don't be angry with me, please?" Her chin wobbled as she said this. "I can't stand it."

Milla looked at her friend. She could see how hurt she was, and how sincere. She realized she'd never spoken to her in anger before.

"All right." She gave Tarya a small, shaky smile. "I'm sorry for being horrible. I didn't mean it. I know you didn't invent the rules."

They hugged each other, then, all three of them. The dragons growled approvingly, sending little curls of smoke into the air.

"If we want the island to be peaceful, maybe we start with us," Tarya said. "If I'm Norlander; Vigo, you're half-Norlander, half-Sartolan . . ."

"But I don't know what I am!" Milla wailed.

"We're all Arcosi," Vigo said. "That's the point. We live

on this island. We love this island. And it belongs to all of us. Right?"

"Right!" Tarya said.

"Of course," Milla said, stroking Iggie's blue scales lightly. But she would bet her dragon's life that the duke would see it differently.

CHAPTER TWENTY-NINE

I sak didn't return to the dragonhall that night. Milla spent the hours of darkness sleeplessly repeating their argument in her mind.

Iggie didn't sleep either. Finally, he came and nosed at Milla in her bunk, whiffling and tugging at her sleeve, till she got up, grabbed her jacket, and followed him.

Fresh air would help.

She pushed the dragonhall doors open and said a friendly, "Morning! Is it morning yet?" to the startled sentry.

It was cold outside. Milla found her hat in her jacket pocket and tugged it low over her curls. They wandered slowly through the deserted palace gardens, Iggie flying low and then circling back to check Milla was still following.

"Where are we going, Ig?" she asked, curious to see what he had in mind.

Behind the palace, there was a stand of wind-bent trees and a little rocky hill that sheltered the palace from the north wind. The hill fell away into sheer cliffs below, where no one but seabirds ever went. Iggie made his way there, and Milla climbed after him, breathlessly.

Finally, they stood on the highest point of the island, just as the long night started fading. Milla looked southward over the whole island, the little dots of light from night fires and lanterns down in the city. This high up, they would be invisible, hidden in the shadows and the mist.

Milla turned to her dragon. "What is it, Iggie? What are we doing here?"

Iggie flapped his wings once. Then he fixed Milla with his intense emerald stare, came two steps closer and knelt on his front legs. *Craaak?* That was a new sound, like he was asking her something. He folded his wings flat and looked up, to see if she understood.

"What?" She puzzled over his actions.

He gestured over his shoulders.

"You want me to get on?" she asked.

Iggie *aark*ed, blinking in delight.

"You *don't* . . . ?" she asked incredulously. "You *do*? You want us to fly!"

A wild reckless impulse possessed Milla.

"We can't," she said. "Can we?"

Iggie just stared at her steadily.

"Oh, Iggie. I know you want to cheer me up after last night, but it's not allowed. I think Duke Olvar might actually explode with rage if he found out."

Iggie *harrumph*ed disdainfully, making Milla laugh out loud and clap a hand over her mouth.

She knew it was forbidden, but this was Iggie's idea. He wanted to fly. With her.

If this worked, Milla would be a dragonrider of Arcosi. Like the murals in the dragonhall. Like Karys Stormrider.

"Really? You sure, love? What if you're not strong enough? What if I'm too heavy?" She might hurt him. What if they both tumbled into the sea, or worse, over the cliffs? They'd be smashed to pieces.

Iggie snorted so violently she got a face full of smoke.

"All right, all right," she coughed. "I'm coming!" Excitement and fear made her clumsy and awkward. She fumbled around, trying to climb on his back without bashing his wings. In the end, she seated herself sideways, then leaned back and hoisted one leg over his ears. She'd rested against him. She'd even sat on him. This felt different. This was about total trust.

Milla looked down. Her fingers touched his iridescent blue scales lightly, tracing their ridged edges. He was as blue as a dragonfly, blue as a peacock, bluer than the sky on a perfect summer's day. Iggie's strong back held her easily, and she knew she was light. She gripped a little harder with her thighs, feeling his ribs and the muscled strength of his sides.

"Where do I hold on?" she asked. "Sorry, Ig, but I don't have wings of my own."

He lifted his long neck and turned back toward her. He lowered his ears and purred at her, reassuringly.

"I know, you won't let me fall! But can I hold your neck while you fly? Can you still breathe?"

He nodded and turned back. Milla leaned forward, trying to balance between his shoulders so she didn't interfere with his wings. She bent low against him and passed her arms around his strong scaly neck, clasping forearm to forearm and shifting her weight forward.

"I'm ready, if you are?" she whispered, seeing Iggie's ears twitch at the sound. She could feel his heartbeat speeding up, and it made hers do the same.

Iggie stepped forward to the very edge of the boulder they stood on, then crouched low. Below them, the gardens were shrouded with pearly mist in the gray dawn light. It was damp and cold and very quiet.

Milla felt the taut clench of his muscles, bunched and gathered, waiting. Behind her back, Iggie unfurled his massive wings.

I trust you, she thought, shivering in the cool air. And if they died, at least they'd die together.

Then Iggie sprang. He strained. She felt the pull and lift of it. She gasped. Eyes screwed shut. Hands clinging, clammily.

They didn't fall. They weren't falling. They were flying!

Milla looked. The bare treetops, rocks, and grass receded below them as they rose. "There's the dragonhall!" She stared through the mist, everything unfamiliar from this bird's-eye view. "Oh, Iggie, we did it!"

She held tight, feeling each beat of his wings begin in his strong chest muscles under her hands.

They flew over the palace, its four towers as spindly and small as a child's toy beneath them. Then they passed over the palace walls and . . .

"Oh!" Milla's insides cartwheeled inside her. And then louder: "Ohhh!" she cried.

The rooftops of Arcosi stretched out below them, disappearing into the mist in a jumble of red tiles and flat roofs, chimneys, bell towers, washing lines, and spires. There were the wharves and the warehouses and the marketplace—ridiculously small, little toytown squares, still deserted.

"Look—the harbor!" Through the fine cloud she saw boats moored, no bigger than the pond skaters in Nestan's favorite fountain. A few were headed out to sea—fingernail ships crossing smooth pale water. Was that Thom's ship? If he looked up now, what would he think?

The wind rushed past Milla's face, pulling tears from her eyes. She laughed out loud and hugged Iggie's neck, screaming, "Iggie-eeee! You're amazing!"

Then they left the island behind them. The world was just wind and sea and sky and the speed of it. And they were one, like they'd never been before. She held Iggie tightly with her arms and her legs, feeling his power and determination and delight.

He soared, wings spread, and they curved around. To the east, ahead of them, the sun rose above the horizon, a sliver of burning coal, getting warmer and brighter every moment. The mist began to burn off.

Milla looked back at Arcosi, seeing it as a true island for the first time. A rock in the sea: so small and self-contained. Beyond it, in the distance, the mainland sprawled like a fish laid out on a slab, with the forked tail of Sartola pointing south.

A strange new feeling possessed Milla. She felt completely calm. She felt light and free. She felt like nothing—a speck in the wind—and part of everything, all at the same time. She could fly all day. Up here, there were no troubles. No one to answer to. Just Iggie and Milla, and this perfect motion, going on and on forever.

Here at last, she felt at home. Home in the sky? She laughed again and screeched aloud, "Eeee-eeee!"

It felt like a weight lifting.

It felt like freedom.

She could feel Iggie's deep, deep joy, matching her own.

It was bitterly cold up high, and Milla started shivering so hard she could barely hold on. With regret, she felt Iggie turning slowly back toward Arcosi. He started to flap his wings hard again, steering them homeward.

Her heart felt heavier in her chest.

She didn't want to go back. She didn't want to face Isak's disapproval. She wanted to fly forever.

Iggie circled the island and they came in from the north, aiming to stay concealed.

Milla peered down, looking for the Yellow House, wondering when she could tell Kara what had happened. She needed to ask her advice.

"How do we land?" Milla asked, suddenly afraid. She tried not to look down at the rocks that loomed up, or think what would happen if she slipped now.

Iggie knew what to do. He soared in and dropped over the palace gardens, circling in tighter and tighter circles, till suddenly the palace towers were above them again and there was the grass coming up to meet them, too fast, too fast and then—"Oof!" Milla slammed against Iggie's neck, with a hard jolt that winded her, banging her cheek as she slid forward to land in a heap at his feet.

Gasping, she put out both arms, facedown, and embraced the solid ground, wondering if she was going to throw up.

Instead, she started giggling, laughing uncontrollably into the blades of damp grass.

Iggie breathed warm dragon breath on the back of her neck, whiffling gently in concern.

"I'm fine. I'm . . ." She hiccupped, then she wobbled up and threw herself at him. "Thank you! Wonderful dragon."

Milla's legs were trembling violently and her vision swam. "Our secret?" she asked him. Flying was wonderful. Flying was what she was for. She and Iggie, together.

Iggie rumbled back at her, and they stood there in a long hug.

Only now did she remember her fight with the twins last night. It didn't seem to matter quite as much anymore. Milla thought she could bear anything, if only she and Iggie could keep flying together.

CHAPTER THIRTY

Three months later. Betrothal Day: Springtime

What if I mess up?" Tarya mumbled into Heral's scaly neck. The large red dragon gleamed crimson in the warm spring sunshine that poured through the open double doors of the dragonhall.

"You won't," Milla said. "We've practiced a dozen times. Get off me, Iggie." She gently batted her dragon's head away. "Look this way? Last pin, I promise. I want to get it in your hair, not Heral's neck." She tried to keep the tension out of her voice, but if they didn't hurry, Tarya would be late for her own betrothal blessing.

"I keep saying it wrong," Tarya said. "I'll disgrace Vigo. Everyone will see me."

"So what if they see you? You look amazing, if I do say so myself." Milla had never known Tarya this nervous before. "Done! Now, stand up, let's see you?"

She'd piled the front sections of Tarya's thick fair hair up high, plaited the sides with waxflowers, and let the back hang loose. Tarya wore a traditional Norlander gown. It was cream, not red, but Milla had added red flowers embroidered down the front of the bodice as her gift to her friend. She'd included a tiny red dragon, too, low down where no one would see it.

"Perfect!"

Tarya only frowned, looking anxious.

"Listen: today, it's all just for show. You and Vigo know how you feel about each other, don't you?"

Tarya nodded, listening.

"So all this, the betrothal ceremony and the holiday, it's for the city. To give people something good to celebrate."

"What do you mean?" Tarya's blue eyes were wide and bright.

"You know it's not been an easy time for most people. They are just glad of a day's rest. That's all," Milla said. The rioting in Arcosi had simmered all winter, between the storms. "Look at the pair of you: Norlander and Sartolan together: you're the perfect symbol of peace and unity. Now, if everyone could just copy you, we'd be fine." She kept her tone light. She didn't say the dragons' lives might depend on it if the words of the poem were true.

"I know. I've heard what you said about how Norlanders treat everyone else, and I'm doing my best to speak out when I notice it. So far, it's only making the duke and Isak angry."

"They're not angry with you," Milla said. "They love you. And you're probably the only person they could hear it from."

Certainly, Isak wouldn't hear it from Milla. He'd barely spoken to her since their fight, and she was too hurt to keep trying. "When you and Vigo are in charge, things will be different, but I'm not sure my friends can wait that long."

Tarya pressed her hands on her stomach, as if the thought of being duchess one day made it churn.

"Will they accept me?" she whispered. "What if I'm not pretty enough?" Her tone grew sarcastic now. "Not graceful enough, like a good Norlander maiden?" Then, in a rush of real feeling, "What if they realize I'd rather be holding a sword than a needle?"

"And that's why Vigo loves you! You're brave and bold and brilliant." She was touched that Tarya confessed her fears. She hadn't realized she worried about the small things, too. "Be yourself, and they'll love you like I do. I promise."

Now Heral turned and put his huge red head over Tarya's shoulder, whiffling softly.

"And like he does."

Tarya smiled at her dragon. "I'm sorry you're not coming, my Heral."

Milla turned to Iggie then and leaned against his neck, yawning. They'd woken up far too early so they could squeeze in their secret flight over the sea before everyone else got up. Milla didn't know when she was going to tell the others. She hoped they wouldn't be jealous that Iggie was the first dragon who had tried to fly beyond the confines of the palace. All she knew was that flying was good for Iggie and good for her, and she would fight anyone who tried to make her stop.

Tarya patted Heral's scaly nose. "I know, it's tough being left behind. Every time my father went to sea, I hated it. But we won't be so long, I promise. You will stay here with Finn; I'll be back later."

Heral growled softly, *Mraaa . . .*

Right on cue, Nestan and Richal Finn appeared in the doorway.

"Dad!" Tarya ran and threw herself into Nestan's arms so hard that he dropped his best silver-topped walking cane.

"Look at you!" Nestan's smile was wide and wobbly at the edges. "Beautiful! If your mother could see you now." He held his daughter close.

"Mind that hair. It took me hours!" Milla mock-scolded Nestan, smiling at them both.

"And, Milla: thank you, you've done her proud." Nestan came over and hugged her, too.

She felt him freeze as he spotted the dragons behind her.

"Oh, my stars. How big?"

Nestan hadn't seen them for a month. He released Milla and stood his ground as all four dragons came to greet him eagerly, not realizing how intimidating they were these days. All except Belara stood way taller than him now.

"H-h-hello there. Oh, how you've grown. Is it still all right to touch them?" Nestan asked nervously.

"Don't be silly, Dad! It's just Heral. You know him." But Tarya pushed Heral back, telling him, "Give my father some space! You're bigger than his horse and you're scaring him."

Iggie was also acting strangely, blowing smoke toward the men, with a muffled *mraaa.*

"Iggie, behave. You don't need to warn us about these two," Milla ordered her dragon. She put herself between him and the men, dismissing the shiver of unease that made goose bumps appear on her bare arms. "It's Nestan! It's Finn. You know him perfectly well: we've been practicing for this."

"We'll be fine, Milla. Don't you worry," Finn reassured her.

Iggie just didn't want to be left alone, she decided. He always knew when she was going somewhere without him.

"Come here." She looked up at her dragon, feasting her eyes on his perfection. His scales in the sunlight were dazzling jewels. Filling her vision, he took her breath away.

"Hey," she whispered, to console him, pressing her forehead against Iggie's nose, reaching up to pull each ear. She let the flood of love wash over her, as it did each time she was near him. "I will be back before you know it, promise." She checked that no one could hear her. "And we'll fly again at dawn, all right?"

His eyes were large spheres of green fire, wise and ancient. He blinked, his lower eyelid moving up over his bright iris, slashed with a thin black pupil. Iggie growled to her, and she felt the heat building in his chest.

"Goodbye, Ig. I need to rush. There's a city waiting."

But Iggie reached out very deliberately and took hold of her skirts in his teeth. It was a fine silk dress, given to her by Serina. The delicate turquoise fabric made a slight ripping noise at the waist.

"Hey! Stop it. You can't do that . . . Iggie!" She prodded at his mouth with her fingers.

Iggie held on.

She tried lifting his lips, revealing those huge teeth, white as seashells, sharp as razors. She tapped on his closed teeth with her fingernail. "Hey, open up. Let go."

"Milla, we need to leave!" Tarya called over. "The horses are ready."

"All right!" Milla squeaked. "You go, I'll catch you . . ." She watched them ride away, with a growing sense of panic. If she wasn't at the ceremony, it would look like an insult to her friends and their families.

"Milla?" Richal Finn had taken position in the doorway. "Aren't you leaving, too?"

"I'm trying," she panted, "but Iggie doesn't want me to." Should she listen to him? What if Iggie knew something she didn't? But she had a duty to Tarya and Vigo today, and she needed to go. "Please, Ig!" she begged.

Finally, he released her, with a low grumble of discontent, closing his eyes and settling onto the floor with a *whoosh* of hot air.

"Good luck, Finn!" she called as she hurried from the dragonhall without a backward glance. "Guard them well."

Milla had to hurry if she was going to arrive before Tarya and Nestan on their horses. She took the steepest shortcuts she knew, knowing they'd have to take the long wide road on horseback, finally emerging near the harbor. Cursing, she elbowed her way through the crowds, toward the waterside shrine. All the citizens of Arcosi were packed tightly in the narrow streets like pickled sardines. She felt ready to scream with frustration, slowed by her long skirts that shivered in the light breeze.

236

"Hey, what's the rush? No one's in a hurry today, girl," someone yelled over the noise of the city bells as she barged past.

She paused for a moment to catch her breath and spotted Rosa and Thom just ahead. They were laughing together, and she felt a sudden pang of loss. She missed them terribly. But here was proof: they were fine without her. She changed direction so she wouldn't have to speak to them. If she was forbidden from mentioning Iggie, what else did she have to say?

Milla joined the small group gathered in the waterside shrine, feeling self-conscious as people stared at the latecomer. Shaded by a carved marble dome, it was cool and airy among the slender white pillars, with a backdrop of blue sea on three sides. A long causeway linked it to the island, lined with armed guards: the duke's soldiers alternated with a special honor guard of Sartolans brought by Vigo's uncle Carlo.

"Hello, Milla, is everything all right?" Serina spun around from her place next to Vigo and the duke.

"Yes, Your Grace," Milla said breathlessly. "She'll be here. Any moment now, promise!"

She slipped in next to Josi, and they each put an arm around the other's waist, without having to speak.

Isak was on Josi's other side, but he didn't greet her. Months now, and the chill distance between them still hurt afresh each day.

A tall man next to Serina glanced around, curious. He noticed Milla's leaping fish necklace and smiled at her.

Milla guessed he was Vigo's uncle Carlo, Serina's royal brother visiting from Sartola, so she made him a bow.

Carlo, the king of Sartola, looked like an older, broader version of Vigo himself, with twinkly eyes, bright copper in the sunshine. And that handsome young man must be Luca, his son.

Vigo stood at the front. Milla could see him shifting restlessly from foot to foot. A short distance away, Duke Olvar faced straight ahead, unmoving.

Time slowed to a crawl.

The air grew hotter.

Everyone gazed back along the causeway.

Milla's stomach was as knotted as a tangled fishing line. "Where is she?"

Josi squeezed Milla. "She'll be all right."

"She'll be late," Isak muttered. "My sister's always late. He might as well get used to it."

"Well, it's not my fault," Milla shot back. "She should be here by now."

"I didn't say it was your fault," Isak said stiffly.

This was how it was now, between them. What did he see when he stared back at her: Someone ungrateful? Someone lesser? Someone not of Norlander descent? Milla searched his profile for the answer and found none.

The crowds crammed along the shoreline in both directions erupted into loud cheering.

"Here she comes!" Milla cried. She jumped on the spot, pointing and grabbing Josi's sleeve. "Look!"

Tarya and Nestan rode along the causeway toward them.

"Heral should be here, though! And Petra. I can't believe they had to miss this," Milla hissed to Josi.

The sunlight turned Tarya's hair to spun gold, long curls dancing loose in the wind, and her eyes were vivid blue, like the sea. Her face lit up with happiness when she caught sight of Vigo waiting for her.

Milla hoped she'd find someone, one day, who made her smile like that.

Tarya slid down from her mare.

Vigo slipped through the ranks of guests waiting in the shrine and went out into the sunlight to meet her. With a wide smile on his face, he looked quite different from that young man Milla had met at the ball last year. Now she knew him well; she saw his kindness, quick intelligence, and his awkwardness with new people. He'd never been arrogant: just shy. He and Tarya were well matched. Their opposites balanced, Milla thought, her heart overflowing with joy for her friends.

Tarya and Vigo started walking along the causeway toward the shrine, waving at the crowd. Everyone clapped and cheered.

When the screams began, there was so much noise that it took a moment for people to realize.

CHAPTER THIRTY-ONE

Milla sprang forward and grabbed Tarya's arm. "Wait! Listen!" She pulled her under the roof of the shrine, searching for the source of the danger.

People were screaming in terror.

In packed streets, people scrambled away from the shore.

Milla's heart leapt into her mouth as a large, familiar shape passed overhead, blocking out the sun. "No. Not now. Not here. No, no, no."

She stared, craning her neck. It circled and the sun was in her eyes. Who was it? Which one?

The dragon soared and she saw him clearly, light glinting on bloodred scales and streaming through the fine webbing of his scarlet wings.

It was Heral, come for Tarya.

How had he gotten out? Where was Iggie? Was he in danger? Questions filled Milla's mind and for a moment she was paralyzed.

The duke's army knew about the dragons. The visiting Sartolan honor guard did not, and to them, a dragon was an enemy. Milla watched in horror as they aimed at Heral and fired a hail of arrows over the sea.

"Stop!" Tarya cried.

"No!" Vigo leapt forward, arms waving a cease-fire.

It was too late. One arrow buried itself in Heral's side. He screamed. A plume of fire shot from his open mouth.

Tarya sped toward the Sartolan guards, yelling. An arrow missed her head by an inch.

"No, Tarya!" Vigo and Nestan bellowed together, throwing themselves after her.

Milla came back to life and followed them.

Heral turned sharply, banking east. He flew back, faster, lower, and let out another jet of fire.

Now the archers screamed, arms raised in feeble defense. Milla saw bows burning, arrows torched to ash midair. A man leapt into the sea, ablaze.

"Hold!" Tarya cried out to her dragon.

There was complete confusion. The city streets were emptying. People were caught in the crush. On the shrine, people dove for cover. Some fell in the sea, others ran along the causeway.

"Come on!" Milla cried to Vigo. "We've got to stop them."

They climbed up on the stone-and-flint wall of the causeway, putting themselves in the line of fire as Heral circled lower, searching for Tarya.

"Do not shoot on the dragon," Vigo shouted in Sartolan,

241

his loud voice carrying clearly over the commotion. "Cease your fire! I command it!"

Duke Olvar echoed these words in Norlandish.

No one wanted to shoot the duke's son on his betrothal day. The archers lowered their bows. Soldiers froze, swords in hand.

Tarya moved fast. She kicked off her shoes. Hitching up her long skirts, she began to climb up the white carved pillar nearest her, using its spiraling design as a ladder. She reached the domed roof of the shrine and clambered up. Tarya rose slowly to her feet and lifted both arms, beckoning to Heral.

The screams stopped. Everyone who had not already fled now stopped to watch, mouths agape.

Heral landed clumsily on the roof of the shrine, wings outstretched for balance. He roared his pain and confusion, sending dark smoke and a flurry of sparks skyward.

Tarya opened her arms and stepped toward him.

Behind Milla, everyone gasped. A Norlander woman in a gray silk gown fainted, crumpling to the floor of the shrine.

Tarya embraced Heral.

Milla saw her lips move, soothing her dragon.

Heral bowed his head to Tarya and squawked more gently, letting himself be calmed. She patted his neck and leaned forward to whisper in his ears.

Traveling her hands steadily lower, Tarya pulled the arrow cleanly from his flank: a shallow wound, but a bloody one. Heral roared again, but he didn't lash out. Tarya ripped a stretch of fabric from the bottom of her blood-soaked dress and tied it around Heral's flank. Then she bent forward and slid one leg across Heral's back.

"She's not . . . ?" Vigo's voice died in his throat.

"Yes, she is!" Milla said. It was a stroke of brilliance from Tarya—how else to get her injured dragon past the panicking crowds?

The dragon gathered himself and with a great leap, Heral jumped down from the roof, over the sea. It looked for a moment as if they'd hit the deep water beyond the shrine. Heral's wings flapped wildly. Then, at the last possible moment, his flight changed. The wingbeats slowed and grew deeper, and he swooped upward with strong powerful strokes, heading out to sea.

"She's done it!" Milla whooped.

She watched them fly in a long curving arc, turning slowly and heading back to the palace of the four winds that topped the island city.

Tarya crouched low over her dragon's back, her pale dress in stark contrast to his deep-red flank. Her hair fluttered out behind them. Then they disappeared over the hill, out of sight.

For a moment, there was a stunned silence.

Milla held her breath and waited for the reaction. Did this mean she and Iggie could fly openly now, too? Kara said dragons belonged in the city. Well, the city certainly knew about the dragons now. The secret was out. Everything was going to be different.

Wide-eyed, people stared at their neighbors, as if released

from a spell. Then the entire island of Arcosi erupted in hectic gossip.

"Quick." Vigo grabbed Tarya's black mare and sprang up into the saddle. Pulling her head around and urging her forward, he shouted over his shoulder, "Isak? Milla? Back to the palace, now!"

Then he was galloping down the causeway after Tarya.

CHAPTER THIRTY-TWO

At the shrine, the scattered guests stared at each other in stunned silence.

"Let's get back to the palace immediately," Olvar called out, in a voice that shook slightly. "Before they riot. I'll order a new curfew."

Milla moved closer, so she didn't miss a word.

"My dear, why not let the people have their holiday? Let them get used to the idea of the dragons?" Serina suggested. "Look, they're calmer now. No one is rioting."

King Carlo waited a polite distance away, listening to his sister.

Any other day, Milla was sure Duke Olvar would have ordered his army to clear the streets, but the presence of visiting royalty restrained him.

"Very well." Olvar's voice sounded tight and effortful. "Guards! Let it be known that the holiday will continue."

Milla watched them go.

The royal carriages parted the crowds, heading straight back up the main street to the palace.

"That's done it," Josi commented dryly. "I'd better get back to Kara, and let her know her wishes might be coming true."

"I need to get back to Iggie. But I'll see you soon?" Milla embraced Josi and Nestan. Then she used the secret steps and the shadow gate to avoid the packed streets, but it was slower going today, and she got caught in foot traffic every time she crossed the main roadway.

By the time she finally reached the dragonhall, the duke and his family were already home. Milla found Vigo arguing loudly with his father, while Serina tried to interrupt.

Iggie welcomed her loudly and glided down from the perch.

She went straight to her dragon and put her forehead to his, holding his head with both hands. "It's all right. Everything's all right," she told him, hoping it was true.

Iggie rumbled his reply, unsettled by the mood in the room.

"You can't deny this is happening! The secret's out," Vigo was shouting. He had one hand out to restrain Petra at his side.

The green dragon was standing next to Vigo, glaring down at the duke for upsetting her person.

"Don't you see?" Vigo tried. "It's a chance to do the right thing! And unite the city. Don't we need that?"

Heral had a fresh bandage, but seemed otherwise fine after his flight over the island. Tarya was running her hands over him, checking every scale, still wearing her bloodstained dress. Isak and Belara huddled by the stove. The golden dragon crouched low, with her ears flat, as though raised voices hurt them.

King Carlo and Luca hung back awkwardly by the door with a few Sartolan guards, all looking dazed. The dragons had been kept secret from them, too. Last time people rode dragons, Sartola had burned.

"Milla! At last," Vigo said, turning to her.

"What's going on?" Her eyes darted from Vigo to his father and back again. Today, the balance of power between them seemed different.

"Didn't you see as you came in?" Vigo asked.

She blanked the question, unwilling to mention the shadow gate.

"Come on, follow me."

Leaving Isak with the dragons, she followed Vigo as fast as she could to the palace gates, the others running to keep up. There, Vigo gestured for Milla to climb the eastern watchtower first. As she walked up the worn stone stairs that spiraled through it, her ears were filled with a strange sound, gathering in strength. She emerged into bright sunshine, hot on her face, and noise broke over her like a wave. Tarya, Vigo, Carlo, the duke, and duchess all stood in a line on the ramparts.

Milla looked down on hundreds of people lining up on the other side of the gates. An ocean of Arcosi citizens, milling, talking, arguing. Children on their parents' shoulders. Elderly couples on little folding stools, fanning themselves in

247

the sunshine. Vendors squeezed up and down with their trays, selling food and drink. The chattering, undulating snake wound its way, six people wide, back down into the heart of the city, as far as she could see.

Milla remembered what it felt like to stand down there, looking at a locked door and burning to enter.

What had Kara said? The dragons belonged to the city. And here was the city, come to see them. The first holiday in years, and they chose to spend it standing in the heat, for the chance of seeing a dragon.

"What can we do?" Tarya whispered in her ear so the duke couldn't hear. "They've come to see the dragons. But there's no way we can get them all in at once: there's hundreds."

Milla stole a glance at the duke. He looked affronted that his people dared come knocking, uninvited.

"Let's open the doors, quickly," Vigo was saying. "Or do you want another riot?"

Carlo looked shocked. "You've had riots? But why? I thought trading was good?"

Serina paled.

Milla guessed she'd seen the results of recent fighting at close hand, working with her healers in the lower town.

"Carlo, I'll explain later. My son is right," the duchess said. "There's nowhere to go. In such close quarters, we cannot risk a riot."

"We need to prove to people that the dragons aren't dangerous—so no one else shoots arrows at them," Tarya said firmly.

"What exactly are you suggesting?" the duke asked.

"We let them in. Let them see the dragons, as they really are." Tarya thought of something else. "Vigo! We could share our betrothal feast with the people?"

"Turn it into a celebration of the dragons?" he said slowly. "I like it." He grinned at Tarya.

Milla nodded. This was it. Finally! Here was the chance to make things right, just as Kara had told them. To heal all the mistakes of the past. "Yes! Let the people of Arcosi meet the dragons of Arcosi, just like—" She bit her lip so she wouldn't blurt out Kara's name.

Duke Olvar twisted his head and stared keenly down at her. He was so tall and thin, Milla thought of a heron, hunting.

"Make it our betrothal gift?" Vigo said to his father.

"It could work." Serina was counting, calculating, with an experienced eye. "We can set up tents. One for food, one for recovery. There'll be heatstroke today."

"Your Grace has a strategy, I'm sure." Tarya appealed to Olvar's controlling nature: let him think this was all his idea. She gestured to the guards all along the palace walls. "What's best, would you say? Swap the guards' shifts double-time so no one gets too hot? Send detachments down with water? Would that need two or three cohorts? And, of course, anyone fighting is barred."

Milla watched Tarya flatter the duke with reverent attention, manipulating him brilliantly as no one else could. Her friend was changing, Milla saw.

It helped that King Carlo was listening. The duke wanted to appear generous in front of his wife's brother.

"I see events have overtaken us," Duke Olvar sighed. "Let it be so. Open the gates, let the people in."

Milla dared to ask, "*All* the people?"

The duke paused.

Carlo cleared his throat and stared meaningfully at him.

Everyone waited. Was Olvar about to insult Sartolans in front of the king of Sartola?

"Yes, yes, all the people of Arcosi. I suppose we must," Duke Olvar said. He stalked away.

Out of earshot of King Carlo, Milla heard the duke amending his orders in a whisper. "But Norlanders first. And when they've seen the dragons, get them out of my palace before we all catch something."

When the palace gates were opened, a line of bedraggled, sweat-drenched Arcosi made their way under the shade of the trees to the dragonhall. Rich and poor, young and old, first Norlanders and then everyone else; they all came in to see the dragons. They filed into the dragonhall and stood staring at what they found: this vast spacious building, with its ancient murals and the four enormous real-live dragons.

Seeing the shocked expressions, Milla went to welcome them in. She remembered her first awestruck impressions on the night of the duke's ball—and there had been no dragons back then.

Iggie glided across to the makeshift wooden barrier and stood, sniffing the air.

Behind the fence, a family of four backed away rapidly.

Milla threw herself after Iggie. "Steady, Ig, steady." How did he look to these people? Huge, vast, lethal?

She glanced over her shoulder: Heral and Petra were watching with interest, while Belara was curled up on the far side of the stove, ignoring them all.

Just then, a girl wriggled out of her mother's arms and ran forward—a skinny little six-year-old with long plaits and a big grin. She pushed her head and shoulders right through the barrier and stretched her arms out. "Hello, dragon!"

"Ella, come back!"

Milla was tense with dread, ready to call Iggie off. Why had she thought this was a good idea? He could break this child so easily. And then what would happen to Iggie? The city would bay for his blood.

But Iggie reached down delicately, whiffling at her palm, like a horse.

"It tickles!" the girl laughed, delighted.

"Well done, Ig. Nicely done." Milla stood at his left shoulder, patting him to calm herself as much as him, and squashing a surge of jealousy. Wasn't this what she'd been arguing for? Iggie wasn't just hers anymore. She had to share him.

The little girl's brother came forward next, stuttering politely, "P-please, my lady . . . Can I pet your dragon, please?" He fixed her with large hazel eyes, hopeful and still a bit scared.

Iggie bowed playfully, then sprang backward, checking to see if they were following.

The little boy flinched and stumbled away.

His mother screamed.

"It's all right. He just wants you to chase him," Milla explained. "Come on, he won't hurt you, I promise."

Slowly, the little boy came forward again, and this time Iggie was gentle and slow, till the boy grew bold and confident with him.

The rest of the day passed in a blur of heat and effort. Three dragons loved it. While Belara slept through most of it, Iggie, Petra, and Heral came to meet the people of Arcosi. They showed off, flying up to the rafters and turning circles in the air. They let children sit on their backs, three at a time, purring contentedly and basking in the attention.

It was late in the afternoon when Milla saw the next people in line were Thom and Rosa. Close up, she noticed with a shock that they had both lost weight recently.

She'd only seen Rosa once, just after the fire. When she visited to check that Rosa was all right, Milla almost got smothered by her parents' grateful hugs. She'd come away laden with gifts of food and wine.

"So that's what's been keeping you away." Thom leaned on the wooden rail and gazed at Iggie with open admiration.

Rosa met Milla's eyes, and it was complicated. There was some hurt there that she hadn't confided in her, but something else, too, closer to awe.

Milla went and hugged her friend over the fence. "I'm sorry I couldn't tell you," she spoke into Rosa's hair. "It wasn't my choice, I promise you." She pulled back and looked up at her face. "I missed you. Can we get back to normal, now that you know?"

The silence lasted a beat too long. Milla wished she'd trusted them with the truth, whatever the duke might have said.

"What's his name?" Rosa said finally. "Aren't you going to introduce us?"

"Iggie!" Milla said. "Ignato, really. Isn't he beautiful? Come on, come and say hello properly."

Aark? Iggie asked, stretching forward to sniff Rosa's sleeve.

"Hey, Iggie, good to meet you finally." She tipped her head back to see his face, lifting a tentative hand. "I can't believe it. A dragon? I must be dreaming."

Iggie whooshed a breath of warm air and slobbered over her fingers.

"Urgh! Except: who knew dragon dribble was so sticky?"

They all laughed, making Iggie blink slowly in delight.

"Come on, come in," Milla said, urging her friends to climb through the fence.

Seeing Thom and Rosa standing with their arms around Iggie's scaly neck, Milla felt tears spring to her eyes. She stretched her arms and rolled her shoulders, as if she'd shed a heavy load.

Near the end of the day, Tarya said, "I think it's actually good for them: Kara was right." She was wearing her usual red clothes again, her bloodied betrothal dress discarded. "Look at Heral: he's never looked so sleek and satisfied."

"My fierce dragon's nothing but a show-off! How did I manage to miss that?" Vigo said, yawning, to Milla as Petra rolled on her back in front of a pair of startled little boys.

"And Iggie adores children—who'd've guessed?" Milla said. And then, "What's the matter with Belara?" she asked, quietly so Isak couldn't hear and take it the wrong way.

The golden dragon, smallest of them all, had not joined the others at the fence. All day she stayed as far from the viewing area as possible. If anyone but Isak or Iggie came near, she turned on them, growling and spitting sparks.

"I've never seen her like this," Vigo said. "If I hadn't backed off earlier, she'd have flamed me."

"I think she's ill," Isak said. He was coaxing Belara with a bucket of water, but she kept turning away. In the end, he gave up. "I'm worried. She's not eating. She won't drink. It's like she's trying to hide. Maybe it's just too much, all this." He gestured at the endless line of people shuffling through the main doors. "Maybe it was a mistake."

Milla was about to contradict him, when she noticed how worried Isak looked. His face was chalky white. He'd cut his blond curly hair shorter so it stood on end, making him seem taller, copying Olvar's style. One of the duke's craftsmen had made him some new eyeglasses, with wire that fitted over his ears, but this wire was thicker and darker. It made him look like someone else. She missed the old Isak.

"Can we stop for today?" Isak asked. "She's really not well."

The sun was setting now, painting the walls of the dragonhall with slanting golden light.

"Let's do it," Tarya agreed. "Everyone's exhausted, me included."

Vigo called the command and the guards stepped forward, breaking the news to the disappointed line just outside the dragonhall.

Milla slid to the floor and stretched out on her back in the sawdust. "Oof! What a day." She felt that old familiar buzz of tiredness in her body, while her mind was racing. "Congratulations, you two. No one will forget your betrothal in a hurry."

Tarya laughed. "Feel free to write a song about Heral and his dramatic timing, Isak."

"They loved it, didn't they?" Milla said, looking over to where Iggie, Heral, and Petra still stood by the fence, watching hopefully to see if any other visitors were coming. She kept her tone light, trying not to start another fight. "You know, Kara said the dragons belong to the city. Do you think we could try taking the dragons down there? I mean, once everyone has met them? They could use the old basking places."

"Why not?" Tarya yawned. "It went better than I expected today."

"I can't believe we just introduced our dragons to the people of Arcosi." Vigo shook his head, smiling.

"Remember that old poem: *walls must fall, peace must reign*?" Milla said. "Maybe this is the start of it. Maybe we can pull it off."

"Speak for yourself, Milla," Isak muttered. "You usually do. We are still here, me and Belara. And in case you hadn't noticed: No, Milla, she didn't love it. No, Vigo, my dragon didn't meet people today. And no, Tarya, it went worse than I expected. Haven't you seen her?"

They all looked over. Belara's scales looked grayish yellow. She was curled up tightly, her back to Isak, ignoring all his attempts to communicate with her.

"It should be quieter tomorrow," Vigo said placatingly. "I reckon we had most of the city through those doors today; maybe she'll feel better then? I think the dragons will like exploring the city. We could start that tomorrow, when they've met everyone."

He was wrong. Next day, there were more new people. The day after that, even more.

On the fourth day, Milla and Iggie went for another early-morning flight. It was a special time of day for Milla. The only time she had her dragon to herself, the only time she felt completely free, just like in the dreams she had before Iggie hatched.

This time, when the mist started to burn off, Milla saw something below her. She gripped her dragon's neck more tightly.

"Iggie, look! What's that?" She stared at the dark shapes in the water below: dozens of them. "Is it fishing boats?"

Iggie flew lower.

Milla nearly fell from his back in shock. It was a flotilla. Boatloads and boatloads of people, all heading toward Arcosi.

Was this an attack?

They flew back to the palace at top speed. They landed right outside the dragonhall. Milla was better at landing already. She threw herself off and into a run, then slammed straight into Tarya tearing the other way.

They gripped each other's arms tightly, both breathless and bursting with news.

"They're coming! Boats and boats, all coming here!" Milla said. "Raise the alarm!"

"No, it's not an attack," Tarya cried. "They sent word. It's the old islanders, coming home. Just like Kara said."

Milla just stared at her.

"There's something else. It's Belara!" Tarya told her: "She's laid eggs!"

"No!" Milla knew she should feel pleased. She wanted the dragons to breed, one day, and secure their future here on Arcosi. She just hadn't expected it so soon.

Who would the new dragons belong to? To these people on the boats—is that why they'd come? It couldn't be a coincidence.

CHAPTER THIRTY-THREE

Later that day, Milla was gathering herbs in Serina's garden, to make Belara a draft that was good for brooding dragons. Isak might barely speak to her anymore, but she could still be useful to him—she had searched out the recipe in one of the library books.

Just then a messenger came to the garden gate and coughed loudly.

"My lady." The young man looked terrified as he conveyed his message. "All the dragon-bonded are informed that the duke has an announcement. Since the eggs must not be left alone, Duke Olvar will honor you with his presence. In the dragonhall. Er, *now*."

Milla jumped up, scattering stems of fennel, and sped through the palace grounds.

She hurried into the dragonhall, her chest tight with dread.

Tarya, Isak, and Vigo were already there, with the duke and duchess.

"My decision is made. I said my people could meet the dragons," Olvar began. "I didn't issue an open invitation to boatloads of strangers."

"But they are the original people of Arcosi. I've been down there, speaking to them. They come in peace. They're just coming home!" Serina cried. "Don't we owe them something? After all, the dragons used to belong to them."

This was what Kara had foretold, back at the duke's ball. What else had she said? Milla tried to remember her exact words.

"I don't care who they are: they are not welcome here."

The other day, Olvar had opened up, just a crack, Milla was sure of it. He'd trusted them and let his people into the palace. But that door was slammed shut once more.

"If we talk to them, we can find out," Serina reasoned. "They might know about the dragons. They could help . . ."

"No. It's already done." Olvar put his hand up when Vigo tried to speak. "I've issued a new curfew: no one on the streets after dark. We must restore order. This has gone far enough. We have the eggs to think of. I'm tripling the guard around the dragonhall."

The eggs. Of course. Milla should have seen it coming. Of course the duke was thinking of the eggs above all else. She'd seen what happened when the duke "protected" his people. How bad would it be when he was protecting a dragon he thought would belong to him? Her stomach started tying itself in new knots.

"Restore *order*?" Vigo scoffed. "You wait and see if it brings order. I don't believe you!"

"Thank you, Your Grace." Isak glanced nervously at his bunk.

Belara had pushed her way in there at first light, as soon as they'd gotten up, and laid two eggs on his bed, in the darkness and privacy behind the curtain.

If anyone looked in, she growled and bared her teeth. If they didn't leave, she started kindling and spitting sparks till they did.

"B-b-but, I don't understand," the duchess said. "What about these people returning home?" She sounded incredulous. "There are hundreds of returning Arcosi just arrived on the island. They'll need food, water, somewhere to stay. The inns don't have space for them all. How do you expect them to obey the curfew if they've nowhere to sleep?"

"Not our problem. We didn't ask them here." Duke Olvar's tone was flat and final. "The eggs come first."

Serina flinched. "And what about your own people?" she asked quietly. "The ones who are still lining up to see the dragons?"

"They can choose: obey the curfew, or stay and be arrested. They have enjoyed my hospitality long enough."

Milla had been nurturing a fragile hope that this could continue: that she and Iggie could spend their days with the people of Arcosi, seeing Thom and Rosa whenever they liked. Now it withered like a seedling in a late frost.

"*His* hospitality!" Tarya tutted quietly, next to Milla. It was Serina who'd set up the rest tents, organizing food and water for all the visitors.

"What about what the other dragons need?" Vigo asked. "Petra loved meeting people."

"It's time we all got back to normal," Duke Olvar said loudly. "The people can go back to their homes. Go back to work. Get out of my palace."

Milla had heard people say everyone had a breaking point. Now she watched the duchess reach hers. Serina sprang to her feet, holding herself tall. "Oh, it's just yours now, is it?" she demanded.

Milla braced herself for the duke's response.

Vigo stared at his mother as if he'd never heard her yell before. Maybe he hadn't. Milla found that hard to imagine, having lived with Josi, who yelled much of the time.

"*Your* palace?" Serina's cheeks were flushed and her eyes were bright with anger. "When it has also been my home for twenty years? When it was my dowry that allowed you to build this cursed army in the first place?"

Iggie leaned on Milla, whining softly. She stroked his neck and down his broad back, trying to take comfort from this contact with her beloved dragon.

"Calm down, my dear," the duke said coldly. "You're not thinking straight. We just need to set an example and everything will soon be back to normal."

A new normal, one that involved the duke bonding with one of these dragons, Milla guessed.

"Have you looked outside today?" the duchess asked.

261

"Thirty boats, I counted! And that won't be the end of it. Well, if you won't let the returning Arcosi in here, I'll just have to take food and shelter to them."

"Mami, just wait a little," Vigo said, squeezing her hand. "He doesn't mean it. We won't close our doors to them. Will we?"

Milla looked at the duke, at the set of his jaw. She was fairly sure he meant exactly what he said; a challenge only made him more resolute.

"The curfew has already been issued," Olvar said curtly. "The troops are clearing the streets right now. And we will close the city gates. They can find shelter down at the docks, or they can leave."

"What?" the duchess cried. "You mean to keep them out of their city? This is madness."

"I tell you what is madness: letting our city be overrun by strangers who think that it belongs to them! Didn't you hear? There are dragon eggs to protect in here."

"And there are people to protect out there!" Serina spat back. "I can't stay here when people need me." With that, she picked up her skirts and marched from the dragonhall.

Milla made a move as if to follow her but jumped back when the duke snapped, "Well? Who else wants to risk their dragon's life out there? Go on! You're free to go! Nobody is making you stay here."

"Well, I'm not leaving Belara," Isak said immediately. "And she can't leave her eggs."

Milla looked around the dragonhall's warm, airy interior. At the well-stocked food bins. At the troughs of Arcosi spring water. At the polished wooden bunks with their colored silk curtains, the comfortable dragonperch and the ever-burning stove. She saw Tarya's and Vigo's miserable faces, and Isak's stubborn one. And she began to understand how firmly they were caught in the jaws of the duke's trap.

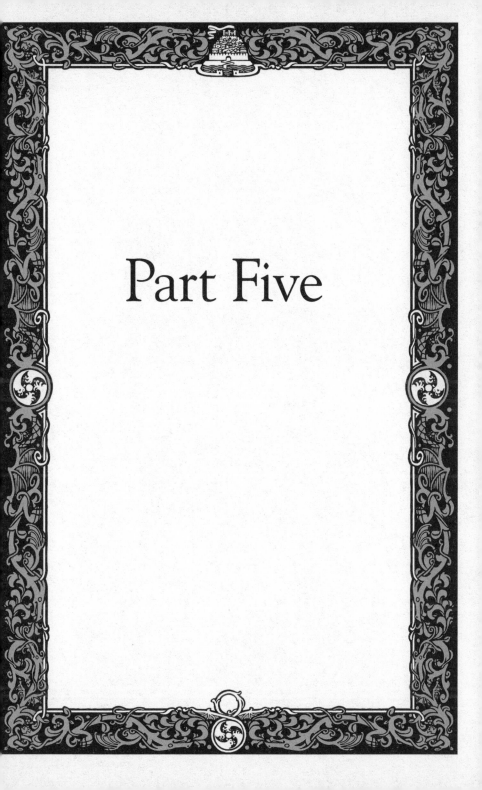

Part Five

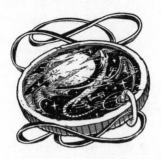

CHAPTER THIRTY-FOUR

Three months later: Midsummer

It was the hottest summer in years. As the sun rose over Arcosi, its rays fell on a city transformed beyond recognition.

Sunlight illuminated the harbor, the dozens of ships moored so closely that hungry rats crossed between them, scavenging for food.

The sunshine traveled slowly across the city gates above the docks, locked and guarded by dozens of black-clad soldiers.

It fell on the people sleeping in the new encampment outside the city walls, between the wharves and the marketplace, now filled with rows of tents and makeshift shelters rigged up from blankets, scraps of rope, and broken crates. A little boy snuggled into the curve of his mother's body, her long black hair pillowing his cheek on the cool cobblestones.

The early shafts of sunlight crept into the largest tent. Duchess Serina was up before dawn to check what was left in her stores and how best to stretch it to feed five hundred mouths that day.

And at the crown of the island, the sun striped the floor of the dragonhall, where screams shattered the calm golden morning.

"Milla! Wake up! *Wake up!*" Vigo's voice cut through the tentacles of her nightmare.

Milla woke, shivering, on the floor of the dragonhall—she'd rolled right out of her bunk.

Aark! Iggie was there, too, nudging her gently, but his warm, smoky breath only revived the terror of her dream: Plumes of smoke rising. A ship alight, ropes burning.

Reaching out for her dragon, she blinked away the horrible images. "Did I scream again?" she asked Vigo quietly. "I'm sorry I woke you."

Isak was curled in a ball on the floor by his bunk, fast asleep under a blanket, and there was no sign of Tarya yet.

Milla stumbled to her feet and went to pour herself a cup of water. Iggie shadowed her anxiously. Water was rationed now, but there never seemed to be a shortage in the dragonhall, and she drank it down gratefully.

"It's fine. Tarya's still asleep. She's exhausted from all the hunting," Vigo whispered, coming to join her with a quick glance to check that Petra and Heral were still fast asleep, curled together on the dragonperch. "Tarya blames herself for all this—the overcrowding, the encampment—just because Heral showed up on our betrothal day."

"That's ridiculous!" Milla hissed back. "She didn't know all these people would come home to Arcosi. And she didn't make the rules—" She stopped short of criticizing Vigo's father directly.

"No, but we could. We could make different ones." Vigo paused. "We need to take a stand," he said, urgent now. "If we don't, who will? The dragons are fully grown now. They give us power. We can use it to stop this."

"What are you saying?" Milla wanted to hear him say it. "That we fight back with the dragons?" she whispered warily, knowing that the whole island felt like a tinderbox in the heat. It would take only a spark to set it all alight.

What did Iggie think? He was listening intently to them both, his eyes huge pools of green fire.

"Yes! Why not? There's got to be another way, if we're just brave enough to take it. The dragons are stronger now. Don't you think it's time? Soon. Before the eggs hatch, and my father . . ."

He didn't finish the sentence, and he didn't have to. The duke was a man obsessed. Olvar would have sat on the eggs himself if Belara would let him anywhere near them.

"Kara said they should hatch in the marketplace," Milla remembered, stroking Iggie's flank.

"Like that's going to happen, with a triple guard around the dragonhall and the city under curfew," Vigo spat. "That's what I'm talking about: this is so wrong."

"What?" Tarya emerged, yawning, from her bunk. "What are you talking about?"

"Nightmares," Milla said, "in my dreams and right here."

269

"We were talking about my father's new rules," Vigo told Tarya, kissing the top of her head.

"It's everything you ever warned us about, Milla, but worse . . ." Tarya tugged at her red shirt, with its little dragon badge sewn on the front. "This? It's a badge of shame, not pride."

The duke had passed many new laws since the spring, but this was the most hated. Anyone of Norlander descent got to wear a black dragon badge on their clothes—the duke's own symbol. Everyone else had to wear a badge in the shape of a ship, to show they were more newly arrived. The ship badge was given to anyone who wasn't Norlander, whether they'd lived here for years, like Josi, or arrived on the lastest boat, and it guaranteed they'd always be last in line.

Milla's fingers jumped straight to the new addition on her shirt, tracing the outline of the boat she'd sewn there, hating every stitch.

"So don't wear it," Vigo said, going over to Tarya and putting his arms around her. "I'm not. Come on, let's rip it off, right now!"

"It's different for you," Tarya said, resting her forehead on Vigo's chest, as if she were very weary. "You won't be arrested."

"Are you sure about that?" Vigo asked, stroking her hair. "When they stormed through the marketplace the other day, the guards weren't checking who we were. They almost took my mother, till someone shouted that she was the duchess."

"It's time for a change, don't you think? Time for us to act?" Milla said, sensing Tarya might be finally ready to hear this.

"Wait."

The three of them jumped at Isak's interruption.

He sat hunched with worry, white as a ghost, and his hair stood in short greasy tufts. He'd lost weight, so his yellow dragonrider clothes hung from him, creased and dirty. His glasses were fogged with grime. "I think you're forgetting about us, Belara and me," he said. "My dragon is nesting right there, raising the next generation of dragons, or don't you care?"

"Of course we care!" Tarya went to him and tucked her arm through his unresisting one. "How are you feeling?"

Isak didn't answer.

Milla went to fetch a fresh bread roll from a covered basket and offered it to him.

"I'm not hungry." He spoke listlessly.

"Oh, come on, Isak!" Milla snapped. Catching herself, she let out a long breath. "I know it's not easy, all this waiting. But how is it helping Belara if you don't eat?"

"You don't get to tell me what to do," Isak said finally, looking at the three of them with open resentment. "You get to be with your dragons every day. You get to fly away and hunt with them. How do you think that feels?"

Milla had to look away from the suffering on his face.

"Isak, you haven't seen it out there," Vigo said. "The city gates are shut: no one gets in or out, apart from the duke's soldiers and our dragons. The tents are full. So's the harbor. Water's rationed. Even hunting double shifts, it's not enough. Someone's going to die out there. We need to do something."

"Oh, I see—it's the same old story!" Isak cried. "You think

I don't know what's really happening in the city? That I don't care?" He was exaggerating, but Milla could see the panic in his eyes at the idea they might leave him. "Go on, then. You go off and start a revolution. Save the little people. Don't worry about me and my dragon! Don't worry about the eggs."

"I can't leave my brother." Tarya looked from Vigo to Isak and back again. "Don't make me choose. Let's wait till the eggs have hatched, and Isak can join us?"

"But it will be too late by then." Vigo paced on the spot, gesturing at the nest. "If we wait till the eggs hatch, my father will likely have bonded with a dragon."

"And what's so wrong with that?" Isak hit back. "Doesn't he deserve the chance to bond with one of these new dragons? After all he's done? He is the duke."

"You think you know him, Isak, but believe me, you don't." Vigo stopped abruptly, biting down on his next words as the curtains of the yellow bunk were parted from inside.

"Belara!" Isak called.

Belara pushed her head through the curtain and hissed fiercely.

Isak's expression changed from hope to heartbreak, like a candle being blown out.

"Steady, Belara," Milla said, retreating with her hands outstretched to show they were empty.

Tarya was muttering, "Isak, get back!" while Vigo tugged her backward, out of the dragon's reach.

Isak reluctantly backed away, too, and they all watched anxiously as Belara emerged to eat for the first time in a whole day. Next she drank deeply of spring water, on and on, as if her thirst would never be quenched.

"How can it be enough?" Isak worried. "Look how much weight she's lost. And she's too pale. How long can it last?"

The eggs made Isak a hostage, Milla saw, as Belara climbed back on her nest and rotated the eggs under her soft belly. Isak was trapped here till they hatched. And if they wanted to stay loyal to him, they were trapped, too.

She was sick of waiting, of arguing, of wondering what to do. Burning with frustration, she stopped caring what Isak thought. She had to fly.

"Iggie? Come on, we have a job to do." Milla marched from the dragonhall without a backward glance.

Soon they were crossing the Straits of Sartola, riding the thermals, flying away from Arcosi with all its troubles. The sea was pale and still, far below them. The breeze cleared Milla's head.

What if we just kept going? She was clinging to Iggie with her knees, and her arms wrapped around his neck. She fixed her eyes on the bright horizon.

"There! We could go there . . . We could go anywhere you like!" she shouted into the wind. All they needed was meat and spring water, now that Iggie was grown. They could fly free and sleep safe and fill their days in constant motion.

Iggie *squaark*ed in reply.

She saw islands ahead, lying beyond the coast of Sartola, little jewels in the blue. "Shall we go? Shall we see what's out there, Ig?" They could be free, just the two of them.

He *harrumph*ed a smoky cough, then turned and gave her a hard look through half-closed eyes.

What about her friends? What about the city? What about Serina, waiting for the meat she was hunting? What about the hundreds of people who'd returned to Arcosi in search of dragons? What about Kara, who'd brought Iggie home to her?

Duty pulled at her like little fishing hooks, drawing her home.

"Never mind, Ig. Don't listen to me," she called out. "Let's hunt! *Down!*"

Iggie changed direction, making her stomach lurch as they dropped. She lay low, gripping him with arms and legs, feeling as if they were one creature now.

"Look, there!" Descending over the plains of the mainland, they found and chased down herds of wild goats. Milla usually looked away when Iggie killed, but today she made herself watch.

Iggie swooped in and grabbed a struggling brown goat with his claws. One quick bite, and it was done. Soon they were carrying four limp carcasses back to Arcosi, and the warm wind carried away the smell of fresh blood.

CHAPTER THIRTY-FIVE

Milla told Iggie to dump the meat near the marketplace, where Serina had set up a kitchen and a healing tent. There was already a line forming outside, which scattered as her dragon landed.

They were mobbed by a group of children, from tiny toddlers to a boy as tall as Milla. She climbed down from Iggie's back, stretching the stiffness from her body, and dragged the heavy goat carcasses away before they were trampled.

Iggie lumbered over to one of the crumbling old basking places built into the market square walls, and curled on his side. As the children climbed all over him, he was almost purring, greeting each child with *prrrt*s of delight.

To catch her breath, Milla leaned against a cool stone wall on the shady side of the square, wiping her brow, trying to ignore the slick of sweat down her back. She was tired and hot, and her clothes stank of blood. She'd gotten lazy, too used to flying.

Thom emerged from the kitchen tent, carrying empty fish crates.

"Hey, Thom!" Milla was surprised how pleased she was to see him, her old friend. Someone uncomplicated.

"Milla! Dragonrider now, eh?" His smile erased the tiredness from his face. "I see you sometimes, flying over the *Dolphin*. Hey, Iggie!" he called out to the blue dragon.

Iggie snorted back in a friendly way over the heads of the children.

Milla leaned up and hugged Thom awkwardly around the crates. "How are you managing?" Thom was taller and thinner than last time she'd seen him. He had a little boat symbol stitched on his cotton shirt, too.

"It's tough and no mistake." He grimaced, gesturing at the empty crates. "All these new ships blocking the way—by the time we unload, the catch is nearly spoiled. Still, there's almost a riot to reach us. But we always save some for the duchess and her tent. Who knows when it'll be us in there, the way things are going."

"Be careful, won't you?" She frowned, studying his open, handsome face, tanned to deep brown now from all the summer sailing. "Get word to me, if anything happens?"

"It won't happen. We are careful. Dad knows how to keep his head down and work hard. Don't worry about us." She knew him well enough to hear the fear below his brave words.

"Thom?" She caught his sleeve, just as he was about to leave.

"What is it? Are you all right?"

"What if we just left? You and your dad with the boat—we could bring Rosa, and me and Iggie . . . ?"

Thom's eyes softened, looking down at her. "That tough for you, too?"

She nodded, horrified to feel her eyes filling with tears. She couldn't cry in front of Thom, in front of all these people who had it worse than her. She scrubbed at her eyes with the back of her hand. "Sorry, don't listen to me."

"It'll pass. It can't go on like this," he said. "Arcosi is our home, right? I'm not ready to give up on it. Hang in there, Milla."

She sniffed and stood a little straighter, giving him a damp smile. "You're right. Let me know if we can do anything, me and him." She gestured at Iggie, who seemed to have three children attached to each leg now.

"See you soon." Thom waved and disappeared into the crowd, just as Serina emerged from under the canvas doorway, trailed by volunteers.

"Hope they want goat stew again." Milla made a tired joke, indicating the limp carcasses next to her.

"Thank you, Milla. Thank you, Iggie. We'll eat well tonight." Serina was as graceful as ever in her pink silk dress, with a matching flower behind one ear, but her apron was stained with evidence of a long day's work, and her warm brown eyes were hooded with tiredness.

Grubby-aproned volunteers appeared. A stout gray-haired man hoisted a goat over one shoulder; two young women took another between them.

"Tarya's worried about you." Milla stayed with the

duchess, keeping her eyes on her dragon as the children swarmed all over him. "She thinks you're working too hard. You and Vigo both. Did he come straight here, or is he hunting already? Me and Iggie can go out again now if you need us to." She hoped Serina would say yes, just so she could fly again.

Before Serina could reply, a voice interrupted.

"Traitors! What are you feeding them for? They don't belong here. It's 'cos of them I can't get back into the city, stuck down here with the dregs." A passing Norlander woman hissed abuse at the volunteers. She had a pinched face with a sharp chin. She raised her voice. "And what do you do? You bring food for *them*?"

Mraa! Iggie roared a loud warning across the marketplace.

Milla was stunned at this open hostility. She darted to Iggie's side. He hated tension.

"It's all right," she soothed him, one hand on his chest so she could feel if he started kindling flame. She shooed the children away. "Go on, go back to your parents. The dragon needs some space, all right? Go!" she urged, and the children moved away, reluctantly.

There were four young men slouching against the wall, but they got up now and surrounded the Norlander woman. "Who is *foreigner*?" one asked, with a strong accent.

"Our family is ancient Arcosi. Before you. We've come home," the other said.

"Why don't you go back where *you* came from?" The third young man looked down at the woman. "If Norlands are so special, you go there!"

278

Milla watched with gathering dread, smoothing Iggie's neck and murmuring wordless sounds to keep him calm.

Mraaa, he told her again, stamping and pacing on the spot.

"I know, I know . . ."

"Arcosi is my home, not yours," the Norlander woman spat, undeterred. "And you are the ones who should leave . . ." A few other Norlanders heard the argument and they came to stand with this woman, murmuring their support.

Now there were two groups, facing off against each other: Norlander women who lived in the dock area, clutching their baskets of shopping, versus the young men who'd been lining up for some food.

"Go home! Leave our island. We were fine before you got here," the Norlander woman said. "Go on, go!" She pointed toward the ships.

"Peace, friend. All are welcome in this tent. I've always made that clear." Serina broke across the dividing line. She stepped toward the Norlander women with her hands open. "The offer is for anyone. You bring what you can, or you stay to help, and everyone receives a meal."

The woman's leathery face was still angry. She turned away, scorning the duchess's open hands. "Not surprising you take their side . . ."

"She isn't taking sides!" Milla shouted over. "She's trying to help."

"Course she's taking sides. She chose these filthy dock rats, fresh off the last boat. She chose you!" the Norlander woman said, sounding bolder now that she was surrounded

279

by her friends. "Keep your food. I'd rather starve than share with them!" Their high-pitched laughter filled the air.

"Dock rats!" Some of the other women joined in. "Throw them in the sea."

"Norlander bullies, Arcosi is ours!" the young men shouted back.

The two groups shouted insults at each other, getting louder and louder.

Iggie rumbled, a low growl, and Milla felt the heat starting to build in his chest. "Shhhh," she told him. "Hold! We don't need flame."

But as she watched the street descend into chaos, she began to doubt her words. The two groups met and pushed against each other, shoving, first this way, then that. Soon it was a moving, struggling wall of bodies. Someone would be crushed.

She couldn't even see the duchess anymore. "Serina! Where are you?"

There was no answer. Serina was lost in that hate-filled mob.

"Fire!" Milla gave the command, flinging her arm out. The air grew hot as her dragon kindled. Iggie tipped his head back and roared out a long orange flame, sending it high over the heads of the crowd.

It worked. People screamed and threw themselves out of range. They stopped fighting, pulling back into their original groups.

Milla saw their shocked faces as they scattered, individuals once more.

"Serina? Duchess, where are you?" Milla called out.

It was as if a spell had been broken. The Norlander woman who'd started it all looked dazed, glancing around her as if she had no idea how she got there.

"What have you done?" Milla yelled at the woman. "Where is the duchess?"

"It's all right, I'm here," Serina called out, scrambling her way through, past the ones who'd been fighting. Her face was ashen and her pink robe was askew.

"Are you all right?" Milla rushed forward. "Quick, she's going to faint . . ."

Serina fell backward, hard, before she could catch her, and Milla heard the crunch as she landed on her left wrist.

"Your Grace? Serina?"

It was too long before there was a response. Milla's head pounded painfully in the silence as she reached for her.

Serina gasped and tried to sit up. Her face was drained of blood. "It's only my wrist." She cradled it awkwardly. "I think it might be broken. I can set it. I need bandages and plaster, but not here. Our stores are low. I have more at the palace."

Iggie lifted his head up and let out a high-pitched *aaark* of distress.

"Steady, Ig, steady," Milla called.

He opened his wings and flapped them, a huge canopy above them, making people cringe and back away farther. Then he knelt and gestured at the duchess. He stretched his neck toward her, making himself vulnerable, then tilted his head and asked gently, *Prrt?*

Milla understood: Iggie wanted Serina to sit on his back. They'd never flown with anyone else before, but this was Iggie's choice, and the duchess wouldn't weigh much.

"Your Grace, will you come with me on Iggie's back? We can fly you to the palace. It's the quickest way."

The duchess hesitated for a long moment, studying Iggie, then made up her mind. "Thank you, Iggie. Show me how."

Milla climbed up first and gestured to the duchess, showing her how to mount in front of her. Then she wrapped her arms around Serina's waist. "Hold on with your legs!" she told her.

Iggie flapped hard—harder than usual—and Milla held her breath, waiting to see if this would work. And then the marketplace fell away beneath them, and they were in the air.

"Ohhh! This is wonderful," Serina called. "But don't let go!"

"I won't," Milla promised.

Above them, the skies were darkening, and the sun was blotted out by gray-blue clouds rolling in from the west. It felt hotter than ever. The air crackled with tension, and it grew darker and darker as they approached the palace.

CHAPTER THIRTY-SIX

The duchess's medicine store at the palace was a simple whitewashed room with high windows, lined with cupboards all labeled in the duchess's neat script.

"Will you tie this bandage for me?" Serina was asking Milla. "Don't worry, I'll tell you exactly what to do."

Milla nodded, praying that she didn't cause her any more pain. She was still shaken from witnessing the hatred of the Norlander women. Her fingers felt huge and clumsy as she tied off the two ends of the white cotton around the duchess's wrist. Following Serina's careful instruction, she smeared sticky gray plaster over the top.

"Vigo usually does this for me," Serina said absentmindedly, suppressing a wince of pain.

Milla wondered exactly how many bones she'd broken.

They both froze as loud footsteps echoed in the corridor.

"My dear, they tell me you're hurt! How bad is it?" Duke Olvar rushed to greet his wife, frowning with concern.

Milla wanted to flee to the dragonhall, to find Iggie. But she hung back, waiting for Serina's instructions, feeling the plaster drying on her fingers.

"You were pushed? By one of these rabble off the boats?"

Milla realized he was gleeful. Here was the excuse he'd been waiting for.

"No. It wasn't like that. There was a scuffle. Norlanders were involved, too," the duchess explained.

"That's the last straw!" The duke's voice rose over Serina's, not listening to her. "I've had enough. Didn't I say it would come to this?" he said. "It's gone on long enough. We are just one small island. We cannot feed everyone indefinitely."

Milla braced to hear the duke's retribution. Non-Norlanders were already marked, like branded goats. What would he think of next?

"Have pity, Olvar." Serina held her injured wrist across her chest and said calmly, "There is space for everyone. These newcomers are ordinary men, women, and children. They've traveled far to see the dragons."

"And they've seen them, haven't they? Dragons fly overhead every day, as those children insist on hunting . . ." Duke Olvar's gaze flickered over Milla.

"If you opened the city gates and let them in, we wouldn't have to hunt so much!" Milla cried. "They'll starve otherwise."

"What do they expect? The dragons don't belong to them. So why don't they leave?" The duke's fury built and he started pacing by the doorway. "I tell you why: they want our land. They say it's theirs!"

It was theirs, Milla thought. She had spoken to the families in the tents. They were descendants of the original islanders.

"Maybe it once was." The duchess said it for her.

Milla held her breath.

"What?" Olvar stopped pacing. "You *believe* them?" His tone changed, grew suspicious. "I should have realized where your loyalties lay. You chose them the day you left here."

"Don't be ridiculous," Serina cried, her scorn now matching his. "I am the Duchess of Arcosi, and I would give my life for our people. I just don't label them. Or divide them. How dare you doubt me now?"

She looked magnificent, Milla thought, with her dark eyes flashing.

"We have to start talking to them," the duchess reasoned in a quieter voice. "Give them proper shelter, not makeshift tents. There are empty dwellings: those ruins in the shadow strip can be used now. With a few adjustments, we can all live together."

"Live together?" The duke laughed, and it was a hard, cold sound. "And when they keep coming? Are you suggesting we invite them in here?" He gestured around the room, coming closer and closer to Serina. "Will you share your bedroom with those unwashed beggars? Will you give your medicine room over to their hordes? Who'll do your good works then?"

The duchess looked at him, aghast.

Milla glanced at the door, but no one came to help.

"No, see? No one else wants to share, either. Nor should they. This. Is. Our. Home." The duke slapped his hand on

285

the wooden worktop to emphasize each word. "My father was brave enough to risk a long voyage, and the stars led him here. Arcosi was empty. If it was theirs, they abandoned it! They can't change their minds now!" The duke was roaring in Serina's face, his cheeks flushed hot and red. "The island is ours. I was born here. We deserve our homeland."

"Maybe those people deserve it, too." The duchess's bottom lip jutted out stubbornly.

Milla had backed away from the duke's fury, but Serina was undaunted.

"They've traveled a long way, too," Serina said. "They survived a difficult voyage to return here. A little boy was born in the harbor this morning. Isn't he Arcosi now?" She seemed to forget her pain in her passion to persuade the duke.

It didn't work.

"No!" Duke Olvar hissed.

"How is that baby different from you? When you were born here, your people had nothing. You'd just arrived. You were just like him."

He took one step back, shocked by her words.

"Arcosi was taken from them, they say," she went on. "They didn't leave by choice. They fled in fear for their lives."

"How do you know they are telling the truth?" the duke roared at her.

"How do I know your father was telling the truth?" Serina finally lost her cool and shouted back. "How do I know they didn't murder the citizens of Arcosi as they slept and take this island by force?"

The duke stepped in and struck his wife across the face.

Milla screamed, "No!" and threw herself forward, grabbing the duke's upraised hand and clinging to it so he couldn't strike again.

"Milla, no. Stay back," Serina gasped, pressing her uninjured palm to her cheek.

Olvar growled and shook Milla off. "Get out! This is none of your business."

She fell backward, hard, and scrambled to her feet, trying to put herself in between Serina and Olvar.

But the duchess had had enough. "Come, Milla, let him go. We're leaving. This is no place for us now." Without a backward glance, Serina strode from her room.

Milla scurried after her.

The duchess walked fast, muttering under her breath, "Should've left years ago. As soon as I saw his true colors. I only stayed for Vigo. To keep him safe. I managed that, at least."

They ran down the stone steps and out into the courtyard. Above them, the sky was low and leaden, purple and heavy with the coming storm. The air was warm and full of flies.

Serina paused as she crossed the dragon mosaic, adjusting the wrapping on her hand.

"Please, wait, Your Grace." Milla caught up with her. "Let Iggie take you—you're injured and the streets are full."

Serina shook her head. "I'll be fine. I'll take the shadow gate and bribe my way down to the docks. I'm not coming back." She reached out and touched Milla's cheek in farewell. "Find Vigo for me? Tell him what happened. My son will find me in the tents." Then she turned and continued walking swiftly toward the shadow gate, her long silk skirts swishing with each stride.

She was right. Vigo was the only one who could intervene now. Milla ran to the dragonhall. Isak barely glanced her way. Tarya must be out hunting.

Iggie flew down immediately, whining and nudging at Milla's side, sensing her distress.

"Quickly, Iggie." She urged him outdoors. "We must find Vigo and Petra. They'll be heading home before the storm." She was on Iggie's back and in the air in moments, barely registering what they did. She saw the soldiers pouring out of the barracks gates and guessed they were on storm defense duties.

As Iggie flew up and over the island, Milla saw the approaching storm clearly. The clouds had turned the color of a fresh bruise. There was a dirty yellow streak along the horizon where the sun should have been. Lightning flashed in the distance: shockingly white, splitting the dark clouds.

Then the rain began.

CHAPTER THIRTY-SEVEN

It was hard to fly in driving rain. Heavy raindrops blinded Milla and soaked her clothes. She didn't know how long Iggie could fly in this before he got dangerously cold. Below them the sea was iron gray, and the sky was darker still. When the lightning came again, she saw a glint of bright green ahead of them.

"There!" Milla shouted, pointing. "There's Petra."

Iggie had to circle in carefully and keep position just below Petra. Soon their wingbeats matched, and they flew apace.

Milla craned around to see Vigo.

"What's wrong? Is it Tarya?" he yelled across the gap between the dragons, his face twisted with worry. Petra's green flanks were silvered with rain and her sides were heaving with effort. She clutched two goats in her claws, their fur dripping pinkly.

"Your mother broke her wrist," Milla screamed back,

clinging to Iggie's neck, now wet and slippery. "There was a fight at the tents. Then she argued with your dad."

"Where is she?"

"Back at the dockside tents."

Vigo nodded, looking grim. His short black curls were flattened against his head, and his wet clothes stuck to him, dark as moss. He gestured forward, and Petra started to lose height, dropping her catch in the sea so they could fly faster.

The dragons came in over the harbor. The gray sea hurled itself against the high wall, sending salt spray into the air. Milla tasted it on her lips. Inside the curved arms of the harbor wall, the broad dockside area looked strange. Milla stared, trying to work out what she saw. She wiped the rain from her face and shook her head. There was a moving, crawling, black-and-silver mass, fanning out over the stone.

Blinking hard, she saw more clearly: the duke had already sent his soldiers to put his words into action.

"Vigo, look!"

Armed soldiers corralled a mass of scared people—new arrivals of all ages, huddled in a knot—forcing them forward, toward the boats.

"What's going on?" Vigo roared.

"Your father! He's had enough, he said," Milla guessed. "He's sending them away." She lost sight of Vigo behind Iggie's broad blue wing.

"In this storm?" he shouted. "Impossible!"

The soldiers were driving the people, like frightened sheep, forward onto the dock. Milla was reminded horribly of a recent nightmare. Something was different this time, though. She looked again.

There was another group, a mismatched, multicolored band of men, barring the way of the soldiers. She saw people she knew, Thom and Simeon Windlass among them. *Oh, Thom, you said you were being careful!*

"Look, it's the sailors and the fishermen. All the ships' crews," she shouted to Vigo.

They were all massing along the harbor wall, facing the oncoming soldiers. They made a barrier. Six men deep, ten across, dressed in blues, reds, and greens, the ordinary tunics, hats, and jackets of sailors home from sea.

Soon the two groups would meet.

"Hurry!" Milla yelled. "They need us!" She squeezed Iggie tightly with her knees as he began to dive. She wouldn't leave Thom to face this alone.

Iggie and Petra angled steeply down, aiming for the narrow stretch of harbor wall in between the two groups.

Iggie alighted. He slipped slightly on the wet stone. Milla slid off and patted him. Then she pointed to the sky: "*Fly!* Keep moving, Ig. Don't get cold."

He disobeyed. *Mraa!* he growled, refusing to move.

"Fly! You have to go. Keep warm."

Iggie flicked his tail in displeasure, but he did as he was told.

She watched both dragons fly off, feeling suddenly as vulnerable as an insect, alone and unarmed, as the mass of people edged toward her from both directions. She'd be crushed if they couldn't stop this.

Vigo took the lead. He strode forward to the nearest captain.

"What do you think you're doing?" Vigo bellowed.

"Duke's orders, Your Grace." The captain stood tall, but he still had to look up at Vigo. "To clear the island of the new arrivals." He was a broad, middle-aged man, with blue eyes and a short blond beard. Behind him stood a line of black-clad soldiers armed with sword and shield.

"Where the hell are you going to clear them to?" Milla yelled. "Nobody's going to sea today. He can't have meant today."

The captain's gaze passed over her briefly, but he didn't answer.

"And them?" Vigo gestured over his shoulder at the motley band of boatmen. They held homemade weapons: fish knives, oars, a net to throw over the guards.

"We will block the harbor to stop them, Your Grace," Simeon Windlass shouted.

"There's no man here who's fearful of foul weather," a gray-haired sailor added next to him. "But this is no day to sail."

Milla felt choked with pride for Thom and his father, risking arrest to protect these strangers.

"Quite right, too." Vigo stepped closer. He towered over the captain. "Tell your men to stand down. No one is putting out to sea in this storm. Your orders are impossible."

"But the duke's orders—"

"I am the duke's son, and I will answer to him!" Vigo was shouting in the man's face. Milla noticed that he sounded just like his father, suddenly.

Vigo looked up so the rain dripped down his face. "Look at it. You can't send them out in that." He tried a different tack, softening. "Do you have a daughter? A son?"

The man nodded, the fight leaching out of him.

"Would you send them to drown out there?"

"No, sir." The captain looked half-ashamed, half-terrified at the idea of disobeying a command. "But if I disobey . . . You know the punishment."

"Listen to me," ordered Vigo. "How long do you think you would last against two dragons?"

Everyone within earshot looked up. Petra and Iggie circled, like hungry seagulls, listening for the word to land. Or to flame.

Milla felt nausea rising, and she swallowed it down. Could she give that command? Take one life to save more? She clenched her fists and prayed she wouldn't have to choose.

"Not long," the captain said, "Your Grace."

"Exactly." Vigo's face was flat and hard. Milla had never seen him like this. "So you take your unit back to the barracks. You tell the duke exactly what I said. Or else you burn where you stand."

No one moved.

Milla tensed, ready to leap for her dragon, watching the captain's face, trying to read the thoughts behind his eyes.

"Go!" Vigo flung his arm forward, pointing. Petra swooped down.

"Retreat!" The captain came back to life suddenly. "New orders. Back to barracks. March!"

Reluctantly at first, the soldiers relinquished the dockside,

293

leaving dozens of frightened exiles where they stood. The troops regrouped into neat ranks and then turned, beetling away up the main road that led to the top of the island.

Behind Milla, the fishermen broke into loud cheering.

Vigo looked at the group of people left behind, sodden and shivering. "Follow me," he called in Sartolan. "Let's get you warm and fed." He started leading them back toward Serina's tents.

Milla felt cold, her wet clothes clinging to her. Wiping the rain from her face, she looked for Iggie and called him down to her.

"Oh, Ig." She threw herself at her dragon, grateful she hadn't had to ask him to become a weapon. Not today at least. "Let's get home, quickly. We need to get you warm and dry."

She flew home, realizing that the storm had most definitely broken on Arcosi.

CHAPTER THIRTY-EIGHT

Where is he?" Tarya asked for the tenth time. "I should go and look for him."

"Vigo will be at the camp, with his mother," Milla whispered. "With the people he rescued from the duke's soldiers." It was almost midnight at the dragonhall, and neither of them could sleep. They each sat leaning on their dragons, curled back to back like two huge scaly half-moons. "As soon as it's light, we'll go and look."

"What about Petra? She needs to roost, or she'll catch cold." Tarya ran one hand over Heral's neck ridges, then along his flank. "It took you ages to get Iggie warm again."

That was why they kept coming back: with its endless supply of heat, food, and spring water, the dragonhall had kept them safe so far, but maybe it was time to risk an alternative.

"They have fires down at the camp," Milla said. "He won't let her get cold. Come here . . ." She leaned over and hugged her friend, over the necks of their dragons. Then they lay back, watching the stove burn low.

Milla could feel Iggie's heartbeat, slow and steady, as familiar as her own.

In the days that followed, Milla would be glad of those wakeful hours she'd spent with her dragon. She held the memory of their closeness like a blanket around her against what happened next.

They must have dozed, because next thing Milla knew, the darkness had turned ashy gray, and she was jerking awake to the sound of marching feet.

"Tarya," she hissed, trying not to wake Isak. "Wake up. Something's happening." She held her breath, listening. Distant cries floated up from the city. Men's voices, issuing commands.

"What is it?" Tarya woke and jumped to her feet in the next breath. She slid the doors open, letting the chill dawn air into the cozy dragonhall. "Oh no!"

Both Iggie and Heral woke at that, raising their heads and sniffing the air. Iggie growled, a deep, bass rumble: *Mraaa.*

That was enough. Without waiting to hear more, Milla began preparing to leave. Somewhere, deep down, she knew she'd been waiting for a day like this to arrive. Trying to ignore the tremble in her hands, she slung a water flask over one shoulder, and fumbled around for her warmest clothes.

Isak sat up, checking on Belara before he did anything. "What's happening?"

"Smell that?" Tarya said, turning from the doorway.

"The city is burning. Vigo is down there somewhere. I have to go." She called for Heral and pulled her red jacket on.

"Almost ready," Milla called.

"You're going to leave me?" Isak said, blinking, bewildered. "Both of you?"

Milla's heart sank. She watched to see how Tarya would react this time.

"Isak, you and Belara are safe behind palace walls. Vigo and Petra are down there alone—I think they need us more."

However much it hurt Isak, she knew Tarya was right. They had to go where they were most needed. She gestured Iggie to her side.

Tarya was already pushing the doors wide and leading Heral through. "Hurry, Milla!"

Milla looked back, just once, and wished she hadn't. The dragonhall looked strange, empty but for Isak leaning on his bunk, with Belara nesting behind its yellow curtain.

She searched for the right words. "Be careful, Isak," she said at last. "Remember, the duke has always put himself first. Maybe you should do the same?"

He was staring at her with hurt and confusion etched on his face.

"I don't understand why you have to leave? Why you'd put your dragon in danger?"

"I know. But I still have to," she told him. "Goodbye." Milla and Tarya launched their dragons immediately, springing from a standing leap. They flew over the palace gardens, full of armed soldiers in tight battle cohorts, waiting for the command to move. They flew over the palace gates. The air was gray and damp, and Milla felt the first drops of rain start to fall.

Sounds rose from the city below them: breaking glass, screams, a child wailing for its mother.

Milla urged Iggie onward, flying next to Tarya on Heral, her face set in grim determination.

As they flew lower over the streets of Arcosi, they saw total chaos. Piles of furniture were being flung out into the street and set alight. Soldiers encircled a family. Milla saw a woman sobbing and pleading with them.

"What are they doing? They've gone mad!" Tarya yelled across to Milla. "The duke's soldiers, attacking the city?"

Milla guided Iggie lower. "Look! See who they target? It's not every house." She pointed, shouting to Tarya.

Here, in the lower streets, where the soldiers hadn't yet reached, some houses were stamped with the duke's black dragon stencil. Other doors were blank. As they watched, the soldiers kicked down any blank doors.

The duke's soldiers were attacking anyone who wasn't of Norlander descent.

"Tarya. We need Vigo! Let's go find him. He can stop them," Milla yelled, remembering how the soldier had listened to Vigo yesterday.

They urged their dragons on and, moments later, reached the marketplace.

"We're too late!" Tarya screeched, circling.

The small open space in front of Serina's tents was a riot of movement. Milla saw a sea of dark-uniformed soldiers closing in on the tents. A mass of people defended it. Sartolans, some

Norlanders, and returning Arcosi exiles fought together, united against the duke's army. They fought to save the duchess's sanctuary.

Then Milla saw them and her heart skipped a beat: Vigo and Serina, fighting side by side. Vigo fought like a warrior, swift and lethal. She saw him slicing with his sword. Serina no longer looked like a duchess. She was indistinguishable from those she defended. Her fine robe was sodden and ripped, the soft rose silk now splattered with mud, her injured arm across her chest. She had a smear of blood down one cheek and her hair flew out in bedraggled black strands, but she was fierce and beautiful as she fought.

Milla just had time to wonder where they'd learned to fight like that, and then a hail of arrows flew toward them.

She screamed to Iggie, flattening herself against his neck, and somehow they weren't hit.

She prepared herself to jump down. One thing was clear to her: Iggie had to stay safe. She would join him later. She brought her right leg over and slipped from Iggie's back. She landed hard, stood, and commanded him to go. "Fly! Iggie, fly!"

He circled above her, bellowing, *Mraaa! Mraaa!*

But it worked: the archers lost interest in him as he flew out of reach.

"Fly! Up!" She turned away, unable to watch Iggie leave, and almost stepped on a dead soldier. A man in the duke's black livery, on his back, staring sightlessly at the gray sky. Rain ran over his open eyes, like tears. It seemed wrong, so she bent and closed them.

Trying not to look at the man's wounds, she bent down and removed the sword from his fingers, already cold and stiffening. "Thank you," she whispered, then took his shield, too, harder to tug free.

She started crossing to her friends, and then she was part of it, caught up in the current of fighting and tugged along. A sword crashed down on her shield with such force that she fell, winded, then rolled to avoid the next blow.

She jumped up. Suddenly, her blood surged with the need to survive. She let it fill her and prayed she'd remember all those hours in the practice yard, fighting with Tarya and Finn.

She struck back, catching the soldier low, in his thigh. She slammed her shield in his face and he fell, lost under feet that danced and stamped and leapt to stay alive. She ran forward, shield lifted, glad of her small size. She ducked under swords, mainly dodging blows, and only hitting out at black-clad knees, feet, or bellies, whenever she found her way blocked.

Time behaved strangely. Moments expanded, flowing slowly, like a wave stretching itself out along the sand.

She seized a quick glance, daring to look across to the tent, shocked to see she was only halfway there; then time seemed to halt altogether.

There was Vigo, slumped against the wall. He was holding a mass of pink silk, stained and muddy, dotted with darker red patches.

Milla felt something change, like the turn of the tide. Fighting ebbed and slowed. People retreated into the tent. The duke's soldiers backed off, edging to the far side of the square, swords still raised.

Milla felt the wind and the impact of another dragon landing behind her.

"No!" It was Tarya's voice, barely recognizable, stretched to breaking point.

Through a blur of rain and tears, Milla watched Vigo rocking, head thrown back, clutching his mother's body to him.

"Mami!" His mouth was pulled wide into an anguished scream, and the rain drummed hard on his bare head and on the slender, limp figure he held.

Milla felt the blast of heat from behind as Heral stretched his head up into the air and let out a massive jet of flame, ready to attack.

Lightning flashed, and barely a heartbeat later, the thunder came again, drowning out Vigo's sobs.

Then something jabbed her hard in the back, sending Milla toppling forward. She landed on her sword and shield. Fingers crunched. A point of metal in her stomach. She tried to roll. Someone stood on her. She was pinned, unable to move. Crushed against her weapon. She tried to raise her head. She tried to call out. Light vanished, fast as a curtain fall.

Darkness won.

CHAPTER THIRTY-NINE

When Milla woke up in a prison cell, everything hurt. She opened her eyes, but it was still dark.

"Iggie?" she moaned. "Iggie, where are you?" There was no answer, and that hurt most of all.

She rolled, gasping in pain at the movement, and slowly pushed herself to sitting.

"Ig?"

He wasn't here. Milla reached out, trembling. One hand banged into cold metal bars, the other felt matted straw beneath her fingertips.

"Iggie!" she screamed.

She remembered fighting. Sending Iggie away. Vigo holding his mother in his arms. Serina's body, limp and broken.

In despair, Milla curled herself in a tight ball on the dirty straw. "No, no, no," she sobbed.

Was Iggie dead, too? Injured? When she reached out for him, she sensed only a terrible blankness. Iggie wasn't there.

She wept on and on, crying till her bruised rib cage screamed for rest, only stopping when she was utterly empty.

Time passed in a painful blur. No guards came. Did they know who she was? Was this Olvar's revenge? Anything could be happening on the island. It was torture not to know.

Milla's hand flew to her neck. The necklace and the leaping fish pendant were gone. Her gift from Serina. The soldiers must have stolen it. Then thrown her in here with all the others.

How many were here? Now that she listened out, she could hear people shifting, whispering, coughing all around her. These were returning Arcosi: they spoke a dialect of Sartolan she could understand. The air was full of the stink of people in captivity: sweat, vomit, worse.

In the darkness, she thought of Iggie. She pictured his huge green eyes, full of life and humor, the sheen of his scales by firelight, the way he would swish his tail with a quick, sinuous flick when he was irritated.

Be strong. I'm alive. I will come for you.

She sent her prayer up into the night, hoping that somehow her dragon would hear.

The next day was worse. The absence continued, that gaping space when she reached out for Iggie with her mind. The pain of missing him blended with the pain in her body. Milla folded herself tight around it and tried to endure. Hours passed. She knew she should start making plans. Making alliances with the prisoners around her. Trying to bribe the guards. But she was sinking fast. For Iggie's sake, she made herself sip the cup of water and eat the crust of bread that was shoved with an insult through the bars. Then she curled up again and fell back into a stupor of pain.

She only swam back to full consciousness when she noticed something unusual and shocking.

Silence.

It was impossible. All these people in close proximity, coughing, talking, bickering, crying, snoring, sneezing. But now silence spread along the cells, blanketing the watchful prisoners.

She froze, like all the others, listening harder than she had in her life.

There was a dull *thud*, like a bag of grain hitting the floor. Then a crash, like a chair upturned.

Milla pressed her face to the bars, straining to see down the building. There was daylight and movement—swift and furtive—giving her a spark of hope.

She inhaled, waiting.

She heard the sound she'd been dreaming of: a jangle of keys. Hope ignited into little flames.

She heard voices she knew: Rosa and Josi. Was she dreaming?

"Milla?" Josi yelled.

Hope blazed inside her.

"Here! I'm here!" she tried to scream, feeling her dry lips crack and bleed.

"Milla! Where are you?" Rosa yelled back.

Milla shoved her arms through the bars, ignoring the pain in her sides.

Josi was there with a bunch of keys in her hand. "Let's get you out." She started trying keys one by one in the lock.

The prison erupted, as every single person started baying for their freedom. It was deafening.

"Free everyone!" Milla said. Then, "How did you know where to find me?"

"Of course we won't leave anyone in here. We didn't know where you were, so we've freed hundreds along the way," Josi told her, in a rush. "We wouldn't give up till we found you, alive or dead."

"How did you get in?"

Rosa answered with a wicked grin, "We baked treats for the guards—a special reward for their hard work, sent from the barracks, we said. They didn't look too close at our uniforms. Too busy reaching for the cakes. Not our fault they're stupid *and* greedy."

"Are they dead?" Milla asked, as Rosa backed away with her hands full of keys to start on the other cells.

"Nah. They'll sleep all day, sore head tomorrow. Josi knows her poisons, doesn't she?"

Josi met Milla's eyes, full of all that was unsaid.

"We've got lots to talk about," she said. "First, let's get these people out of here."

CHAPTER FORTY

They streamed outside, blinking in the warm afternoon sunshine. Milla's ribs ached badly and her legs felt stringy and weak, but freedom was a powerful remedy spreading through her battered body.

"What's going on?" Milla said to Rosa, as her friend supported her weight.

There were crowds of freed prisoners heading across the wharf area, moving toward the docks.

"The island is at war: we must leave," Josi said grimly. "Tarya left for Sartola yesterday with Vigo. She told me what happened. They took Serina's body home."

Milla stumbled, remembering.

Rosa caught her elbow. "We'll get you out, don't worry," she said. "Simeon and Thom have promised us safe passage to Sartola."

"They're at the harbor now," Josi said. "We'll meet Nestan and Kara there."

"And Iggie? Will he be there, too?" Milla could see the docks now, the boats' masts in the distance.

And just then, on the light wind that blew over the island from the north, Milla heard a faint noise. "Stop. Shhh. What's that?" She closed her eyes, one hand raised, listening.

Mraaa! Mraaa!

"It's Iggie. It's him." Tears flowed down her cheeks. "He's alive!" The sound was faint but unmistakable. Up at the dragonhall, it would be deafening.

"What's he saying? Is he hurt?" Josi asked. "No one's seen him since . . ."

"No, that's his warning cry. He's telling me there's danger."

"Of course there is. Come on, Milla," Rosa urged her forward. "We don't have time."

Milla kept moving. She didn't want to slow her friends down, but as soon as they were safe on the *Dolphin*, she would go to Iggie.

When they reached the harbor, Milla barely recognized it. The rows of houses facing the harbor were smoke-stained, their windows cracked or broken. The old marketplace was deserted. Where Serina's tents had been, now there was only ash and strewn rubble, blackened and burned.

The dockside was a heaving mass. Everyone jostled toward the remaining boats. There, right at the end, the *Dolphin* was moored. She could see Thom, blocking the gangway, arguing with Simeon.

"Josi!" Nestan's voice carried over the din.

He pushed through the crowd toward them, leaning on

307

his cane, half dragging, half sheltering Kara on his right side. He would reach the boat before them.

Then Milla saw something that made her blood turn to ice in her veins.

Behind Nestan, three soldiers dropped down from the harbor wall, closing in on him. Someone must have seen Nestan leave with Kara. Someone must have betrayed them.

"Soldiers!" she screamed to Nestan. "Behind you."

Simeon saw them first. He rushed across the gangplank, grabbed Kara from Nestan, and shoved her roughly behind him, onto the deck. Then he darted back to join Nestan.

"Catch!" Thom threw Simeon his staff.

Nestan drew his sword, but he swayed as he did so, his left leg faltering, just for a moment.

The soldiers closed on him, sensing vulnerability.

"Oh no. They will not have him," Josi muttered, next to Milla. "Get on that boat. Now. Both of you." She withdrew two blades from hidden sheaths in her sleeves, using one to slice down the seam of her skirt so she could move more freely. "Don't wait for us."

"Milla! Get on board." Thom beckoned to her, releasing ropes.

Milla wasn't leaving. She wasn't. She was staying here with Iggie.

But Iggie was warning her off. With all his strength, he was telling her to stay away.

And Kara was there, all alone. She looked small and frail, cowering in the stern.

Who needed her most?

"Take Kara. Go now!" Josi yelled without looking back.

Milla heard the clashing of steel, followed by a scream of pain. She twisted to look. One man lay on the floor. Nestan was upright, clutching his sword arm, dark red blood seeping through his fingers.

Simeon was trading blows with another soldier. Instead of a sword, he had his stout wooden staff that he used to parry and block. With a grunt, he twisted it around and landed a hard blow in the man's gut with one end. The man bent forward, and Simeon slammed the broadside into his chin. He slumped to the ground, unconscious.

Josi was terrifying. She whirled with a blade in each hand, astonishingly nimble. She kicked out sideways, sending the last man sprawling. He crawled away, and staggered back to his feet, still holding his sword.

"Come on!" Milla yelled. But just then she heard footsteps approaching from behind. She turned, her heart pounding.

A dozen more black-clad soldiers were running toward them.

Milla felt paralyzed. She couldn't decide what to do.

"Go!" Nestan gasped, now leaning against the harbor wall, still pressing his wound. His face looked gray. "Take Kara and leave."

They were fighting for them. So they could escape.

"Move, Milla!" Rosa screamed in her ear.

I'm sorry, Iggie. I will return for you!

With a terrible wrench, the choice was made.

Her breath came in ragged gasps now, and she hobbled with Rosa along the worn stone of the harbor edge.

The boat pushed off, leaving a stretch of inky-dark water between them, growing broader every second.

"Now!" Rosa shouted. She jumped for the boat.

Milla leapt, half expecting the icy embrace of deep water. But she landed, stumbling, aboard the *Dolphin*, feeling the deck shift below her feet. She moved toward Kara, shocked at the change in her.

"Dad!" Thom yelled. "Jump! Come on, you can make it!"

But Simeon and Josi were guarding the injured Nestan, facing the third soldier together.

"Dad! We need to catch this tide."

"Go, Thom!" Simeon shouted. "Don't wait for me."

Thom spun around, looking grim. "All right." His eyes sped across the harbor, reading every nuance of wind and light and sea. "Do as I say, we might just make it. Get her below." He nodded toward Kara.

Milla guided Kara into the small dark space belowdecks. It stank of damp and fish, but she made a bed out of three empty crates and Kara huddled there, silent now. She could hear Thom yelling to Rosa, "No, that one! Quickly!"

She felt the *Dolphin* gather speed. They were leaving Arcosi.

She had to see. She went up on deck to watch her island home recede in the *Dolphin*'s wake. Black smoke hung above the city. She saw a flock of gulls circling. Smaller and smaller Arcosi grew, till it was just a dark mound in the vast sea. Tasting salt on her face, she wondered if she would ever return. If she'd ever see Iggie again.

CHAPTER FORTY-ONE

When Thom no longer needed them, Milla and Rosa went belowdecks to check on Kara. She seemed feverish and confused.

Milla slipped one arm behind her back and lifted her gently. Rosa held a flask of water to her lips. "Hello, I'm Rosa. Here, drink this."

Kara didn't reply, and water spilled from the edge of her mouth.

"How long has she been like this?" Milla asked quietly as she felt Kara's brow.

"I don't know, Josi didn't say. Who is she?" Rosa asked.

"Kara. One of the old Arcosi: the Returned," Milla explained, dampening her sleeve and using it to cool Kara's forehead and cheeks. "But she got here last year. She's the one from the duke's ball—remember?"

"Wow." Rosa sounded impressed. "That was her?"

"Oh, believe me, she's a real tempest, this one." Milla

smiled down at Kara. "And you will be again, soon as you're better."

"Dear Kamilla," Kara whispered, opening her eyes.

"It's Milla." She tilted her head to ask Rosa, "How long till we reach Sartola?"

"Hours yet," Rosa said, her anxious face confirming Milla's fears.

Milla peered outside, but no land was visible now: the ocean held them in its vast, dark embrace. She pictured the boat from dragonback. It would be a tiny speck, alone on the Sartolan Straits, vulnerable and small, leaving Iggie farther behind every moment.

"Did we do it?" Kara asked urgently. "Did we bring the eggs home safe?"

Rosa raised her eyebrows.

"Yes, you did," Milla said, with a nod to Rosa. "Don't you remember? You met Iggie." It was a tender relief to say his name, to speak of him, when he occupied her every waking thought. She wondered if she looked as raw and incomplete as she felt without him, like a bird without wings.

"Ah, yes, of course. Cato's son," Kara murmured.

"Is he?" Milla asked, leaning in.

"I hoped it would be me," Kara was saying, half to herself. "Selfishly. All my life, I wanted to be the one to bond with the next dragon. I saw what my mother had with Cato, and I wanted it so badly, but the time never came."

"Your *mother*?" Milla bent close. "Are you the daughter of Karys Stormrider? Did she survive?"

"Cato saved her." Kara's eyes opened wide, focusing beyond

Milla. "The dragons knew. They always do." Her voice was faint and gravelly. "Cato sensed my uncle's intentions. He wasn't dangerous. Cato only did it to protect my mother."

"What did he do?" Milla prompted her. "Did Cato stop Rufus?"

"Yes. Both dragons were there when Rufus killed Silvano. He would have come for Karys next. But Cato flamed him. Karys watched her dragon kill her brother, to save her life . . ." The words died in her throat. "Oh, the horror."

Milla closed her eyes, trying not to see it, but her mind was filled with terrible images.

"My father, Gallus Dorato, he was their dragonguard. He found Karys afterward. They took both dragons and they fled. Aelia almost died, but she bonded with my father eventually."

"Where did they go?"

"Islands . . . off the coast of Sartola." Her voice was so faint, Milla had to keep her face right next to Kara's, to catch each precious word. "They hid there. They sheltered in the caves, hunted wild goats. Later, when they were all strong again, they took turns to find the Arcosi, buying them back with Rufus's cursed gold, and freeing them."

"What happened to the dragons?"

"As a child, I played with Cato and Aelia. They were so gentle with me. They lived free, in exile, until the end. And then it was given to me to guard their dormant eggs. My life's work . . ." Kara's voice was fading now.

"You did well. You brought them home to hatch. But I don't understand," Milla said, ignoring Rosa's frown. "Why

313

did they have to hatch on Arcosi? Why couldn't they stay on the other islands and hatch there?"

"The spring water: didn't I tell you? Young dragons only thrive on Arcosi. But when we were ready to return, someone had taken our island for their own. And brought another war upon it, too. We waited, but time was running out. The eggs were getting old. All those years at sea, playing cat and mouse with the duke's men . . . But we did it. I wish Josiah knew. We'll be together again soon enough."

Milla didn't like the sound of that. The old guilt stabbed again, at not preventing Josiah's death. "I'm so sorry," she said. She took Kara's hand, and stroked it gently. Kara's eyes closed. Her breathing came in rattling gusts.

"You're like her," she said at last, without opening her eyes.

"Who?" Milla asked.

"Your mother."

Milla froze. Did Kara even know who she was right now? Was this the fever talking?

"You knew my mother?"

"Oh, yes," Kara wheezed, with something that might have been a laugh. "*Karys. Kara. Kamilla. Milla.* You see? I knew you by the necklace. And your face. You are my grand-daughter. Dragon daughter."

Milla heard Rosa's intake of breath next to her. Everything leapt into sharp focus: the light filtering through gaps in the wooden deck, the foul brackish water slopping around their feet, her own fingers squeezing Kara's arm, spindle-thin through her old cloak.

314

"Where is my mother?"

"Milla, gently!" Rosa warned, one hand on her arm.

"Where is she?" she asked again, full of urgency.

Kara's expression smothered any hope.

"No," Milla said, "no, no, no."

"They died. I'm sorry," Kara murmured, eyes half-closed now. "When you were a baby. We were at sea, sickness burned through our people, taking half from us. We took it hard."

Milla's parents were dead. It hurt more than she expected, after all this time.

"We sent you ahead to Arcosi, with your aunt."

"My aunt?" Milla said, confused.

"With Josi."

Josiah and Josi. Kamilla and Milla. It fitted the same pattern.

Memories jostled for attention, asserting the truth: Josi weeping in the kitchen the day after her father was murdered, just steps from where she worked. Josi's shock when Milla burst into the kitchen with Kara on the night the eggs hatched. Josi staying to fight so that her niece and her mother could escape.

"Why didn't anyone say?" She had seen her grandfather killed before her eyes. She could have saved him. Milla was faintly aware that tears were rolling down her cheeks now and dripping from her chin. She wiped her face absently. "All this time, I didn't know."

"It was safer that way. For you. For us. For the eggs. You were hidden in plain sight, ready for the day we could return. Josi loved you and raised you, didn't she? But she didn't tell

315

you, so you'd still be safe even if she was betrayed. She recruited Nestan to our cause. They both protected your secret."

Milla sat in shock, letting the truth sink in. After a while, she felt Kara's grip slacken, as she drifted off into sleep. She sat there, oblivious to the crick in her neck as she watched Kara rest, oblivious to the throbbing ache in her side where she'd supported Kara's weight against her cracked rib.

Her grandmother. She had family.

She knew where she came from, after all this time.

"You're descended from Karys Stormrider? I don't believe it!" Rosa's voice was trembling with excitement and wonder.

Milla stared at Rosa, unable to speak.

It changed nothing real: Kara was still desperately ill. Karys was still dead, just like her parents. She'd still left Josi and Nestan fighting for their lives. Her city was still at war. Every second away from Iggie still hurt more than she thought possible. And they were still sailing into the unknown, gambling on finding Vigo and Tarya.

And yet, and yet . . .

It changed everything.

She had a family, however broken. She was loved. She'd always been loved. She knew who she was! At last.

Milla crawled into the little gap next to Kara. She curled herself around her grandmother's sleeping body and fell asleep, holding her.

But by the time they reached Sartola, Kara was no longer breathing. She'd slipped away before the turn of the tide.

CHAPTER FORTY-TWO

They buried Kara next to Serina. Vigo's uncle Carlo led the speeches honoring her.

"This is how we bear witness. This is how we heal," King Carlo said in Sartolan. "We honor Kara, daughter of Karys Stormrider. Our ancestors fought each other, but today we form a new alliance in their names."

"Rest in the earth, Kara Seaborn," Milla said next, using the name she'd found among Kara's papers. She swayed, but her friends held her up: Tarya had Milla's left hand, Rosa her right. "Your work is done," she went on. "You devoted your life to the dragons of Arcosi. They survived because of you. We thank you for your courage." It wasn't enough, but it was the truth.

Heral and Petra flew in circles in the pure blue sky above them, but Milla couldn't look at them. Missing Iggie felt like a huge stone on her back. Every moment they were apart, an invisible hand added another rock, and another, till the weight of it threatened to crush her.

They were standing on a narrow grassy spit of land that reached out like a pointing finger into the blue-green waters that lapped the coast of Sartola. The sun was bright and hot, and the colors were so vivid that they hurt her eyes. All around them were the ornate marble headstones of the Sartolan nobility, making a little city of the dead. But in the sunshine, with yellow flowers marking the rows, with orange butterflies flitting between blossoms, and the distant noise of the waves, it felt peaceful enough, and Milla hoped Kara would approve.

Milla stared out across the water, where Arcosi was just visible in the distance as a pale bump on the horizon, with tiny spirals of smoke staining the sky above it. It looked small and very vulnerable. Was Josi alive over there? Was Nestan?

"They'll be all right," Tarya whispered, guessing her thoughts. "Josi is a survivor. My father is a fighter. The duke needs Isak and Belara. They will be fine until we reach them." And more softly, "I have to believe that. It's the only thing that stops me riding Heral straight back there and flaming the palace today . . ."

Milla went over to Vigo when the ceremony was done. She could see her own pain reflected in his face. "I'm sorry I wasn't here when you buried your mother." She put her arms around her friend in a careful hug and was surprised how tightly he clung to her.

"I can't believe it." Vigo spoke into Milla's hair. "I can't believe she is down there. Isn't that stupid, after everything?

I saw her body. I carried her. We buried her, two days ago. But I keep thinking any moment I'll wake up and it'll all have been a bad dream and she'll be stroking my head, like when I was little."

"I know." Milla pulled back, looking up at his tear-streaked face with her own eyes brimming.

"This is for you," Vigo said, putting something in her hand and closing her fingers around it. "She always wore it. It matched my sister's necklace that she gave to you."

"It was stolen."

"I know, that's why she'd want you to have this one now."

She looked down. There in her palm was a silver chain with a dangling fish pendant: identical to the one Serina had given her.

She tried to say thank you, but it was lost in tears.

"I'm sorry, too, Milla. To lose your grandmother, on the day you truly knew her . . . We're going to make my father pay," Vigo said, wiping his eyes. "Uncle Carlo has almost as many men at his command. But my father doesn't have his own dragon. Yet. And we have two. Four when we rescue Belara and Iggie."

Milla's heart leapt at those words.

It was the first thing she had said to Tarya and Vigo: "When can we rescue Iggie?"

The other dragons had sensed her arrival. Petra and Heral had brought Vigo and Tarya to the Sartolan harbor, already crowded with fleeing Arcosi, just as the *Dolphin* moored. They had found Milla weeping over Kara's body.

Tarya tried to prise Milla away.

"Back off, lady! Can't you see she's grieving?" Rosa removed Tarya's hand from Milla's shoulder and pushed her way between them.

"Who are you anyway?" Tarya bristled, challenging Rosa.

Rosa squared up, ready for a fight. "Her friend Rosa," she snapped. "Who are you?"

"Her friend Tarya."

Milla's friends were evenly matched: both tall, both strong, both fierce.

"Which makes us allies . . ." Tarya stepped back, with a tight smile. "Come on, let's get everyone safe inside, and Milla can do all the grieving she needs . . ."

For a long moment, Rosa paused, assessing Tarya from head to toe. "All right," she said finally. "But I'm staying with her."

Milla sat vigil all night, watching over her grandmother's body. Rosa and Tarya stayed with her, an uneasy truce between the two of them.

They wrapped Kara in the finest blue silk, in honor of her mother, Karys, and her dragon, Cato. They laid her in state, surrounded by lilies and candles, in a cool marble-lined vault below the Sartolan palace.

Milla was holding Kara's belongings, which she'd found hidden in her cloak: Kara had been wearing her secrets the whole time. There was a small fortune in gold coins sewn into the fabric, a map showing where the rest of Rufus's gold was hidden, in a secret cellar at Villa Dorato. And its key. Milla turned it over and over, feeling its weight and shape, till it was warmed by her skin.

"That's where you found that coin, last year," Tarya said. "Do you remember? It must have dropped from the main hoard."

"Villa Dorato! That's why Kara hid there. Of course. It must've belonged to her father, Gallus. They must have hidden the gold there before they left. Karys and Gallus always meant to return."

Milla's eyes rested on the silk-wrapped figure laid out in front of her. It looked too small to contain Kara: all her energy and defiance.

"What will you do with the gold?" Rosa asked her. "It's yours now. You are the heir to the Arcosi throne." Her eyes were dark and unreadable. "I should say, Your Grace."

"Don't be daft," Milla said quickly, uncomfortable with the way they were both looking at her. "And it's not mine."

"It is yours," Tarya said. "Let me fly to Arcosi and return it to you here. I can do it tonight if you like?"

"It's Sartolan gold," Milla answered. "Stolen in the burning war, melted down for Rufus's hoard of coins. It's blood money. It's tainted." She didn't want to have anything to do with it. "It feels cursed and I don't want to bring that upon us."

"So you can redeem it now," Rosa said.

"Carlo said he can't afford a war. But you can," Tarya agreed, picking up Rosa's argument. "Use this money, pay his soldiers, and we can retake Arcosi. We can get Iggie back. And my brother. And the eggs. Didn't Kara say the dragons needed to live in the city? Let's do it for them . . ."

Milla stared at the flickering candles, wrestling with

temptation. She wanted Iggie back more than anything. She spent every free moment planning how to break into the dragonhall and steal him back. Was this the way? She wasn't used to making decisions that would affect hundreds, maybe thousands of other people.

What would Kara say? It was her gold, really.

Suddenly, Milla knew what Kara would want. She would want the dragons of Arcosi to belong to the city. Any future eggs must hatch in the marketplace, as they used to.

The words of the prophecy floated up from memory.

Daughter of the storm, three times reborn,
Who bears the sign of the sea.
When four seasons wane, for this bright dawn
She will be given the key.

Karys Stormrider. Was she daughter of the storm? Her great-grandmother. Karys. Kara. Kamilla. Milla. Three times reborn. And the end of summer was in sight. That made four seasons since Iggie hatched. Was this the bright dawn they were waiting for? She gripped the key.

With a shiver, she felt something shift inside her.

She made her decision and spoke the words into the cool scented air, like a vow: "I will use the gold to pay for our war. And Carlo must be offered his share. Let's win our home back. There's just one condition . . ."

"When do we leave?" Milla asked now, blinking in the bright sunshine as they turned to leave Kara's grave. "I can't be away from Iggie much longer."

"Before sunrise. You saw what my father was doing," Vigo said. "There won't be much left of Arcosi if we don't act soon."

They started walking back toward the Sartolan palace, through the gardens that spread as far as the cemetery. Tall palms shaded the pathways, and to their right, a large circular fountain bubbled with clear water—it tasted pure and fresh, Milla knew, but lacked the distinctive metallic tang of Arcosi water.

So much was different here: everything sprawled out, across the lush mountainous ridges and the lowland plains beneath. They approached the palace buildings, built high above the city and surrounding villages to give a clear view of approaching danger. The sunlight glinted off the pale domed roofs—some still bore the scars of old smoke damage—and a light breeze blew through the intricately carved windows that looked like lacework turned to stone.

"It's so beautiful here," Milla said.

Rosa squeezed her arm. "Didn't I tell you so?" She looked down at the city where her parents had sought shelter with their families.

"Are you tempted to stay, Rosa?"

"I must admit, it's a relief to be somewhere where everyone looks like us and talks like us, and no one is sticking badges on me. But no, Milla. Arcosi is my home, and I'm going to fight for it."

"Same." Thom was standing behind them, next to Luca, and he called over, "No question! I need to get back to my father. I'm with you. I'm going home."

"Yes. Tarya and I agree on that," Vigo said. "Even though this was my mother's first home, and her ancestors' for a thousand years before her."

Milla's new knowledge of her own heritage still felt dangerous, incendiary as firepowder. She circled it warily. But one distant day, if they won this fight, she resolved to sit in the palace library and read every book, every sentence, every word that had ever been written about Karys Stormrider and her family.

"My father always hated that my mother knew her roots and was proud of them. He used to put her down, endlessly, when no one else could hear." Vigo sounded coldly furious. "Deep down, he knows he's no duke. He's no more right to rule than anyone else. That's why he built that army. Always so afraid someone would come along and take it all away."

Tarya said, "Well, let's bring his worst nightmare."

Milla looked at all the faces surrounding her: at Thom, Luca, Rosa, Tarya, and Vigo.

"Olvar's right, in a way," Milla said. "None of us have a *right* to rule. How can anyone call me Your Grace? I'm the same as I was when you shouted orders at me."

"What are you saying?" Vigo asked.

They were all listening now.

It was interesting to Milla how people did that more now.

"Just that, if we win," she said with fierce determination, "the dragons must belong to everyone. The new eggs must hatch before everyone. We have to do things differently. Or what's the use in fighting?"

CHAPTER FORTY-THREE

W ake up," Tarya hissed, shaking Milla awake, her face lit from below by her lamp.

Milla scrambled into her borrowed clothes, all blue. At last the separation was almost over. By the end of today, she would be back with Iggie, or she would have died trying to reach him. Either way, she wanted to be dressed in his colors.

"Are you ready for this?" Tarya asked, as she buckled Milla into a leather breastplate. With her injuries still healing, she wasn't strong enough for full armor like Tarya wore.

"I've been ready since the day I left Iggie," said Milla, realizing she'd never seen Tarya look so calm, or so focused. She was made for this.

"Your tools, Your Grace," Tarya said with a smile, handing over some long metal lockpicks and a sharp dagger that Milla sheathed at her waist.

"Stop that nonsense." She nudged her. "I'm Milla, same as I've always been." She tucked the tools away. Milla had dreamt about Iggie in chains. She could scarcely believe it, but she wanted to be prepared for the worst.

"Come here," Tarya said, pulling her into an awkward hug as their armor met.

"If anything happens to me," Milla said, "will you look after Iggie? Find him someone good to bond with? He seemed to like Rosa." She could barely say the words.

"Shhh. It's not going to happen. But yes. Of course. Will you do the same for Heral?"

Milla pulled back and they looked at each other in the circle of golden light from the lantern. "You know I will. You're my sister."

For a long moment they held each other's gaze.

And then it was time.

They met Heral on a flat stretch of the palace rooftops, the full moon casting milky pools of light around them. Tarya went to her dragon first, patting and checking him over. "Milla?" she called eventually.

Milla had known this was coming. She gathered all her strength and crossed to them.

"Hey, Heral," she said, holding out one open palm for him to sniff. It wasn't his fault she'd been separated from Iggie. It wasn't his fault that she compared him constantly to Ig, noting all the differences between them: how his head was larger, his neck more curved, his nature more restless.

The red dragon gave a deep rumbling *whoosh* of hot air, and touched his nose to Milla's forehead.

He understood. Heral was telling Milla that he knew.

"Thank you." Her chest felt like it might burst open, with

painful longing for her dragon. But she blinked her tears away, and climbed on Heral's back behind Tarya, tucking a quiver of arrows to the side so she didn't squash them.

Milla flew with Tarya on Heral's broad back. They left the lights of the palace behind, and soon Sartola was no more than a few pinpricks of light, no brighter than the stars. The full moon guided them, its reflection bright and shivering on the sea below.

At first she and Tarya murmured to each other for reassurance, but as Arcosi grew large before them and they could count the harbor lights, they fell into silence.

Peering hard at the sea below, Milla spotted darker textures in the waves. There! Carlo's ships, like shadows within shadows, sleek shapes headed for the harbor.

To the east, the sky grew pale.

Vigo and Thom would be landing Petra on the harbor wall. While Petra kept the guards at bay, Thom was in charge of this part: he knew the harbor better than anyone.

As they soared closer, more lamps were lit on the harbor wall. Nothing unusual in that. But then they blinked, fast, three times: the signal that Carlo's soldiers were ashore. While Vigo and Petra caused a diversion, a small cohort of Carlo's best soldiers would tackle the city gates, led by Thom. The rest waited, ready to head for the palace, guided by Rosa. She knew the secret ways of the island almost as well as Milla.

So far, everything was unfolding just as they'd planned it, talking late into the night over maps of Arcosi that Milla and Rosa had drawn, showing all the hidden paths, right up to the shadow gate.

Tarya let the wind carry them way out west and then Heral circled in from the north. He lost height, dropping in over the cliffs, and then one last burst of speed, to plummet into the palace gardens.

Milla squeezed Tarya's hand and whispered, "Good luck," and then she was tumbling from Heral's back before he launched again.

Milla rolled and hid behind some bushes. She waited, listening for danger. Her heart was beating so loudly, she couldn't hear anything else. This was not the time to be fearful. Iggie was out there, waiting for her. Thinking of him gave her the courage to move, one more shadow in a dawn of cool blue shadows, slipping to the secret door of the dragonhall, to avoid the guards.

She opened the door a crack, just wide enough to ease herself through, listening, listening, listening. She stayed hidden beneath the tapestry.

She peered around the heavy fabric.

There, curled on the dragonperch, was a single dragon.

Head down. Pale blue scales glinting dully.

Iggie.

He was here!

Her dragon was alive.

Joy bloomed inside her.

There was an explosion of noise inside the dragonhall, loud clanking and whining. Iggie saw her. Her dragon went wild, frantic to reach her, but something was stopping him. He seemed joined to the dragonperch by one of his hind legs.

He was chained, the shackle fastened around his leg with a huge padlock.

Her racing heart stuttered.

"Shhh! Easy, Ig! I'm here, it's me." Milla left the shadows, moving toward him, hands outstretched, alert for danger.

By the dim orange light of the stove, she could see the metal bite into his flesh, cutting through the outer scales, so blood ran down his foot. She'd come prepared, but it still hurt more than she imagined.

His scales were too pale. His green eyes, watching her every move, had lost some of their fire. She could count his ribs. But he was alive.

She sprang for Iggie, throwing her arms around his neck, finally holding his precious head against hers, breathing in his scent of smoke and blood and cinders.

"Oh, my love. My Ig. My dragon." Her eyes were squeezed shut, but the tears flooded out anyway.

Aaaark! Iggie's greeting was the sweetest sound in the whole world. He almost knocked her over, rubbing his head against hers, nudging at her, wriggling every inch of his frame in greeting.

She ran her hands over his scales, over his neck and back and too-thin ribs. "Are you all right? Oh, Ig. You have to eat. You have to live."

Aaark, aaark, aarrrk, he told her.

"I've so much to tell you. But now, be still." She pulled the lockpicks from her waistband and patted her way down his flank, letting him know what she intended. Keeping her emotions in check, she knelt to release the evil chain from his hind leg. She carefully placed the metal picks in the lock and felt for the mechanism of the padlock. With a crisp metallic *snap*, it sprang open, and the chain pooled harmlessly on the floor.

Iggie was free! The shackle left a terrible wound, but at least he was free.

"Can you walk?" she asked him, backing away, wiping his blood on her clothes.

Iggie threw back his head and trumpeted his pain. He limped forward and almost fell.

Milla threw herself at him, trying to support his vast weight. "What have they done to you?" She cursed herself for not reaching him sooner. What did anything else matter, next to him?

Then a voice spoke from behind her.

CHAPTER FORTY-FOUR

I sak!" Milla spun around, keeping one hand on Iggie behind her.

For a long moment, they stared at each other.

Isak threw himself forward.

Milla braced, unsure of what he would do.

Then he was hugging her. "Oh, Milla! You're alive. I didn't know. When Serina was killed, I thought . . . No one told me anything."

Milla held him tightly, her legs suddenly wobbly with relief.

He pulled back, searching her face. "Tarya? Vigo? Tell me my sister is all right!" he demanded.

"She's fine." By the stove's dim light, Milla could see how stained and torn Isak's clothes were now. There was a crack across one side of his new glasses, but his face was different. Alive again.

"She's better than fine," she corrected herself. "She's on a mission. You'll see. We've come to take back the island."

"Good." Isak was vehement. "Milla, I'm so sorry. I was wrong about Duke Olvar."

Milla froze. For the first time she thought of Belara. Her glance jumped to the back of the dragonhall, where Isak's bunk stood empty, its yellow curtain hanging, torn.

"What has he done? Where is she?" she asked.

Tears filled Isak's eyes, but he looked grimly determined, speaking fast now. "Remember you told us about the mad duke of Arcosi? The one who killed his cousin?"

"Rufus?" Milla said, bewildered.

"The duke found his journal," Isak said. "He showed it to me." He was struggling to find the words. "Terrifying . . . the ramblings of someone . . . murderous . . . awful. I can't even . . ."

Milla recalled the last part of Kara's story. She shivered. "What did it say?"

"Something's happened to Duke Olvar since you saw him. Maybe reading that journal made it worse. The eggs are late: they haven't hatched yet. He's become . . . *strange*." Isak ran a hand through his greasy hair, making it stand on end. "He won't sleep. Won't eat. Won't see sense."

"Tell me, Isak. What did he do to Belara?" Milla urged.

"Duke Olvar found instructions in Rufus's journal. Poisons. For people." Isak hesitated. "And for dragons."

Milla's hand flew to her mouth. Her heart felt like a stone in her chest. She leaned on her dragon, making him stagger back.

"He poisoned Belara." Isak's voice came in broken gasps.

"In her water. And when she moved off the eggs to drink . . ."

"She's not—?" Milla couldn't say the word.

"Dead? No." He shook his head, a bitter note in his voice now. "Not yet. He needs her too much, don't forget. The poison wore off after half a day. She's in the palace, in the hall. In chains." Isak met her eyes, looking ashamed. "And, Milla, Olvar did it to Iggie, too. Dosing him to sleep—it's the only way they could have chained him."

Iggie, poisoned? That explained the terrible blankness she'd felt in prison. When she reached for him, for their bond, and there was nothing.

She spun around and laid her head on her dragon's broad, scaly chest, her arms reaching up around his neck. "Oh, Iggie. I'm so sorry." Tears came fast now, turning to steam as he kindled lightly, whiffling smoky breath over Milla's hair. "I was in prison. I couldn't get to you. And then Kara needed me. But oh, I should never have left. I'm so sorry." On and on, she murmured, telling her dragon everything, till she felt his forgiveness wash over her and make everything all right.

Finally, she turned and faced Isak again. "How dare he?" she asked.

Her mood had shifted. Now she felt her anger rising like hot lava. "Come on, Iggie, let's get you safe." She wanted to get on Iggie's back and ride him away from here. She started checking him over, assessing the damage.

He fixed her with his strong green glare, lowering his head and opening his wings. They unfolded, with a rustle, still proud, still perfect. He flapped twice, scattering sawdust in a pale cloud, making Milla sneeze.

"I see," she said. "You can't walk, but you can fly!"

Iggie growled, sending sparks into the air.

"Then let's go."

"Please, Milla." Isak's voice stopped her. "You have to help me. I need my dragon back. You don't know what it's been like, these past months."

She felt some of the old defensiveness return. But she bit her lip and waited.

"I can't go near Belara. I can't even help her," Isak was saying. "The eggs should have hatched by now. If they don't hatch, the duke will blame Belara. If they do hatch, he won't need her anymore."

"The duke wouldn't hurt a dragon . . ." Milla said slowly, but her fingers were sticky with Iggie's blood, and she knew it wasn't true.

"We've got to get Belara out. With your help, we can do it. The duke still thinks I'm loyal. Please, Milla. Will you help me?"

Milla rested her head for a moment on Iggie's chest, asking him to understand why they weren't fleeing from here this moment.

"All right," she said finally. "And there's something else you should know. The duke's not the only one who has learned past secrets. Kara's dead. Before she died, she told me something important."

Listening to each other, thinking fast, Milla and Isak made a new plan.

CHAPTER FORTY-FIVE

Isak left first. When Milla crept out of the dragonhall's secret door, it was fully light and there was no escaping the horror of battle.

She watched, staying hidden.

This was her doing. She'd broken her promise to Serina: she'd shared the knowledge of the shadow gate.

The green-clad Sartolan soldiers poured through the shadow gate in single file and ran silently through the gardens, unchallenged. All the duke's men were massed around the main gates, expecting an attack from below.

There was a *whoomph* of huge wingbeats from the opposite direction.

Milla looked up as Heral soared overhead, kindling.

Tarya shrieked, "Fire!"

Heral opened his mouth and spat a blaze of fire, right at the gates. They burst into flame. Then he flew up, circling.

The fire devoured the wooden gates. Milla could feel the heat from here.

The duke's men fled from the stone watchtowers, back into the palace grounds.

Tarya was waiting for them.

The rising sun glinted off her helmet and breastplate, and Heral's bloodred scales. She let her arrows fly faster than ever, her arm reaching and nocking the next almost before the first had hit its target. Tarya fought with a light Sartolan bow and white-fletched arrows, spare quivers strapped to Heral's shoulders. Her aim was deadly, backed by his blasts of flame.

Vigo came next, on Petra, fresh from fighting in the lower city. Together, he, Tarya, and the dragons were unstoppable, working in deadly symmetry. They cut through the duke's forces, leaving a trail of ash and black-clad bodies so that Carlo's army found their way clear.

Then came the surge of foot soldiers attacking from inside and outside the gates at once. The noise swelled and broke like waves. The scent of blood, the screaming and grunting, made Milla think of slaughter time, only these were people.

She bent, retching.

"Join us! Leave Olvar and fight for the allies, Arcosi-Sartolan combined!" Tarya yelled, tossing down green armbands for any who were ready to switch sides.

Tarya would expect Milla to take Iggie to safety and wait for the all clear. But Milla had given Isak her word. She would take her dragon into danger, to rescue his.

She stole forward, beckoning Iggie to follow. "Ready, Ig?

Can you fly?" She slipped onto his back, feeling how much muscle he'd lost these past days.

She held her breath while he gathered his weight and sprang from his powerful haunches, flapping hard to gain height.

"Brave Iggie." She urged him onward. "That's it."

They flew over the battle, drawing attention.

"Down!" she screamed, ducking low to avoid a black arrow.

They banked hard left. Her stomach lurched again, but she gripped tight, feeling Iggie battle a sudden gust of wind. "Come on, my Iggie," she coaxed him, sensing how weak he was. "You're Cato's son. You can do this. Almost there!"

He caught an updraft and glided toward the palace, with its stonework like the arching ribs of a giant dragon, its four towers standing tall and proud.

"Land!" she told Iggie, pointing to the courtyard with the black dragon mosaic.

He touched down clumsily, bellowing in pain.

Milla winced, at his pain and hers. She rolled from his back, asking, "Can you walk with me?" She kept one eye on the main doors, expecting an attack, but none came.

Iggie flinched and folded his wings. He limped toward her, head bowed, snorting smoke through his nostrils at each step.

"I know, I know," she soothed. "But you heard the new plan. We're going to rescue Belara." She reached up and pressed her forehead to his, trying to pass all her love and strength through her skin and his scales.

Iggie growled softly.

She went to the huge double doors and pushed. They swung open. The vast hallway with its elegant staircase was dark and deserted. The servants must have fled, as Isak had guessed.

"Come on, Ig, this way." She hated to see her dragon's awkward shuffling gait as he obeyed her.

She blinked hard, adjusting to the dimness.

Isak was already there.

Ready? he mouthed, darting to her.

They stood together on the threshold of the palace. Milla held Isak's glance, praying she was right to trust him, praying they would succeed.

She nodded. "Quickly, take my hand."

Isak took it.

They each put their free hand on Iggie.

"Now focus hard on our plan," Milla whispered. "Everything we discussed. Send your thoughts to Belara—we are close enough. I'll tell Iggie, and he'll let Heral and Petra know. All four dragons should be enough to stop them."

"Are you sure?" Isak's face was grimly determined, half in darkness.

"It's what Kara said: *The dragons knew. They always do.* And Petra and Heral came to greet me on Sartola. We're all connected. We can use that."

She closed her eyes and reached out for Iggie. Although she'd only just begun to name this link, now she realized it had been there since before he hatched. An invisible silken thread that bound them for life. She passed all her love and courage and all the details of their plan from her mind to his, trusting he would do the rest and summon Heral and Petra to help them.

Iggie made an impatient noise, scratching his claws.

Milla opened her eyes and knew that her dragon understood. "Let's do this. Hide here till we call for you?"

Iggie whined in the back of his throat, but he folded his wings tight, crawled across the hallway, and curled up in the shadows under the great staircase.

Isak nodded and beckoned Milla forward.

Milla took a deep breath, ignoring the sudden tremor in her legs, and followed him.

"I've got Milla!" Isak shouted, pushing open the door to the great hall. "She thought to steal her dragon, but I've got her, Your Grace." His voice was harsh and loud in her ear.

He forced them forward into the great hall.

This was where everything had begun for Milla and Iggie. Would it also be where it ended?

Just as before, a huge fire burned in the hearth. Morning light streamed through the tall windows. A crimson rug covered the floor. A massive four-poster bed had been placed in the center of the room where the table had once been. Hung with thick black velvet curtains, it made the perfect nest for Belara and her eggs.

"Ah, Milla," a voice spoke from inside the room. "We were wondering when you would join us." Duke Olvar strode forward, away from the nest.

As soon as he looked at her, Milla felt her courage peel away and shrivel up. She felt like an impostor. She might be the descendant of Karys Stormrider. She might have inherited a fortune in gold. But when Duke Olvar looked down his nose at her, she felt very small indeed. Just like that frightened child hiding in an orange tree, unable to move.

Suddenly, her arms were twisted behind her back. Isak pushed her forward, and her injured ribs burned in agony.

"Let go!" she hissed. Black dots danced before her eyes, and she struggled not to pass out. She felt him remove her dagger and throw it down. She thought of Iggie, hiding just outside and sent him a wave of reassurance. She prayed he would understand everything she'd told him: that this was a disguise, that Isak was still their friend.

"I've got this. Focus on the nest, Your Grace." Isak released the pressure slightly. "Give it up . . ." he muttered in her ear, forcing her into the center of the room.

He sounded so convincing, she wondered if this was a new trap.

Just then, Richal Finn strode into the room, pulled his helmet off, and saluted the duke. "Your Grace, I bring news."

Isak had told her Finn was the duke's man. Always had been. She pushed away the shock and anger, resisting the urge to turn over old memories to spot his treachery.

"Finn?" Milla asked, pretending she didn't know he was a traitor. "What are you doing here?"

He ignored her. "Your Grace, you must hear this. Your forces are overwhelmed," Finn said. "We need to leave, now."

"Don't be a fool!" Olvar snapped. "We're not giving up now, after everything. We must wait for the eggs to hatch."

"Your Grace, the situation has changed: your son and the Sartolans will be here very soon."

"The timing couldn't be worse," Duke Olvar said. "We

340

don't need the distraction, not on hatching day." His pale blue eyes were red-rimmed, and his hair was a greasy mess, flat against his scalp.

His voice had a strained quality to it that made Milla feel even more afraid. How many nights had he gone without sleep?

"The hatchlings should have emerged by now. The moon was full last night. Maybe our calculations were wrong, Isak?" Olvar paced by the nest-bed.

"No, no, they can't be, Your Grace," Isak said. "We've been through this. We double-checked."

"I've heard them tapping! They *will* hatch, any moment." Duke Olvar looked at the velvet drapes, as if saying it would make it happen. "This is our time. And I will not run. We must wait."

"But for how long, Your Grace?" Finn asked. "They'll be here soon. Then the new dragons will belong to your enemies. You've waited so long. These eggs are yours—do you want to lose them now?"

Milla saw these words hit home.

"Of course not!" Olvar said. "But what choice do we have? I will not leave them."

"We could take the eggs with us, Your Grace. Keep them warm."

"It could work, if we also bring spring water . . ." Olvar seized on these words like a drowning man. "We will need a hostage." He nodded at Milla. "So we can demand safe passage—for us and the eggs."

Finn drew his sword in response.

"They won't give you safe passage!" Milla said. And Iggie would never let them leave. *Just a little longer*, she thought hard in his direction.

"Keep quiet!" Isak said. But he released her arms, keeping only the lightest pressure on them. "Ready?" he whispered in her ear.

This was it. Milla tensed every muscle, waiting. They had to judge the moment perfectly.

Finn cried, "Time is running out, Your Grace."

"You deal with the dragon," Olvar ordered. "I'll take the eggs."

"I'll do it," Finn replied. "I will distract it. Your Grace can use the bag!"

Milla spotted it: the beautiful silk egg carrier that once held Iggie's egg and the other three, hanging on a chair near the fire.

"Listen to me, Finn." Olvar headed for the bag. "You will have to kill the mother. Leave the girl till it's done."

"*Kill* the dragon?" Finn paused, closing in on Belara's nest with his sword lifted, looking horrified. But he only said, "Yes, Your Grace."

Olvar picked up the bag and started walking toward the nest.

"*Now!*" Isak hissed.

Now! Milla sent the thought to Iggie.

Isak sprang forward and tripped the duke. Olvar went sprawling on the floor, holding the bag.

Milla grabbed a chair and flung it at Richal Finn, aiming for his sword arm.

He stumbled, but didn't fall.

Just then, Iggie burst through the door and swiped at Finn, flooring him with his powerful tail.

Finn struggled, swearing and spitting, still gripping his sword, though he couldn't escape Iggie's bulk pinning him down.

Milla pounced. She pulled out her lockpicks and brought them down on Finn's sword hand. The thin metal skewers bit into the skin, disarming him.

She grabbed Finn's sword, heavy and unfamiliar, and scrambled to her feet.

Finn cursed in disdain. "You think you can fight now? You forget, I know you." And he kicked out viciously, catching Iggie square on his leg wound.

The wound gaped open, right down to the bone: it gleamed palely through, making Milla feel sick.

Iggie bellowed in pain and curled up, a defensive instinct that allowed Finn to spring free.

Milla lifted Finn's sword, but her arm was shaking. She would resist as long as she had breath.

From the corner of her eye she saw that Olvar was on his feet again, facing down Isak.

"You will not stop me now," Duke Olvar was saying. "I will have my dragon."

Despair rose, swamping Milla. The plan hadn't worked. The other dragons hadn't heard Iggie. Why had she believed they could win against the duke?

CHAPTER FORTY-SIX

S uddenly, the room grew dark, as if a cloud had covered the sun.

Then, with a loud crash, it erupted in light and noise. The huge glass windows shattered into pieces. Everyone dove for cover. Dropping the sword, Milla rolled under the nest-bed. She looked up.

Through the shattered windows she saw Heral spin in the air, with astonishing control. Then he broke through, feet-first, like a bird of prey, snapping the broken window frames like twigs and landing right there. Heral flapped his huge wings and roared at them.

"Get back!" Tarya screamed from Heral's back, with an arrow nocked and pointed at Duke Olvar. "Get away from my brother!" Her face was spattered with dried blood, but Milla guessed it wasn't hers.

Milla crawled toward Iggie, slicing her palms and knees on the broken glass that covered the rug.

"Ig," she moaned. Her hands found hard black claws, scaly blue feet, slippery with blood from his leg wound. She pulled herself up, using him for support, hand over hand: his knobbly knees, his broad chest, the heat and gust of his smoky breath.

Aark, Iggie said, telling her he was all right.

Milla leaned on him gratefully.

"It's over," Tarya shouted.

The balance had shifted. Milla stood in a line with her friends: Isak nearest the nest, with Tarya and Heral by the broken window.

Olvar froze, the empty egg pannier still gripped in his hand.

Finn was on his feet again. He took one step toward the nest, crunching on broken glass, then paused as Tarya aimed at him instead.

A strange noise broke the tension, startling them all. It came from inside the velvet drapes.

A breathy, gasping *tac-tac-tac*, like a cat stalking birds.

Everyone listened.

Then it came: the light crack of an eggshell.

Duke Olvar moved first. He darted to the bed, pushing Isak aside, and drew back the velvet curtains, letting light fall on the nest.

Belara was shackled by a long chain, as Iggie had been. Weakened by her long brooding season, she lay curled on her side, giving the eggs air and space. They sparkled slightly in the sunlight: one was palest orange, like an apricot, but speckled with green dots; the other was creamy white, like parchment, covered in black lines as if someone had scribbled on it.

"Belara!" Isak called to her.

But the golden dragon only gazed down at her two eggs, near the end of her strength.

Duke Olvar fell on his knees in front of the nearest egg, the apricot-colored one. If they didn't intervene, soon there would be a baby dragon seeking a human to bond with.

"No," Milla cried, "you don't get to do this. Not after everything you've done." Her courage flooded back now, stronger for its absence. "Your men killed Serina. Kara's dead. The city half-ruined . . . This is not your reward."

But Olvar wasn't listening. This was the moment he'd been waiting for all his life.

A larger zigzag crack split the egg in two. Soon the egg would hatch.

"Get back from there!" A new voice spoke from the doorway. It was Vigo and Petra, followed by a group of green-clad Sartolan soldiers.

"Arrest my father!" Vigo ordered.

"No! Let me see the dragon," Olvar begged, on his knees. "Please! Just let me see . . ."

Now Milla was reminded of the night Iggie hatched. She squirmed uncomfortably, seeing the roles reversed. Hadn't she begged to stay and see Iggie hatch? Hadn't the duke let her stay? Just when she needed to be strong, she was moved with pity for him.

Vigo's men approached.

In a blink of an eye, everything changed.

Olvar saw his final chance vanish. His face distorted with murderous rage.

"No! If I can't have it, no one can!" The duke grabbed Finn's discarded sword from the glass-covered floor. He stood and lifted it high, poised to bring it down on the eggs.

"No!" Milla screamed in warning.

Isak was closest.

He threw his whole weight at Olvar and pushed him aside. The blade buried itself deep in the wood of the bedpost. Duke Olvar pushed Isak away, sending him staggering backward. Then he tugged at the sword with both hands.

Milla watched from the edge of the room. It felt like a recurring dream, where everything turned horribly slow and deliberate, unfolding with awful inevitability. She had to do something.

She thought out for Iggie, for her friends, for their dragons. She felt the bonds connecting them, humming with life and strength. She saw bright tendrils of colored light—blue, yellow, red, and green—swirling out from each dragon and each of their people. Like a rainbow, it bound them together, all eight. She sent out a wave of love and protection and saw it pass from her, like bright blue fire, into Iggie and Belara, Heral and Petra.

Duke Olvar pulled the sword free. He lifted it again.

Mraaa! Iggie bellowed.

The dragons knew. They always do.

Finding new strength, Belara drew herself up tall, kindling . . . Her golden chest blushed orange with heat.

"Get back!" Milla yelled. "Get back!"

Everyone except Olvar and Finn obeyed.

Then Belara acted to protect her brood of eggs. She blasted

Duke Olvar with a massive stream of fire. Olvar caught the worst of it, but Finn's clothes also burst into flame. He fell to the floor with a hideous shriek.

Milla grabbed the edge of the thick crimson rug, wrapping Finn's burning body in it and rolling him back and forth to put out the flame.

"You stopped the fire spreading," Vigo said, as he bound Milla's burned hands in the dragonhall afterward. "How did you know what to do?"

"Working in a kitchen, you learn to douse flame," Milla said. "Your father?" she asked, though her throat felt raw and skinned.

She was leaning on Iggie: his leg had been treated first. She found she was unwilling to be apart from her dragon, even for a moment.

He shook his head.

Milla only felt numb. "And Finn?"

"He might live. He was the spy in Nestan's house," Vigo said. "My father suspected Nestan's loyalty: he was paying Finn to report to him. So when the man brought the eggs, Finn was there, ready to strike, and steal them. Except the man hid them first. As you know."

So Finn killed Josiah. Finn was the cloaked assassin. Piecing it together, Milla realized Finn must have circled around the Yellow House and climbed back up the wall to the practice yard, using Tarya as an alibi. Only Milla and Tarya knew he'd been late to Tarya's sword practice that day. She shuddered, suddenly cold, as she understood he'd been there all along, so close to those she loved, like a snake under the bed. She'd even left Iggie in his care.

She half closed her eyes and leaned back on Iggie, keeping her injured hands outstretched. "Did you see it?" she murmured. "Did you see the light? The connection between us? Like a rainbow."

"What light?" Vigo frowned in concern. "You mean the fire?"

Why hadn't he seen it? It was so bright. But she whispered, "Never mind," and promised she'd ask Tarya and Isak later.

It's over," Vigo said firmly. "We are safe now." He was gentle as he tied the ends of the bandages.

She watched him work, remembering what Serina had said about all the times her son had tended to her injuries. She didn't ask how Serina had gotten those injuries. She didn't need to.

"What do we do now?" she asked her friend. The task ahead of them seemed overwhelming.

"Funny. I was going to ask you the same thing . . ."

The dragonhall doors opened then, and Tarya walked in, arm in arm with Isak. Her face was clean of blood. "Word came from my father: he and Josi are alive. They'll be here soon. Rosa and Thom are with Simeon: hurt, but not badly."

Milla found relief more overwhelming than fear. She sank down and turned her cheek to Iggie's scaly back to hide her tears.

"We'd just reached the big question," she heard Vigo telling them, "of what we do next."

"For the hatchlings or the island?" Tarya asked shakily.

"Both."

"Belara's tending them well, but the hatchlings need people. The books say they should bond within a week," Isak said. "They can wait longer than our dragons because their mother is alive. So do you fancy organizing a bonding ceremony, Milla?"

She looked at him, through her tears. She sniffed, sat up and wiped her face against her upper sleeve, trying not to get tears in her burns. Had Tarya told him everything?

"I mean, down in the marketplace of course," he added quickly. "Like Kara told us."

Iggie rumbled his approval and Milla felt some of her fears dissolve. "Like in the old days?"

Isak nodded and flushed. "We'll invite the whole island this time."

"Time to do things differently," Tarya said.

"We'll work it out between us"—Vigo put his arm through Tarya's—"using the old books as a guide."

The three of them stood there in a row, waiting.

Iggie growled impatiently, so deep and loud, she could feel it reverberate through her ribcage.

Milla smiled at her friends through a blur of tears, feeling the salt sting her burns. "All right. Let's get to work."

EPILOGUE

A year and a half later

T he second Hatching Ceremony fell on a warm spring morning, and the air was clear and fresh. All six eggs were already tapping eagerly. Under the watchful eyes of Petra and Heral, with a full complement of guards in their new uniforms, the eggs were slowly transported down to the marketplace in a special carriage.

Milla stood in the front row, behind Iggie, ready to listen. She had helped Vigo write his speech, but Milla could see him shuffling the parchment sheets anxiously. She might be the most trusted of his elected councillors, but she still felt a mixture of nerves and excitement. Her fingers played restlessly with the gold chain around her neck. The golden pendant dangling from it was a mixture of both she'd lost: on one side it had a leaping fish, and on the other, an outline of a dragon and a full moon.

She put the other hand out, touching Iggie to calm herself. His peacock-blue scales shone brightly—she'd spent the early morning polishing them. As she stroked his gleaming back, the sun's warmth soaked through the fabric of her blue jacket.

The young duke stepped up to the wide, open space where the eggs waited on their cushions, circled by the six dragons of Arcosi, enclosed in turn by a huge audience.

"Citizens of Arcosi, our guests from Sartola"—Vigo nodded around at the combined crowd—"I welcome you warmly and most sincerely to our Hatching Ceremony."

Milla spotted her aunt Josi and Nestan in the crowd.

Josi was lifting up Joe, her small restless son, so he could see. Now that he could walk, he wanted always to be in motion. He had bright blue eyes like his father, Nestan, and a shock of thick dark hair that stood up in a tuft at the front like the tail of a duck.

"Egg?" Joe asked loudly. "Egg?"

Milla laughed, glad the tension was burst by her little cousin. She had a cousin! Joe was the link between her family and Tarya and Isak's, and she adored him.

"Go!" Joe threw himself right out of Josi's grasp. He tottered unsteadily across to his half sister, Tarya, who scooped him up.

"Yes," Tarya whispered. "Eggs! You're right. They're going to hatch today. That's why we're all here." She lifted Joe up and showed him the gathered crowd, dozens of rows deep, using the streets above the marketplace as a kind of amphitheater so everyone could see. "And you see those big boys and girls?"

Milla looked to where Tarya pointed at a queue of nervous teenagers in their best clothes, half of them Arcosi, half of them Sartolan, all aged between eleven and eighteen. Any child of the right age—from either city—was eligible, and today that meant there were thirty of them, Rosa and Thom among them.

Rosa looked anxious. Milla winked, and Rosa flashed her a quick nervous smile. Thom had his eyes fixed on the eggs.

Good luck, she mouthed silently.

"They're the Potentials, Joe," continued Tarya. "Six of them—we don't know who—are going to bond with the hatchlings."

After the bonding, the six hatchlings would return with their humans to the new dragonhall in the palace gardens. And once the dragons were fledged, there was another building waiting for them. Today it still smelled of newly sawn wood and fresh paint: the Dragon School of Arcosi, where the dragonriders would instruct the newest six.

"Eggs?" Joe said again.

"That's right, Joe. Dragon eggs! When they have hatched, the baby dragons will choose their people. Like me and Heral." She pointed to each in turn, moving round the circle. "Like Vigo and Petra. Like Isak and Belara. Like Milla and Iggie. Like Luca and Caithas. Like Lanys and Ravenna."

Milla recalled that first Hatching Ceremony, here in the marketplace, among the wreckage of the city. How nervous they'd been, inviting everyone in. How relieved Vigo had been that the little dragons, Caithas and Ravenna, had chosen two people from the different tribes—one Sartolan; one

Norlander. It helped the rebuilding of the city and the reconciliation process.

If she was honest, she still couldn't believe that Ravenna had chosen Lanys. Out of anyone on the island? She sighed. She couldn't even avoid her: the dragons saw to that. So Lanys and Milla still clashed, with depressing regularity. Milla was trying very hard to respect the way she and her little black dragon did things differently, she really was. It didn't seem to help.

Milla watched Isak exchange a glance with his new friend, Luca, Vigo's cousin, seeing the warmth and reassurance that passed between them.

Everyone waited in hushed silence. They'd waited this long for a new brood—no eggs were laid at all last year—and when it finally came, it was a healthy size. She took it as a good omen: that this peace on the island would last.

Milla patted Iggie, sending a wave of affection toward him.

He looked up, and asked if she was all right, with a soft *Aaark?*

"I'm fine," she whispered. "We're ready."

This morning she'd woken from a vivid dream with tears on her face. She guessed it'd be the last time she ever dreamt of Karys Stormrider. It felt like a farewell and she was grateful for the chance to say goodbye.

Karys sat on the dry sand at the top of the beach, wiggling her feet deeper into the warm golden grains. She squinted out to sea, where they'd left their boat tethered, dancing on the sparkling blue. How she loved this bay. It would be hard to say goodbye. Not yet, she told herself. Let the dragons heal. Let us heal. Just a little longer.

Aelia and Cato were basking near the caves. They'd hunt at dusk, when no one could see.

She closed her eyes against the hot sunshine, letting one hand fall slack, while the other rubbed her belly idly. She lifted her shirt, letting the sun fall on the round dome of it. From deep inside, she felt an answering blow against her palm. From inside and outside, both at once: she knew this baby already.

"Ha! Feel this, Gallus. It's a strong one, this child. There—put your hand there. Feel it?"

And he did: she saw the incredulous grin spread across his face.

"I felt her! I did. Karys, that's amazing. Our daughter is strong."

"How do you know? It might be a son!" she teased, but she felt he was right. It was a daughter. Dragon daughter. She would call her Kara. She closed her eyes and prayed for the day Kara could return to Arcosi on a dragon of her own.

Milla wished Kara could see this. She was glad she hadn't had such a crowd for her bonding. Or maybe, in the moment, it wouldn't have made any difference. She studied the faces of the Potentials: some were calm, some looked terrified, one or two were grinning with pride and waving to family in the crowd.

Crraack! The first egg broke in two.

A little nose appeared, pushing away the top of the egg. Then the shell fell clean apart, leaving a small damp wriggling creature.

"Ohhh!"

Hundreds gasped as one.

The children lurched forward, in spite of their training.

Petra growled, ready to step in, and they drew back. As soon as the ceremony was over, she'd collect the hatchlings under her and keep them warm and safe. The dragon-bonded would live near them in the new quarters.

Isak gestured to the children. "Come forward, Potentials. Slowly, calmly. Remember our practice or you will be excluded."

Milla watched as the young people filed carefully forward, eyes fixed on the new hatchling. They sat in a perfect circle around the hatching cushions, no one nearer than anyone else, in total equality with one another.

Who would it be? she wondered, looking from one eager face to another, hoping it would be Rosa or Thom.

"You may call quietly. Or sing. Or whistle. As your heart instructs," Isak reminded them. Serious but kind, he was the perfect person to be the first official Dragonguard of Arcosi, training up several apprentices. He and Belara flew together now, but Isak made it clear he never wanted to fight.

The baby dragon stretched and yawned, drawing a long breath. Like Caithas, Luca's apricot-and-lime dragon, this one had two colors. It had a red back and a yellow underside.

Isak leaned in and tossed it a piece of shredded chicken.

The hatchling growled and bit the scrap of meat, shaking it to and fro like a terrier with a rat.

One little girl laughed louder than the others. She looked about eleven years old, with glossy chestnut plaits down her back, a wide dimpling smile, and eyes that glittered with mischief.

Let it be her! Milla thought. She reminded Milla of herself, when she had nothing and wanted everything.

The girl pulled a little pipe from the pocket of her dress and played a three-note trill. She stopped, listening.

The dragon raised its little head high and fluted the notes back to her.

And Milla saw their fledgling bond: a ribbon of crimson-and-yellow fire that danced out from each of them. It met in the air and redoubled, stronger now, passing from one to the other.

No one else seemed to see the dragonbond as Milla did: careful questioning had proved that. She didn't know what that meant, so she kept it quiet for now.

The girl put her hand out, calling, "Charo?"

The dragon trotted clumsily over to her and climbed onto the girl's lap. She bent her head, whispering to him, tears in her eyes.

The rest of the young people sank back on their heels, disappointed.

"Don't give up!" Isak told them. "There are five more today. Be patient and listen to your heart. Soon, there will be another clutch of eggs. Soon the Dragon School will be full again."

Milla thought of Kara and whispered, "You did it. The dragons are back for good."

Iggie rumbled his approval.

ACKNOWLEDGMENTS

Thank you to my brilliant editor Rosie Fickling, who has worked very hard with me on this. If you hadn't loved this book so much and believed in it so deeply, we wouldn't have reached the finish line.

And everyone at David Fickling Books (in alphabetical order this time): Bronwen Bennie, Cecilia Busby, Jasmine Denholm, Phil Earle, Caro Fickling, David Fickling, Alison Gadsby, Anthony Hinton, Sabina Maharjan, Simon Mason, Carolyn McGlone, Bella Pearson. I count myself so lucky to work with you all.

Thank you to Angelo Rinaldi and Paul Duffield for the stunning artwork that graces the cover and interior of this book. I'm dazzled by your talents.

Thank you to Sam Palazzi for your energy and enthusiasm, and to everyone at Scholastic who helped my dragons fly across the Atlantic, and become *Legends of the Sky*.

Thank you to my agent Ben Illis, for years of support.

Huge thanks go to Tara Guha, for arranging the writing retreat where this story began, and for reading dozens of drafts along the way. And my other writing group friends: Sally Ashworth, Brianna Bourne, Kate Sims—thank you for your insight and encouragement. Thank you to my dear friend Elizabeth Bananuka for all your support, and for our conversations about representation and diversity: you're an inspiration to me.

Thank you to all the bloggers, teachers, librarians, and booksellers who have supported this book from its early days.

Thank you to Sophie Anderson and her daughter, Nicky, for reading and responding to this when it mattered most, and especially for the wonderful testimonial! Thank you, Francesca Chessa for beta reading for me and advising on Italian names: *Grazie mille*! To my fellow BIA writers, Lu Hersey, Karen Minto, and Kirsten Wild: thank you for reading and sending me your thoughtful feedback. And to Tiffany Murray, thank you for reading it way back when: it got there in the end! And to the wonderful and talented Chloe Daykin, thank you for the friendship, support, and many sanity-saving emails and phone calls; you are such fine company on this writing journey.

Thank you to all my friends, especially to Angela, Helen, Jennie, and Kirsty for years of encouragement and Friday lunchtime chats. Thank you to my beloved family: especially to Molly for painting the island of Arcosi so beautifully; and to Hanna for reading this over and over and telling me exactly what you thought, for the Minecraft version of the island, and for the gorgeous felt dragons. Thank you, CK, for everything, down to imagining the geology of this world—what would I do without you?